POLAND

POLAND

Marc E. Heine

HIPPOCRENE BOOKS
New York

To My Mother
and
the Memory of My Father

Published in the USA in 1987 by
Hippocrene Books, Inc.
171 Madison Ave.
New York, NY 10016

ISBN 0-87052-380-5

CONTENTS

LIST OF MAPS

LIST OF ILLUSTRATIONS

PREFACE

There are very few English-language guide-books on Poland, and fewer still written by 'Anglo-Saxons' specifically for 'Anglo-Saxons' (the term under which the Poles lump together all Britons, Americans and other English-speaking peoples). So, although Poland is hardly virgin territory, it is at least relatively un-discovered, certainly when compared with the main tourist areas of Western Europe and the Mediterranean. It is also a big country — as big as the United Kingdom and Ireland combined — and no travel guide can hope to describe all the attractions of such a large area in a couple of hundred pages.

Therefore I have had to select, which naturally means leaving out as well as putting in, although I have tried to include everything of real importance, as well as a number of, perhaps, less important sights which a traveller might ordinarily overlook, but which possess an element of charm or 'Polishness' (and not infrequently both) that makes them well worth a visit. Also, with so much territory to cover, I have concentrated largely on those parts of Poland which a foreign traveller is most likely to visit, namely the south-east (i.e. the Warsaw-Lublin-Cracow triangle), which for various historical reasons is particularly rich in fine buildings, as well as the larger towns generally, where most of Poland's hotels are located, making them the best centres for excursions into the surrounding coun-tryside. By the same token, I have included only a limited amount of information regarding travel to and from Poland, hotels and restaurants, passports and visas, customs regulations etc., on the assumption that most travellers, particularly those who have never visited Eastern Europe before, will contact a travel agent or the Polish Travel Office 'ORBIS', which has branches in many of the world's major cities, including London, New York and Chicago. I have, however, added a chapter on Polish food and drink at the end of the book.

Almost certainly, anyone who knows Poland well is going to note the omission of one or two of his or her favourite towns, villages, palaces, churches or whatever. I can only apologize, at the same time partly excusing myself on the grounds that any travel book is bound to reveal the author's preferences and tastes, no matter how much he may try otherwise. And, may my reader forgive me: I have kept one or two secrets to myself. I can only hope that the reader, too, will discover one or two secret places. I wish him luck — and pleasant travels in Poland!

ACKNOWLEDGMENTS

For their advice and assistance the author is indebted to ORBIS and Polorbis Travel, London; Stelp and Leighton Agencies Ltd., agents for Polish Ocean Lines; and the Zrzeszenie Gospodarki Turystycznej (Association for Tourism), Warsaw.

Illustrations 1, 4, 5, 7, 9, 12, 13, 15, 18–21 and 23–25 were kindly supplied by the Polish Tourist Information Centre, Warsaw, while 2, 3, 6, 8, 10, 14, 16, 17, 22 and the back cover were provided by ORBIS, London. The rest come from my own collection.

GUIDE TO PRONUNCIATION

The Poles are usually immensely flattered when visitors make an effort to speak a few words of their (admittedly) difficult language, but a total lack of Polish is hardly an insurmountable problem for the traveller. English is by far the most popular foreign language in the country, and many Poles, particularly the younger generation, have studied it in school or at university. German can be useful in the north and west of the country, and amongst the older generation. French, however, is less often encountered, although many educated Poles speak it, or at least understand it.

The present book sticks by and large to the Polish form of Polish names. Indeed, as Poland has always been fairly unknown to the English-speaking world, few Anglicized equivalents exist. As for the rare exceptions, such as Warsaw-Warszawa and Cracow-Kraków, I shall provide the Polish version but rely on the English one. In the case of Polish personal names, I shall invariably choose the form which the Poles themselves use. To call King Jan Sobieski 'John Sobieski' has always seemed to me as bizarre as to write Shakespeare 'Szekspir' and Chopin 'Szopen', as the Poles curiously—and frequently—do.

To most non-Poles, the Polish language must—at least on first encounter—appear a daunting hodge-podge of strange consonant clusters and precious few vowels, arranged in words of terrifying length. Place names like Szczecin and (even worse) Szczebrzeszyn seem almost purposely created to frustrate the foreign visitor, while words like *taksówka* and *kawiarnia* (for 'taxi' and 'café') only emphasize the exotic flavour of so much that is Polish. The basic problem is that the Latin alphabet, which English and Polish share, was not originally designed to cope with the Slavonic languages, and the Poles have had to adapt it to fit their own phonetic system, in some cases using combinations of consonants to denote single sounds, and adding diacritical marks to alter the pronunciation of certain letters.

Nevertheless, in Polish, spelling corresponds to pronunciation far more consistently than in English, while a number of letters—*b, d, f, k, l, m, n, p, q, t, v, x* and *z* —have roughly similar phonetic values in both languages. For the other letters, the following guide may prove helpful:

a	= a shortened version of the 'a' in 'father'
q	= a nasal vowel, like the 'own' in 'sown'
c	= 'ts' in 'cats'
cz	= 'ch' in 'church'
ć (*ci* before a vowel)	= a softer version of the English 'ch'
dz	= 'ds' in 'beds'
dź (*dzi* before a vowel)	= a softer version of the English 'j'
e	= 'e' in 'bet'
ę	= a nasal vowel with no close English equivalent; pronounced as a non-nasal 'e' at the end of a word
g	= 'g' in 'get'; never the 'j' sound of 'George'
h (ch)	= weaker form of 'ch' in the Scottish 'loch'
i	= 'ee' in 'feet'
j	= 'y' in 'yet'
ł	= 'w' in 'wet'
ń	= 'ny' in 'canyon'
o	= a shorter, clearer form of the 'o' in 'go'
r	= always trilled
s	= 's' in 'set'; never as 'z'
sz	= 'sh' in 'show'
ś (*si* before a vowel)	= a softer version of the English 'sh'
u (ó)	= a shorter version of the 'oo' in 'food'
w	= 'v' in 'vat'
y	= a cross between the 'i' in 'sit' and the 'e' in 'set'
ż (rz)	= the 'zh' sound in 'azure'
z (zi before a vowel)	= a softer version of the English 'zh' sound

Polish words are almost invariably stressed on the penultimate syllable.

Obviously, the above can provide only a rough approximation to Polish sounds, but it should at least enable the reader to pronounce the personal and place names in this book with some degree of accuracy. Berlitz provide a cheap and useful ten-minute $33\frac{1}{3}$ rpm recording, reproducing the sounds and rhythms of Polish, and they also offer an extremely comprehensive phrase-book, *Polish for Travellers* (Editions Berlitz S.A., Lausanne, 1973). The phrase-book is widely available, but the record is distributed solely by Travellers Shopping Service, Postmark House, Cross Lane, London N8. For further study, I can recommend from personal experience *Beginning Polish*, by Alexander M. Schenker (Yale University Press, London and New Haven, 1966), available through good booksellers or directly from the publisher at 20 Bloomsbury Square, London W.C.1.

Baltic Sea

Słupsk
Gdynia • Sop
Gdańsk

Kołobrzeg
Koszalin

Świnoujście
Biały Bór
Gniew

Międzyzdroje • Kamień
Pomorski

P O M E R A N I A

Szczecin
Vistula
Chełm

Piła
Bydgoszcz
Toruń

Oder
Noteć
K
U
J
A
W
Ł

Gorzów
Wielkopolski
Warta
Biskupin

Sieraków
Gniezno •

Berlin
Poznań
Konin

W E
Rogalin • Kórnik

GREAT POLAND

Oder
Leszno
Kalisz

Zielona Góra
P
O
L
Siera

Trzebnica

Legnica
Wrocław

Dresden
S
I
L
Czę

Jelenia
Góra
Wałbrzych
Opole

S
U
D
E
T
E
N
Ząbkowice
Śląskie
Paczków
E
S
I
A
Ka

Kłodzko

Prague
M
T
S
Oświ

CZECHOSLOVAKIA

Cieszyn •

— · — · — International boundaries
————— Provincial boundaries
Radom   Provincial capitals (Provinces bear the
names of their capitals)
Sanok   Other towns

C   A   R

GERMAN DEMOCRATIC REPUBLIC
(East Germany)

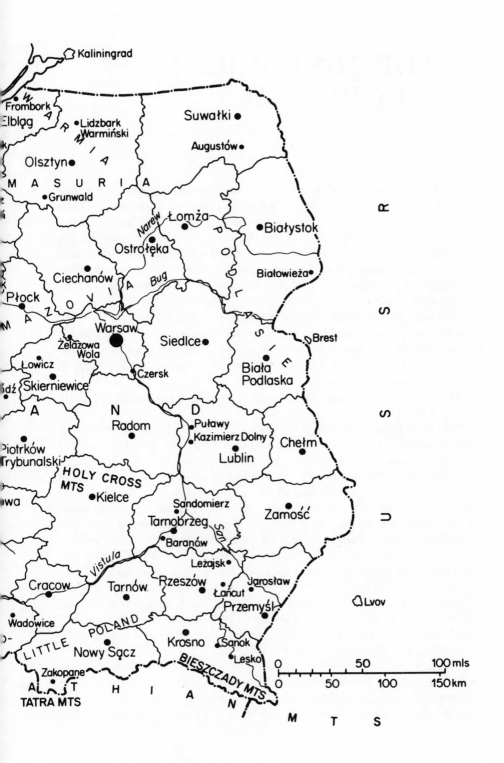

1 THE HISTORICAL BACKGROUND

The history of Poland is a record of human resilience, for few peoples have experienced so many changes of fortune, or such massive threats to their very existence as a nation. Yet, though caught between expansionist neighbours, repeatedly overrun by invaders, and even subjected to a policy of inhuman terror and genocide, as during the Nazi occupation, the Poles have somehow managed to survive, as proud and patriotic as ever, their spirit unbroken, their sense of national identity undiminished.

Poland is, therefore, understandably obsessed by its history, particularly its recent history, and some knowledge of the subject is indispensable to any traveller—even an armchair traveller—who wishes to understand this brave, irrepressible nation. Geography, in turn, provides the best key to Polish history, for the Poles have suffered far more than most other nations as a result of their geographical position.

Modern Poland occupies an area of 312,677 square kilometres, which makes it the seventh largest country in Europe. In size, it is roughly equal to the United Kingdom plus Ireland, though its population is much smaller, thirty-five million, compared with a United Kingdom population of 56 million. Poland is bordered by the Baltic to the north-west, East Germany to the west, Czechoslovakia to the south and the Soviet Union to the east and north-east. As a result of the Yalta and Potsdam Conferences and recent official West German acceptance of the Polish post-war borders, the latter now seem more or less permanent. But this has only recently been the case, for, as we shall soon see, during the last 1,000 years Poland has shifted back and forth across the map of Europe, expanding and contracting as its power waxed and waned, and even, in the 1795–1918 period, disappearing altogether following the infamous Three Partitions.

A brief glance at a relief map of Europe will immediately reveal the cause of this fluidity. Most of Poland lies astride the great North European Plain, which stretches from northern France eastward across the continent, through the Low Countries, northern Germany, Poland and western Russia, all the way to the Urals. The whole of this vast area is virtually lacking in natural barriers, apart from a few great rivers, which represent no real obstacle to a determined army. Consequently, from time immemorial the area that is now Poland has lain exposed to countless foreign invaders. At the same time, in the absence of natural frontiers, such as major mountain ranges or large bodies of water to divide them from one another, Poland and her neighbours, particularly expansionist Prussia (later Germany) to the west and no less expansionist Russia to the east, have been engaged in an age-long struggle to establish advantageous national borders.

Poland is for the most part low-lying, a characteristic borne out by the Poles' own name for their country, Polska, which ultimately derives from *pole*, or 'field'. Yet only the middle half of Poland — stretching from west to east and comprising the former provinces of Great Poland, Lower Silesia, Kujawy, Mazovia and Podlasie — is basically flat. To the north, between the central lowlands and the sandy Baltic coast, lie Pomerania, Warmia and Masuria, three heavily forested regions whose undulating contours and several thousand lakes were formed by the scouring action of glaciers during the last Ice Age. The south of the country — largely corresponding to the historical provinces of Upper Silesia and Little Poland — is predominantly hilly, the central lowlands giving way to a region of highlands and old, eroded mountains, including some of the oldest in Europe, like the picturesque Holy Cross chain, near Kielce, and the Sudeten, on the south-western border with Czechoslovakia. A number of important river basins — the upper Oder, upper Vistula and San — divide this region from the heavily forested Carpathian Mountains, which form most of Poland's southern frontier and rise to a maximum height of 2,499 metres (Mt. Rysy).

Pre-history
So much for geography. The history of Poland is somewhat less straightforward, and precise records are virtually non-existent before the middle of the tenth century A.D. All the same, there is evidence to indicate that primitive man made his appearance on Polish territory well before the last Ice Age, and traces of permanent settlements of hunters and food-gatherers dating back to approximately 38,000–32,000 B.C. have been found in caves in the Cracow region. Much later, with the onset of the neolithic period around 4400 B.C., permanent agricultural settlements began to

appear, coinciding with the gradual arrival of relatively advanced tribes of basically Mediterranean stock via the middle Danube basin. An important feature of this period was the use of flint tools — indeed, 'neolithic' means 'new stone'. The largest and best preserved flint mine in Europe has been discovered at Krzemionki Opatowskie, in Kielce province.

The Bronze Age first reached Poland around 1800 B.C., and five centuries later we find the beginnings of Lusatian culture. This is the name given to various farming and stock-breeding tribes which initially inhabited Great Poland and adjacent regions of East Germany (Lusatia, Saxony) and subsequently spread to other parts of present-day Poland. By 700 B.C. the small, scattered agricultural colonies began to be replaced by larger fortified settlements, like that at Biskupin in Great Poland, first excavated in 1934.

There is considerable evidence to suggest that Lusatian culture was one of the main elements in the formation of early Slav civilization, but it was by no means the only one. During the Iron Age, which began in Poland around 650 B.C., various peoples — Scythians, Celts and numerous Germanic tribes — invaded, and in many cases settled on Polish territory, thereby contributing to the early Slav racial mixture. Towards the end of the last century B.C., the same area began to develop increasing trade contacts with the Roman Empire, thanks to the so-called Amber Route, which ran from the Baltic up the lower Vistula, through Great Poland and Silesia southward via Moravia to the Mediterranean. Besides amber, the Poles and their Baltic neighbours traded in cattle, furs and slaves, receiving in exchange Roman manufactured goods.

Further invasions, notably by the Goths and Huns, occurred during the first centuries A.D., but by the fifth and sixth centuries the Slavs themselves began to expand — into vast territories to the east and west, and as far south as Greece, leaving Poland comparatively empty. However, a number of tribes remained, including the Wiślanie in the upper Vistula basin, the Pomorzanie in Pomerania, the Mazowszanie in Mazovia and the Polanie in Great Poland. It was the last-named who were eventually to unite the territories of modern Poland and establish the first Polish national dynasty, the Piasts.

The Piasts and the rise of the Polish state

According to legend, the first Piast was a wise and virtuous peasant of the same name who, guided by divine voices, became king around the middle of the ninth century and established a Golden

Age of peace and prosperity. However, the first historically recorded Polish ruler was the Piast prince Mieszko I, who was in possession of Great Poland, Kujawy and adjacent areas by approximately 960. Mieszko's reign was marked by an event of paramount importance in Polish history, for after marrying the Christian Czech princess Dobrava in 965, he formally accepted his bride's religion for himself and his people in the following year.

Political considerations probably played a part in his decision, for by the middle of the tenth century most of the peoples of Europe had already accepted Christianity, and by following their example Mieszko made Poland a full-fledged member of the European family of nations. Moreover, the Holy Roman Empire had been trying for some time to convert the Poles by force, and Mieszko's move eliminated the religious justification behind the Empire's continual attacks. But there is another aspect, the full consequences of which Mieszko himself can hardly have foreseen. Polish Christianity derived ultimately from Rome, rather than Byzantium, so henceforth the nation would be tied religiously and culturally with *Western* Europe, a link recently emphasized by the election of Cardinal Karol Wojtyła of Cracow as Pope John Paul II, the first non-Italian to hold that office in 450 years. However, in 988, Poland's eastern neighbour, Kievan Russia, officially embraced the Byzantine, i.e. Eastern Orthodox form of Christianity, a move which added a religious and cultural dimension to the growing political rivalry between the two nations — a rivalry which continued unabated right up to World War II.

Mieszko died in 992, by which time he had succeeded in uniting under his control most of the territories we now know as Poland. His son, Bolesław Chrobry (the Brave), considerably enlarged these territories, but, as so often happened in Polish history, he lacked the necessary administrative resources to control his new acquisitions, and most of them fell away before his death in 1025.

To make matters worse, the Germans (or, more accurately, the Holy Roman Empire) continued to make incursions deep into Poland even after the latter had officially accepted Christianity. The Poles were now clearly on the defensive, and the administrative centre of the country gradually shifted from the Poznań-Gniezno region, in Great Poland, to the less vulnerable Cracow, capital of the province of Little Poland, on the upper Vistula. But Poland faced an equally dangerous internal threat, for the centripetal forces that had plagued Bolesław continued to manifest themselves during subsequent reigns, as the numerous feudal princelings repeatedly sought to assert their power vis-à-vis the central government.

Matters were hardly improved by the statute of succession drawn up by Bolesław Krzywousty (Wry-Mouth) shortly before his death in 1138. Fearing the chaos that might result from protracted disputes over the right to succeed him, Bolesław divided the kingdom amongst his sons, giving his eldest the seniorial province of Cracow and limited sovereignty over Poland as a whole. When the senior prince died, he was to be succeeded by the next eldest member of the Piast dynasty, whose own province would be taken over by the next eldest and so on down the line, until all the provinces had been redistributed. Not surprisingly, this 'musical chairs' formula proved disastrous: not only did it not provide a workable system of succession, but—even worse—it led to the establishment of separate provincial dynasties, so that by the beginning of the thirteenth century Poland had disintegrated into a number of independent principalities.

A dismembered Poland was a weaker Poland, a fact her neighbours were quick to appreciate. A particularly aggressive lot were the pagan Prussians on Poland's north-east frontier (not to be confused with the later, largely German-descended inhabitants of the same area). Finally, in 1226 Prince Konrad of Mazovia (the province which had borne the brunt of their attacks) turned for assistance to the Teutonic Knights, a semi-religious order which had been unemployed since its return from the Crusades, and settled them in the Prussian marches. They were *very* efficient: by the end of the century they had succeeded in subjugating and Christianizing the Prussians, wiping out a large proportion of them in the process. To repopulate the region, the Order encouraged immigration from the Low Countries and (particularly) the German states.

It became obvious with the passage of time that Poland had merely exchanged a lesser danger (the Prussians) for a greater one (the Teutonic Order). The steady influx of German colonists greatly increased the prosperity of the region, and the Order grew more and more powerful, annexing large chunks of northern Poland. Finally, in 1308, the Knights seized the rich trading city of Gdańsk (in German, Danzig) and massacred its 10,000 Polish inhabitants. The Order was now in possession of the whole of northern Poland and would remain so for another century and a half.

To the east, the Mongols (or Tatars, as they are usually called in Polish sources) constituted a no less serious threat. After taking

China, Central Asia and the Caucasus in the first decades of the thirteenth century, they turned their attention to Europe, conquering most of the Russian principalities by 1240. In the following year they swept westward, devastating much of Little Poland and Silesia, and inflicting heavy losses on the Polish forces, who were no match for their superior military skills. The final Polish defeat came later that year at the great battle of Legnica, when Henryk the Pious, the most powerful Polish prince, lost his life. The Tatars then withdrew, although they were to make further bloody forays into Poland for more than a century afterwards.

During the reconstruction that followed, large numbers of foreign colonists (mainly Germans) were encouraged to settle in Poland, especially in the south, where the Tatars had wrought the most damage, but also in Pomerania, the lower Vistula valley and the west. The immediate benefits to Poland were considerable: the new settlers brought with them much-needed professional and commercial skills, and new towns developed, while older ones expanded. There was also substantial rural colonization, par- ticularly in the rich farmlands of Lower Silesia and the Vistula delta. But there were long-term dangers as well as benefits in such large-scale foreign immigration; for while in some areas, such as Little Poland, these new settlers eventually became Polonized, elsewhere (notably Silesia) they remained a race apart, gradually Germanizing areas which had once been solidly Polish. German political influence also increased in these areas, facilitating their eventual absorption by German powers.

During the four decades preceding the Tatar invasion, Henryk the Pious and his father Henryk the Bearded had succeeded in expanding their small principality of Wroclaw to embrace over half of the historic Polish lands, including all of Great Poland and Little Poland. But the former's death at the battle of Legnica led to the disintegration of the new state and the end of Silesian supremacy.

The next attempt at unifying the Polish lands came well over half a century later in the somewhat unlikely person of Prince Władysław of Kujawy, who was so short that he has gone down in history as 'Łokietek' (Little Ell). Władysław seized Sandomierz in 1305, and thus began the slow process of unifying the country, which culminated in his coronation in Cracow as King of Poland in 1320.

To be sure, Władysław's kingdom did not include Silesia, Pomerania or Mazovia; but his son, Kazimierz, who succeeded him in 1333, made Mazovia a Polish vassal and captured vast areas to the south-east in what is now the Ukraine, thereby more than doubling the territory he had inherited from his father. But if Kazimierz was a great warrior, he was also an enlightened monarch, codifying the law, instituting fiscal reforms and promoting the expansion of trade and the economy in general. In the field of education his most memorable achievement was the establishment of Cracow University, the second oldest (after Prague) in Central Europe. He was also a great founder of towns and patron of architecture, and the Poles have a saying that he 'found Poland built of wood and left her in stone'. It is not surprising therefore, that amongst all the Wry-Mouths, Little-Ells and other equally remarkable epithets that Polish tradition has bestowed on its rulers, Kazimierz alone has been accorded the title of 'the Great'.

The Jagiellonian dynasty

Kazimierz left no heir, and on his death in 1370 the crown passed to his nephew and ally, Louis of Hungary, whose daughter, Jadwiga, succeeded him in turn. Jadwiga is mainly remembered for her marriage, in 1386, to the pagan Grand Duke Jagiełło of Lithuania, who as part of the bargain accepted Roman Catholicism for himself and his people, at the same time adopting the baptismal name Władysław. By his marriage, Władysław Jagiełło became King of Poland, thereby establishing the dynastic union of the two nations, which guaranteed the security of Poland's eastern frontier and at the same time opened the way for further eastward expansion.

To the north however, the Teutonic Knights remained a threat, although their defeat by a joint Polish-Lithuanian-Tatar army at the Battle of Grunwald in 1410, when the Grand Master of the Order himself was killed, marked the beginning of their gradual decline. They were finally, and conclusively, defeated in the Thirteen Years' War (1454–66), whereby the Poles regained eastern Pomerania, Gdańsk and part of Prussia itself, while the Order was forced to pay homage for its remaining territories. The Order emitted a last gasp in the next century when Albrecht of Hohenzollern, the last Grand Master, not only refused to pay homage to Poland, but—adding insult to injury—attempted to switch his allegiance to Muscovy. However, after a brief war in which Poland was victorious, a compromise was reached, and in 1525 Albrecht secularized the Order, adopted Lutheranism and became the hereditary Duke of Prussia, owing allegiance to the Polish king. In the following year with the death of its last Piast prince, the vassal state of Mazovia was finally incorporated into Poland. Later, in 1561, Gotthard von Kettler, the Teutonic Grand Master of Livonia (present-day Latvia and southern Estonia), who was under attack from both Sweden and Muscovy, followed his Prussian counterpart's example and secularized his Order, adopted Lutheranism and became a Polish vassal. The dual realm of Poland and Lithuania was now the second largest nation in Europe (after Russia), stretching from the Baltic almost to the Black Sea, and from the borders of Brandenburg on the west to within 375 kilometres of Moscow. It was also a rich mosaic of nationalities, consisting of Poles in the centre and west; Orthodox Ukrainians and Byelorussians in the east; Lithuanians, Latvians and Estonians in the north; Germans in parts of Prussia and along the western frontier; and a fairly substantial scattering of Jews throughout the country.

The sixteenth century was Poland's Golden Age in more than mere terms of power and territorial expansion, for it was also a period of great cultural activity, stimulated by Renaissance influences from abroad. Polish replaced Latin as the chief language of literary expression, and a truly national literature was born. It immediately produced a star of the first magnitude in the poet and dramatist Jan Kochanowski (1503–70), whose exquisite lyrics, virtually unknown outside Poland, are masterpieces of European literature. In the field of science, the great Nicholas Copernicus (in Polish, Mikołaj Kopernik) changed the whole course of astronomy with his monumental *On the Revolutions of the Celestial Spheres*, published in 1543, the year of his death. More and more Poles were studying abroad, chiefly in Italy — Padua, Bologna and Rome were favourite destinations — and also at the German universities, such as Leipzig and Wittenberg. Cities and towns continued to expand, and architecture flourished, largely paid for by the steadily rising price of grain, of which Poland was then one of Europe's main suppliers. Numerous architects and skilled craftsmen began to arrive in Poland from Western Europe, particularly Italians, who were very much in demand after the marriage of a Milanese noblewoman, Bona Sforza, to King Zygmunt (Sigismund) I.

Both he and his son, Zygmunt II August, were great patrons of the arts; Zygmunt I rebuilt the Wawel castle in Cracow and commissioned what is considered by many Polish art historians to be the finest piece of Renaissance architecture outside Italy, Bartolomeo Berrecci's Sigismund Chapel in Cracow Cathedral; Zygmunt

August subsequently embellished the castle with nearly 200 especially ordered Brussels tapestries, the largest and possibly the finest collection of its kind anywhere in Europe. The gentry and nobility were also busy building, and some of Poland's finest castles and country houses (Baranów, Krasiczyn, Pieskowa Skała etc.) date from this period. But perhaps the most ambitious and impressive architectural project was undertaken at Zamość in the years following 1580, when the Italian Bernardo Morando, working for the powerful Chancellor Jan Zamoyski, commenced the construction of an entire fortified Renaissance town, the first of a number of planned towns built for Polish magnates during the sixteenth and seventeenth centuries.

This was also a period of great religious ferment. The Reformation at first made considerable headway in Poland, with many of the townspeople, who were in many cases of German origin, accepting Lutheranism, while Calvinism enjoyed much success amongst the *szlachta* (gentry and nobility). The peasantry, however, who constituted the bulk of the population, largely remained Catholic. The spirit of religious toleration which prevailed in Poland is perhaps best shown by the Warsaw Compact, passed by the Sejm, or Parliament, in 1573, which abolished the privileged position enjoyed by the Catholic Church and at the same time established the equality of all faiths in the eyes of the law. The Poles are justly proud that theirs was only the second country (after Transylvania) in the whole of Europe to guarantee such a high degree of religious freedom. To be sure, in theory this toleration covered only the *szlachta* (approximately ten per cent of the population), but in practice it was extended by and large to the other social classes as well. Yet, despite its early successes, Protestantism never really made any lasting impact on Polish religious life. In 1564, the Jesuits, the 'shock troops' of the Counter-Reformation, arrived in Poland, and within about a century the Protestants were reduced to only a tiny minority of the population, which they have remained to this day.

The elective monarchy and the decline of Poland

By the Union of Lublin (1569), Poland and its eastern neighbour, the Grand Duchy of Lithuania, were finally merged into a single state — the *Rzeczpospolita* (Commonwealth) — after having been linked dynastically for almost two centuries. But three years later, Zygmunt August died, and the Jagiellonian dynasty became extinct in the male line. This posed enormous problems for the country, as no formula of succession had been established during the King's lifetime. However, in 1573, the Sejm came up with a novel solution in the form of an elective monarchy with life tenure, the obvious intention being to strengthen the *szlachta* vis-à-vis the king. The consequences were disastrous, for at each royal election the other major European powers (particularly Russia, Austria, France and Sweden) all tried to place their own puppet candidates on the throne, whether by means of bribery, pressure, or the promise of high office to members of the Sejm. This in turn led to the development of treasonous factions within Poland itself, often involving the great magnate families, at a time when the country desperately needed a strong sense of national unity and purpose if it was going to keep its increasingly expansionist neighbours at bay.

Poland's experience with its first elected king hardly augured well for the success of the experiment. Chosen by the Sejm in 1573, Henri de Valois had reigned for only a few months when news reached him of the death of his brother, the childless French king, Charles IX. Anxious to assert his claim to succeed Charles, he decamped from Wawel castle in the dead of the night and headed back to Paris. No amount of persuasion by the Polish Senate (the upper house of the Sejm) could make him return, and he subsequently ascended the French throne as Henri III.

Its national pride bruised, the Sejm had no alternative but to elect another king, although this time it was luckier in its choice, Stefan Batory, the Prince of Transylvania, who later married the late Zygmunt August's sister Anna. Despite the relative shortness of his reign (1576–86), Batory, together with his brilliant chancellor and commander, Jan Zamoyski, won a number of important military victories over Ivan the Terrible, which resulted in the annexation of a substantial chunk of Russian territory.

Following Batory's death, the crown was offered to another prince with Jagiellonian connections, Sigismund Vasa, the son of Zygmunt August's sister Katarzyna, and heir to the Swedish throne. As Zygmunt III, he was the first of three members of the House of Vasa who ruled Poland uninterruptedly — though by virtue of individual election rather than dynastic succession — from 1587 to 1668. Zygmunt is perhaps best remembered for transferring the royal residence (and thus, in effect, the nation's capital) from Cracow to Warsaw in 1596, a move motivated, according to tradition, by his desire to be closer to the game-rich forests of the north-east. A far more divisive event occurred in the same year at Brest, when a majority of the Polish Orthodox hierarchy accepted the supremacy of the pope, thereby establishing the so-called Uniate Church, linked doctrinally with Rome but retaining the Eastern rite and other traditional practices. The state strongly supported the Union, seeing it as a means of increasing Polish cultural influence in the largely Ukrainian and Byelorussian (and therefore basically Orthodox) eastern half of the country. However, a majority of the Orthodox faithful rejected their bishops' actions, and the great bitterness which developed between the two factions was further exacerbated by the authorities' attempts to impose the Union by force.

Despite growing difficulties at home, Poland remained a power to be reckoned with internationally. Ind ed, in 1610, during the turbulence and confusion following Boris Godunov's death and the establishment of the Romanov dynasty, Polish troops actually seized Moscow, and Zygmunt's son Władysław was proclaimed tsar. Two years later, a Russian army of national liberation recaptured the city, putting an end to Polish hopes of permanently retaining the Muscovite crown, but by the Truce of Deulino (1619) Poland acquired further large chunks of Russian territory, including the great frontier fortress of Smolensk. Poland was now at the peak of its power, comprising a total area of 990,000 square kilometres (i.e. more than three times its present size).

But the rot had already set in, and the seventeenth century was to prove the turning-point in Poland's fortunes. With the growing success of the Counter-Reformation, the spirit of toleration on which Poland had prided herself gradually turned into one of mutual distrust and even fanaticism, pitting Catholic against both Protestant and Orthodox, although unlike Western Europe, the Poles never burned one another because of religious differences. In the political field, the elective monarchy had led to a dangerous weakening of royal (and hence, central) authority, as successive candidates for the kingship bargained away one royal prerogative after another in order to get elected. The victors were the *szlachta*, who had always been fiercely jealous of their own privileges, and were ever eager to acquire more. Indeed, there is an ancient Polish saying which maintains that 'the squire on his fence is equal to the king in his court'. Now, bolstered by such pernicious and absurd institutions as the *liberum veto*, which required a unanimous vote of the Sejm for the passage of any law, the *szlachta* was slowly making effective government well-nigh impossible. Not surprisingly, disgruntled nobles, finding the Sejm useless as a political forum, frequently resorted to armed rebellion. The country had grown too large for its administrative and military resources — the same problem had plagued Bolesław the Brave hundreds of years earlier — and now it began to lose a number of strategically important frontier provinces. Thus, Brandenburg annexed Prussia in 1657, while Cossack uprisings and a series of wars with Russia (1648–67) led to the surrender of Smolensk, Kiev and half of the Ukraine. By the end of the century, Poland had lost well over a quarter of her vast territories.

However, none of these conflicts was as catastrophic for Poland as the war with Sweden (1655–60), known in Polish history as the 'Deluge' and immortalized in the stirring romantic novels of Henryk Sienkiewicz. The origin of this conflict was twofold. First, there was the dynastic issue. Zygmunt III, Poland's first Vasa king, had succeeded his father as king of Sweden in 1592 and ruled the two countries jointly for a time. However, his Catholicism, and the fact that he was a shared ruler, made him unpopular in his native, and overwhelmingly Lutheran, Sweden, and in 1599 he was dethroned by the Swedes and replaced by his Protestant uncle, Charles IX, whereupon the two nations almost immediately went to war. It was a long, intermittent war, ending only in 1629 with Poland ceding most of Livonia to Sweden. Even so, Zygmunt and the two subsequent Polish Vasas — his sons Władysław IV and Jan Kazimierz — still persisted in their claim to the Swedish throne.

This was bound to lead to further conflict between the two countries, particularly as Sweden was rapidly becoming a great military power, with an enormous appetite for territorial expansion (and, in particular, control of the Baltic), while Poland was growing weaker and weaker, which made it ripe for the plucking. Finally, in the summer of 1655, Sweden invaded Poland, and by the end of the year — partly owing to the treasonous capitulation of several noble Polish generals — it had overrun almost the entire country (hence the term 'Deluge'), while the King, Jan Kazimierz, had fled to Silesia. However, the cruelty of the occupation quickly rallied the people to the national cause. Partisan warfare developed on a large scale, several liberation armies were formed, and the King himself returned to Poland the following year. Gradually the tide turned, and in 1660 peace was signed. Poland was left in possession of all its pre-war territories — but it was also left in a state of near-total collapse; most towns had been plundered or burned, agriculture, and indeed, the economy as a whole, was in ruins, while a large proportion of the nation's cultural and artistic heritage had been carted off to Sweden, in whose museums much of it remains to this day. But undoubtedly the greatest loss was human, for largely as a result of famine and disease the population fell by an almost incredible 40 per cent, from ten million to approximately six million.

Poland experienced its last great military success with the Battle of Vienna (1683), when King Jan Sobieski, leading a united Christian army which included a large Polish contingent, trounced the Turks and forced them to retreat, thereby permanently halting their advance into Europe. Sobieski died in 1696, and in the following year the Sejm chose the Elector of Saxony to succeed him as August II (or 'the Strong', because of his prodigious physical strength). Unfortunately for Poland, the period of Saxon rule (1697–1763) coincided with a pathetic decline in Polish strength and prestige, with the country becoming little more than a meeting-place for foreign invaders, its very existence tolerated only because the great European powers (Russia, Austria, Prussia and France) feared to upset the continental balance of power by carving her up. A large share of the blame for this decline must lie with Poland's own rulers. For instance, August II's chief ambition was the creation of an absolute and hereditary monarchy, and he even went so far as to propose a number of partition schemes to foreign rulers, in the hope of permanently retaining at least part of Poland for Saxony.

Meanwhile, to the north, Sweden remained a threat, but what appeared to be a splendid opportunity for settling old scores presented itself when Charles XII ascended the Swedish throne in 1697. A mere fifteen-year-old, Charles — and Sweden — seemed easy prey, so in January 1700 August declared war, to be followed eventually by Denmark and Russia. With so many states lined up against it, logically Sweden (with a population of less than a million) should have lost the war almost immediately, but to everybody's surprise Charles turned out to be a military genius. In 1701, his armies invaded Poland, remaining there until 1709, while the Great Northern War as a whole dragged on and on until the Swedes finally surrendered in 1721.

However, Polish dissatisfaction with August reached its peak well before then, and in 1704 he was deposed by his opponents, to be replaced by Stanisław Leszczyński (the future father-in-law of Louis XV), who had Swedish support. Poland now had two kings, a situation which persisted until 1706, when Charles defeated August in the latter's native Saxony and by the Treaty of Altranstädt forced him to abdicate in favour of Leszczyński. Nevertheless, with

Russian support August soon regained the crown, as a result of Charles' defeat at the Battle of Poltava (1709). Even so, dissatisfaction with August, and with the Saxons in general, continued to manifest itself, as during the civil war of 1715–16, which flared up largely in reaction to the overbearing behaviour of the Saxon troops stationed in Poland.

August II died in 1733, and there were two chief candidates to succeed him: his son, also named August, and (once again) Stanisław Leszczyński. The latter, who had French support, received a majority of the votes, whereupon Russia invaded Poland, thereby setting off the War of the Polish Succession. The succession issue was finally resolved by the Treaty of Vienna (1738), whereby August was confirmed as king of Poland, while Leszczyński was granted the Duchy of Lorraine.

Most of the new King's energies, and much of the resources of both kingdoms, were spent on continuing his father's programme of turning Dresden into one of the most architecturally splendid capitals in northern Europe, a fact which was deeply resented by his Polish subjects. In August's absence, his chief minister, the Saxon Count Brühl, was put in charge, but people living in Poland at the time must have wondered whether anyone was actually governing the country, as it slid deeper and deeper into anarchy. To give just one example, during August III's entire reign only a single Sejm managed to pass any resolutions, all the others having been terminated through the use of the *liberum veto* as a result of bribery by foreign powers and the narrow self-interest of the great landed magnates.

The dismemberment of Poland

August III died in 1763, and following Russian armed intervention Stanisław August Poniatowski, a Polish nobleman and former lover of the Empress Catherine the Great, was elected to succeed him. A great patron of literature and the arts, Poniatowski proved to be a moral weakling and virtually a Russian puppet. Nevertheless, despite Poniatowski's own ambivalent position, the nation as a whole began to be increasingly aware of the dangers threatening Poland. The resultant antagonism between patriots and king turned into armed rebellion in 1768 with the formation at Bar, in the south-eastern province of Podolia, of an anti-Poniatowski, anti-Russian confederation, which soon spread to every corner of the country. The result was four years of civil war and nationwide devastation, leaving Poland in a chaotic state, which in turn provided her neighbours with a pretext for beginning her dismemberment. Accordingly, in 1772, Austria, Prussia and Russia agreed amongst themselves to annex some 29 per cent of Poland's territory and 35 per cent of her population, and the demoralized Sejm had no choice but to ratify this partition formally in the following year.

The First Partition shocked the nation into action and led to numerous projects for the reform of Poland's political, social and economic structure. Finally, in 1788 a special reforming Sejm was convened, in which the patriotic pro-Polish party constituted a clear majority. One of its first acts was to increase the authorized size of the army from 20,000 to 100,000 men and to demand the immediate withdrawl of Russian troops, who were one of the main props of Poniatowski's régime. But by far the greatest achievement of the Sejm was the Constitution of the Third of May (1791), the second written constitution in the world, after that of the United States. Strongly influenced by the ideals of the French Revolution, the Polish constitution was remarkably liberal for its time, its main feature being the creation of a parliamentary monarchy, with the king of Saxony to become hereditary king of Poland after Poniatowski's death. In addition, the *liberum veto* was abolished, while the powers of the rich nobles were curtailed, and the rights of the middle class increased.

However, alarmed by the liberal tone of the constitution and anxious to re-assert Russian influence, Catherine the Great joined forces with Polish conservatives opposed to the new reforms and invaded the country in 1792. The Russian-conservative coalition quickly gained the upper hand and repealed the reforms. Then, early in the following year, Russia and her ally Prussia effected the Second Partition, taking well over half of Poland's remaining territory.

By now the patriotic party had reached the end of its patience, and on 24 March 1794, in the Market Square of Cracow, Tadeusz Kościuszko, a hero of the American War of Independence, launched an armed insurrection which quickly gained nationwide support. But, despite early victories, the outcome of the conflict could never seriously have been in doubt; the Polish forces were no match for the stronger, better equipped Russian troops, and by the end of the year Kościuszko had been defeated. The result was the Third Partition (1795), whereby Russia, Prussia and Austria dismembered the rest of Poland, forcing Poniatowski to abdicate. (He died in St. Petersburg in 1798.) Within a generation Poland had been wiped off the map of Europe.

The loss of independence

The final dismemberment of the Polish state led many Poles to emigrate, chiefly to France, where they joined Napoleon's Polish Legions. Indeed, the Poles as a whole were strongly pro-French, seeing the latter as their sole ally against the three partitioning powers. Their loyalty was rewarded in 1807, when, having defeated Prussia, Napoleon created the Duchy of Warsaw out of the Polish territories previously annexed by Prussia and, as the Constitution of the Third of May had intended, installed the King of Saxony as its ruler. Large areas were added to it in 1809, following France's successful war with Austria, but this last vestige of Polish independence collapsed with Napoleon's final defeat, and in 1815, at the Congress of Vienna, Russia and Prussia divided the Duchy between themselves.

The Poles did not submit peacefully to their loss of independence, and the next half-century was marked by a number of uprisings against the three partitioning powers. By far the most serious were the November Insurrection (1830) and the January Insurrection (1863), both of which led to considerable loss of life, massive emigration and large-scale exile to Siberia, where the largely Russified descendants of many of them live to this day. (The Russian composer Dmitri Shostakovich, whose paternal grandfather fought in the 1863 Insurrection, is probably the best-known present-day descendant of these exiles.) During this period the Polish political refugee became a familiar figure throughout Europe and the Americas.

The catastrophic failure of the 1863 Insurrection, and the harsh repression that followed, forced Polish patriots to reconsider their tactics. Realizing the hopelessness of armed rebellion in the face of the partitioning powers' superior strength, they now began to call for 'organic work', i.e. the rapid growth of the economy, education and culture, linked with a keen development of national consciousness. The success of these measures varied with the region. In Prussian Poland, agriculture flourished, the road and rail network expanded, and heavy industry developed, particularly in Upper Silesia. In the Russian sector growth was more moderate, although a number of important industrial centres developed, e.g. Warsaw, Łódź and Białystok. But Austrian Poland, or Galicia, remained backward economically, particularly in the agricultural sector, although its two great university cities of Cracow and Lwów made it eminent in the field of culture and education. Because of poverty at home, large numbers of Poles began to emigrate, chiefly to the

United States, but also to Western Europe, Canada, Brazil and Argentina. By 1914, over four million Poles lived abroad, out of a total of only 22 million.

The turn of the century was marked by intense political activity, most of it peaceful, and some of it — particularly in Russian Poland — conducted underground. But here, too, the situation varied considerably among the three sectors. Thus, Austrian Poland enjoyed a considerable measure of cultural and even political autonomy, whereas in the other two sectors the use of Polish was suppressed in education, administration and the courts, while thousands of German settlers were moved into hitherto Polish rural areas in an attempt to alter their ethnic character. However, instead of demoralizing the Poles, these measures merely strengthened their sense of identity, and the ranks of the nationalist movement swelled correspondingly.

World War I resulted in enormous destruction and considerable loss of life in the Polish territories, as the front shifted back and forth across the land. Since there was no Polish state, there was no Polish army. Instead, Poles in the Russian sector were drafted into the Russian army (on the Allied side), while those in the other two sectors went into the Austrian and Prussian armies (the Central Powers), with the result that Pole was obliged to fight against Pole. However, the defeat of the Central Powers and the chaos in Russia following the Revolution enabled the Poles to form a state of their own in 1918, and as a result of the Treaty of Versailles, armed conflict with the Soviet Union and newly independent Lithuania, and plebiscites in Silesia and East Prussia, the borders of Poland were finally established by 1923.

The reborn Polish state

The new nation faced formidable difficulties. Apart from war damage, there was grinding rural poverty, a high illiteracy rate, generally low productivity in both agriculture and industry, and all the other problems usually associated with a relatively backward economy. There was also the difficulty of national minorities, for over a third of the population consisted of Ukrainians, Byelorussians, Jews, Germans and other non-Poles, most of whom had strong separatist tendencies and no great love of being ruled by the Poles. Finally, there was the almost unique problem of having to fuse the completely separate administrations, economies, and transportation and communications systems of the three former occupied sectors into a unified whole.

The new state had little more than two decades in which to deal with these massive problems, for on 1 September 1939 Germany invaded Poland, thus beginning World War II. The situation was desperate: the Poles were outnumbered by three to two, and (far worse) they had only about one-fifth the number of tanks and aircraft that the Germans had. Even so, the Poles fought valiantly, but within five weeks the entire country was in German hands.

During the next six years the Poles were subjected to a living hell. Hundreds of thousands of civilians were rounded up on the streets and deported to Germany as slave labourers. Countless others were executed on the spot or sent off to concentration camps, as were thousands of Poles living in areas scheduled for German colonization. All high schools, colleges and universities were closed, and hundreds of professors, lecturers, writers, politicians and clergymen were murdered in a deliberate attempt to deprive Poland of its intellectual, political and spiritual leadership. But it was for the Jews that the Nazis reserved their special hatred, at first confining them in ghettos, where they were systematically starved to death on inhumanly small rations. Finally, in 1942, the Germans began sending them to death camps, such as Auschwitz, Majdanek and Treblinka, where hundreds of thousands of Poles (Jews and non-Jews alike) perished, together with several million others of different nationalities.

Nazi terror met with strong resistance, as thousands of Poles joined the underground movement or partisan groups. In addition, many Poles fought for the Allies outside Poland, distinguishing themselves in the Battles of Britain, Monte Cassino, Arnhem and numerous other campaigns. Two main forces ultimately emerged: the Armia Krajowa (Home Army), which owed allegiance to the government-in-exile in London, and the Armia Ludowa (People's Army), which was more leftist-oriented. Finally, in July 1944, the Red Army, joined by Polish forces, crossed the River Bug and established a Committee of National Liberation in Lublin. The Soviet and Polish armies then continued to push westward across the country, but it was not until 9 May 1945 (i.e., a week after the fall of Berlin) that the last German troops on Polish soil surrendered.

Poland since World War II

The war left Poland in ruins. As a result of war action and Nazi terror, the country lost a higher proportion of its population than any other nation — 20 per cent, or over six million people, including the vast majority of its more than three million Jews. In addition, half a million people were left permanently crippled. Thirty-eight per cent of Poland's material wealth was destroyed, as compared with less than one per cent in the case of the United Kingdom. Few — if any — urban centres came through the war unscathed. In some, the damage was colossal, amounting to 50 per cent in Szczecin, 55 per cent in Poznań and Gdańsk, 70 per cent in Wrocław and 85 per cent in Warsaw. In the countryside, the situation was hardly better; over a third of Poland's farmland had gone out of production, while its livestock supply had fallen by two-thirds. As a result, the country was living near starvation level, and many Poles had literally no roof over their heads.

To complicate matters still further, the Yalta and Potsdam Conferences had awarded Poland's eastern provinces, with their predominantly (though by no means exclusively) Ukrainian and Byelorussian population, to the Soviet Union. In exchange, the Poles obtained the lion's share of German territory east of the Oder and Neisse (in Polish, Odra and Nysa) rivers, consisting of Pomerania, Silesia and the southern half of East Prussia (the Soviet Union received the northern half). In numerical terms, Poland lost 178,500 square kilometres of territory in the east and acquired 103,000 square kilometres in the west. It is bitterly ironic that after centuries of bloodshed Poland's borders are now roughly where they were at the death of Bolesław Wry-Mouth more than 800 years ago.

These radical border changes resulted in massive transfers of population, putting an enormous strain on the post-war Polish state. One and a half million Poles from the former eastern provinces moved westward into Poland, changing places with half a million hitherto Polish Ukrainians and Byelorussians who moved east. At the other end of the country, hundreds of thousands of Germans living east of the Oder and Neisse rivers had fled west with the retreating German army during the last months of the war, and by the end of 1947 more than two million more had been deported to Germany. Their place was taken by four and a half million Poles, including many from the lost eastern provinces. In addition, two million Poles who had been deported to Germany as forced labourers during the war were repatriated, along with tens of thousands of Polish servicemen and pre-war emigrants to Western Europe who now chose to return home. All in all, well over ten million people of various nationalities were on the move, into and out of Poland — an enormous figure, especially when one considers that its 1945 population was only some 24 million.

Despite the massive upheaval which these population transfers created, Poland began rebuilding immediately following liberation, one of its main priorities being the integration into Polish society of its millions of repatriates. Progress was rapid in many areas, though the economy still contains a number of serious weak spots, particularly in the fields of agriculture and housing. After a few years of uncertainty and bitter dissension, leading in many areas to armed conflict, Poland ultimately adopted a socialist system of government, including centralized planning, state ownership of industry, and land reform — though not universal collectivization, three-quarters of Polish farmland remaining in the hands of peasant smallholders. In matters of foreign policy, Poland is closely allied with the Soviet Union and the other countries of the Socialist Bloc, being a member of the Warsaw Pact (the East's answer to NATO) and the Council for Mutual Economic Assistance, or Comecon (a sort of Socialist Bloc Common Market).

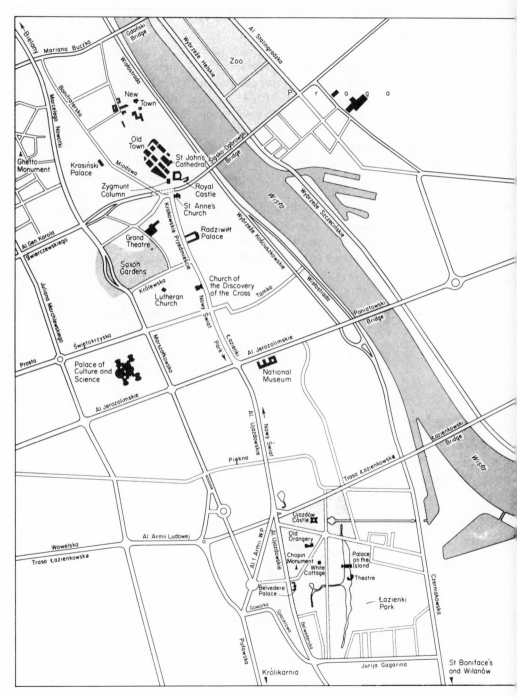

2 WARSAW AND VICINITY

Warsaw lies very close to the heart of every Pole, for during the last war no Polish city suffered such immense loss of life and such destruction, nor has any city been so impressively and lovingly restored. Indeed, for Poles and non-Poles alike, Warsaw has come to symbolize the entire country, rising phoenix-like from the ashes of World War II.

This alone would be sufficient reason for beginning our tour in Warsaw. But there are many other reasons, too. Warsaw is, after all, the capital, a fact which still rankles in the hearts of many Cracovians, who lost this honour to Warsaw in 1596 and still tend to think of the latter as a brash upstart. But this is mere local rivalry, and to any visitor Warsaw immediately feels like a capital, whereas Cracow, stunningly beautiful though it may be, does not.

In the first place, Warsaw is a very spacious city, except of course in the Old Town, whose picturesque narrow streets give it a special character all its own. For the most part, though, Warsaw is a city of long, frequently tree-lined avenues and numerous parks and squares. This is partly due to the last war, for when Warsaw was being rebuilt in the late 40s and 50s the planners took advantage of the fact that most of the city lay in ruins and broadened many streets, at the same time trebling its park area.

Warsaw is also Poland's largest city, with over one and a half million inhabitants, which makes it bigger than Prague, smaller than Budapest, and about half the size of the two Berlins put together. At the same time Warsaw is the country's chief cultural and artistic centre, with some twenty-odd theatres, numerous museums and art galleries, and a thriving musical life. That is not to say that one cannot see equally good theatre or hear equally fine concerts in other Polish cities, particularly Cracow. It is just that there is so much more to choose from in Warsaw.

But perhaps the best reason for beginning our tour in the nation's capital is that this is precisely what most foreign visitors—and certainly most British and American visitors—do. Thus, whatever their point of origin, almost all international flights to Poland terminate in Warsaw. Overland travellers, too, mostly go straight to Warsaw, passing through Poznań, Wrocław or Cracow and often doubling back later to take in their respective charms. Somehow, when one is visiting an area as foreign—even to an experienced traveller—as Eastern Europe, it generally seems a good idea to head for the largest, most cosmopolitan city in a country, to absorb some of its atmosphere, and then to branch out into the provinces. This idea has a lot to recommend it, and it is the approach we shall be following here.

Warsaw lies astride the River Vistula (in Polish, Wisła), which arises in the Carpathians close to Poland's southern border and then carves a 1,047-kilometre long, S-shaped course through the heart of the country before finally emptying into the Baltic. Warsaw proper stands on the higher, left bank, while below, on the right bank, lies the old suburb of Praga, which was joined to the capital administratively as long ago as 1791. In the past, the Vistula was a broad, shallow, capricious river, never quite certain of its proper channel, and prone to overflow its banks, causing serious flooding and loss of life whenever its mountain tributaries gave it more water than it could handle. So, a project is now under way for regulating it over much of its course. But at Warsaw the river still looks broad and shallow, and almost lazy, full of the shifting sandbanks and islets which made it a useful ford for travelling merchants at least as early as the time of the ancient geographer Ptolemy, who recorded it on his world map eighteen hundred years ago.

Strangely enough, for a city which in recent centuries has played such a dominant role in the political, cultural and economic life of the nation, Warsaw took a long time to make its mark. In fact, it did not become a permanent part of the Polish state until 1526, having formed part of the Principality of Mazovia up to that date. But in 1524 Prince Stanisław died, followed two years later by his brother Janusz, the last of their line—their joint tombstone survives to this day in the south aisle of Warsaw's St. John's cathedral—whereupon Mazovia was finally incorporated into Poland.

From that point on, progress was rapid. As we have seen, Warsaw became the capital in 1596, and during the next decades the important noble families and ecclesiastical orders, wishing to locate near the court, embellished the city and its suburbs with numerous palaces, churches and convents. The destruction caused by the Swedish-Polish War of 1655–60 occasioned more building and rebuilding, a process which continued throughout the next century as well. Indeed, by far the most impressive construction programme was undertaken by Poland's last king, the eminently cultured (and politically disastrous) Stanisław August Poniatowski, who went on building right up to the time of the Third — and final — Partition, and even gave his name to a special architectural style, Stanislavian Classicism, influenced by Palladian ideals but softer and more romantic than other forms of Neo-classicism then sweeping Europe.

The suppression of the Kościuszko Uprising and the ensuing massacre of thousands of Warsovians, followed by the loss of independence, sent the capital into a rapid decline. However, the opening of the Warsaw-Vienna railway line in 1845 and its subsequent extension to St. Petersburg provided a vital stimulus for economic growth, and by the end of the century Warsaw had become one of the most important centres of Polish industry. The population grew by leaps and bounds, rising from a mere 63,500 in 1800 to 690,000 in 1900, and passing the million mark in 1919. By the outbreak of war in 1939, the total had increased to 1,300,000, including over 400,000 Jews, which made Warsaw one of the largest centres of Jewish population in Europe.

The year 1939 marked a crucial turning-point in the history of Warsaw. Certainly very few observers in Poland or indeed anywhere else could have anticipated the fate that awaited the city, not even when German bombs began to drop on Warsaw on 1 September 1939, the first day of the Nazi invasion. On 8 September the city was besieged, and although it held out bravely, it was finally forced to capitulate on 28 September.

In the following month the first hostages were arrested, and on 3 November the first death sentence was passed — on two women who had torn down Nazi placards. The day after Christmas the first mass executions took place, in Wawer, a right-bank suburb, claiming 107 victims. In 1940 the pace of the Nazi terror accelerated, and the first prisoners were transported to concentration camps. At the same time, Poland's artistic heritage began to be shipped off to the Reich, although much was saved, owing to the bravery and ingenuity of many Polish curators, who secretly buried or otherwise hid a large proportion of the country's treasures. The year 1940 also saw the establishment of a ghetto in the north-central part of the city, in which all the Jews of Warsaw were to be confined on rations totalling a mere 184 calories a day. This was the first ghetto in the history of Warsaw, for although there had previously been large concentrations of Jews in some quarters, by and large Jews and Gentiles had lived — if not in perfect peace — then at least together.

The following year, 1941, brought the first of the public executions in which thousands upon thousands of Warsovians died. The sites of these executions were never forgotten during the war, and during reconstruction dozens of commemorative plaques were set into walls throughout the city. Even now, more than three decades after the end of the war, they are invariably marked by wreaths and bouquets. Their wording is almost always the same, namely, that this site has been 'consecrated by the blood of x number of Poles shot here on a given date'. They are very moving in their terse simplicity and, perhaps more than any other type of monument, help to give the visitor at least some understanding of what Warsaw endured during the war.

Besides public executions, there were also the notorious 'łapanki' (round-ups). Suddenly, without any warning, a street would be closed off, or a tram stopped and everyone in it would be arrested and transported to concentration camps, or to do forced labour in Germany. Many did not even get that far, thousands perishing in such infamous places as Pawiak prison, at ulica Dzielna (i.e. Dzielna Street) 24/26, and the former Gestapo headquarters at No. 25 in the aleja I Armii Wojska Polskiego (First Polish Army Avenue), still commonly known by its shorter pre-war name, aleja Szucha. Both have been turned into Museums of Resistance and Martyrdom, where — if one has the emotional stamina — one may see prisoners' cells, transcripts of interrogations, execution notices, and torture instruments.

The underground stepped up its retaliations against the Nazis. The first of Warsaw's two uprisings began on 19 April 1943 in the Ghetto, whose population had been reduced — by starvation, disease, public executions and the concentration camps — to only some 70,000. Almost weaponless in the face of German tanks, flame-throwers and repeated air attacks, the Jews nevertheless held out until 16 May, when their leader, Mordechai Anielewicz, and his companions were burned alive in their bunker as they made a last stand against the enemy. The Nazis then razed the ghetto to the ground, at the same time killing or shipping off to concentration camps those Jews who had survived. Today the Muranów housing estate occupies much of this area, but in the centre, on ul. (= ulica) Zamenhofa, on the site of Anielewicz's bunker, the heroes of the uprising are commemorated by an impressive monument by the sculptor, Natan Rappaport, one side of which depicts Jewish fighting men, and the other women and old men being deported from the Ghetto. A few streets away to the south, at aleja Swierczewskiego 79, the Jewish History Institute contains a large and very moving permanent exhibition dealing with the Ghetto Uprising, as well as the history of Jewish settlement in Poland.

Despite the crushing defeat of the Ghetto, the rest of the city was fiercely determined to continue resisting the invader, and on 1 August 1944 bitter fighting erupted throughout the city. This, the second and larger of the two uprisings, lasted for 63 days, until 2 October, when the insurgents finally capitulated. By then, over 200,000 civilians and insurgents had lost their lives, and much of the city lay in ruins. The Nazis then deported the survivors, the insurgents being sent directly to prisoner-of-war camps, and began the systematic destruction of the city. Soviet and Polish forces had succeeded in liberating Praga, or right-bank Warsaw, on 14 September, less than three weeks before the end of the uprising, so it was spared, but throughout Nazi-held, left-bank Warsaw the procedure was everywhere the same. First, special squads removed furniture and all other objects of value from the buildings. Then, armed with flame-throwers and dynamite, commandos proceeded to burn and blow up literally everything, street by street, and house by house. They even tore up the city's tramlines and telephone cables, at the same time destroying its electricity, water and sewage systems. It was the same story in the parks, where tree after tree was uprooted and burned. More than three months later, on 17 January 1945, when the Soviet and Polish armies at last succeeded in crossing the Vistula to liberate Warsaw, the Nazis had still not completed their work, but, even so, the scale of destruction was colossal. Roughly 85 per cent of the capital's housing had been destroyed, that is to say, either totally razed to the ground, leaving entire quarters like the Ghetto as nothing more than fields of rubble, or, at best, reduced to roofless, floorless, windowless shells. The death toll was equally staggering; an estimated 800,000 Warsovians had lost their lives during the German occupation — over 60 per cent of the city's 1939 population. Apart from Praga, which had a population of some 160,000 by the beginning of 1945, Warsaw was virtually deserted.

The reborn Polish state was faced with a serious problem: should it even attempt to rebuild Warsaw, or should it transfer the capital elsewhere? The question was resolved a fortnight after liberation when the Council of Ministers declared that Warsaw would indeed continue as the capital, and that rebuilding should begin immediately to house the thousands of Warsovians and others who had begun to pour into the destroyed city. The difficulties were immense: 20 million cubic metres of rubble had to be cleared, thousands of bodies lying amidst the rubble had to be buried, and — most serious of all — the retreating Germans had left behind some 100,000 mines. People returning to Warsaw that first post-war winter were forced to take shelter wherever they could find it: in trenches and bunkers, in the cellars of burned-out houses, and literally in holes in the walls.

Living conditions were, to say the very least, primitive. Yet, when the Bureau of Town Planning consulted the returning population about priorities for reconstruction, the majority replied that the first priority must be the Old Town, with its narrow, cobbled streets and scores of historic buildings. To aid in the reconstruction, countless pre-war photographs, paintings, sketches and archives were consulted, many submitted by the Warsovians themselves. Finally, a master plan was drawn up, and rebuilding began.

The rubble was cleared by the end of 1945, and by the early 1960s most of the city had been rebuilt, although, here and there, rebuilding continues. Indeed, two of the largest projects — the Royal Castle and Ujazdów Castle, Zygmunt III's country residence in the south of the sprawling city — were begun as recently as the early seventies.

Both in the Old Town and throughout the capital as a whole, the following basic principles have been adopted. First, only historic buildings and architectural ensembles have been reconstructed, for it would have been senseless to rebuild the hundreds of unsightly tenements and other substandard housing that had disfigured so much of Warsaw — and, indeed, most other European cities — before the war. (The latter are gradually being replaced by modern blocks of flats.) Second, it has been general policy to return to the original architecture of a given building, eliminating the accretions of later periods, particularly the nineteenth century. Third, as far as possible, original materials have been employed, which meant painstaking searches through the rubble for usable bits of architectural detail and decoration, such as architraves, cornices, flooring and tiles. Where new material has been used, and by and large it has had to be used, owing to the vast extent of war damage, considerable effort has been taken to make it blend in with the original building fabric. Fourth, reconstruction has been practical, the beautifully restored exteriors concealing modern flats, shops, offices, artists' studios etc.

Looking back to 1945, it seems incredible that the Poles could have even contemplated the rebuilding of Warsaw, for here was a country which lay prostrate by war. But, of course, that was precisely why the project was undertaken. A nation so shattered needed a rallying point, a sense of common purpose; and, like any other nation, it needed a capital that it could be proud of. Above all, it needed to forget the horrors of war — to pretend that Warsaw had never been destroyed.

That is exactly the impression one gets when standing at the Praga end of the Śląsko-Dąbrowski Bridge, which every visitor to Warsaw ought to do at least once, because it offers by far the best view of the city. Directly across the broad Vistula, at the other end of the bridge, stands the massive pink block of the recently rebuilt Royal Castle (Zamek Królewski). To the north, perched above the Vistula, sits the Old Town (Stare Miasto), its five- and six-storey houses dominated by the high-gabled, red-brick St. John's Cathedral. Further to the north lies the New Town (Nowe Miasto), centred on the domed Church of the Nuns of the Holy Sacrament. The district is so called because it is a century or so 'newer' than the Old Town, though it is still very old, dating back to the late fourteenth century. Its present buildings, however, are largely eighteenth-century in style. In the background, alas, a few inappropriately positioned high-rise office buildings are beginning to spoil the view, but even so the whole panorama would be immediately recognizable to Bernardo Bellotto, who, as court painter to Stanisław August Poniatowski, spent a great deal of time in the capital in the middle of the eighteenth century. In fact, his beautifully detailed views of the city, a number of which are in its National Museum, were used as guides in reconstruction.

We shall soon be crossing the Vistula to explore the Old Town in greater detail, but as we are now in Praga, let us explore this often overlooked area. This is one of the traditionally working-class areas of the city, and its 'East End', both literally and figuratively. Like the Cockneys, its people used to speak a racier language than their more prosperous neighbours in other parts of town, but local differences are being ironed out now, partly because the old slums of the area are gradually being replaced by modern housing, and more and more newcomers are moving in. As recently as the early '70s, there used to be a colourful 'flea market' on Saturdays just beyond the tatty old church on ul. Skaryszewska, less than half an hour's walk from where we are standing now. One could buy almost anything there, including delicious *pyzy* (raw-potato dumplings), cooked by fat old peasant women who really looked the part. Most of the goods were second-hand, and bargaining was very much the order of the day; and, if one was lucky, one might just find something that *almost* qualified as an antique — I once bought a splendid old German coffee-grinder there — though in Poland most good antiques are sold privately, or through the state-operated DESA shops. There used to be quite a few spivs, some obvious drunks from the night before, and — or so it was said — enormous numbers of pick-pockets. But, for the most part, the 'flea market' was frequented by ordinary Warsovians in search of a bargain, or of goods which, owing to the vagaries of centralized state planning and distribution, were temporarily unavailable in the shops (the latter remains a recurring problem in Poland). But the area has recently been tidied up, and the market has been moved to Rembertów, on the easternmost outskirts of the city. So the local colour is disappearing fast, which is a pity, at least for the tourist, though perhaps not for the people who have to live in it.

Still, the district has some pretty things to attract the eye, as well as one or two curiosities, all of which lie within a few hundred metres of our present vantage-point at the Praga end of the Śląsko-Dąbrowski Bridge. Just behind us, in al. Świerczewskiego, one of Warsaw's main thoroughfares, we find, somewhat surprisingly, a bear-pit with its enormous, usually very lethargic brown bears that never fail to attract an audience, especially on Sundays, when the avenue is filled with strollers. In fact, the scene is not as incongruous as it might seem, for this is the entrance to Praga Park (Park Praski), directly behind which is the zoo (Ogród Zoologiczny). This is not one of the world's great zoos, but it is a good one, and attractively laid out, so it is worth keeping in mind if one is travelling with children.

Almost directly opposite the bear-pit is the red-brick Neo-Gothic parish church of the Archangel Michael and St. Florian, designed by Józef Pius Dziekoński and erected in 1888–1901. Its tall twin towers have made it one of the landmarks of Praga. A few minutes further along al. Świerczewskiego, on the same side as the bear-pit, and at first glance almost as incongruous, is another well-known landmark, the Orthodox Cathedral of St. Mary Magdalene. Built in 1868-9 and recently restored, its five onion domes give it a very un-Polish appearance, though it should be remembered that Warsaw was in tsarist hands for exactly a century (1815–1915), during which time many Russians (i.e. Orthodox) settled in the city. Many of their descendants still live in Warsaw, and these,

together with the Byelorussians and Ukrainians who have traditionally inhabited Poland's eastern and south-eastern borders,
form the bulk of the country's nearly half a million Orthodox, its
largest non-Catholic minority (about one and a half per cent of the
total population). The Cathedral is the seat of their Metropolitan, a
kind of Orthodox archbishop, and the Sunday liturgy there is very
impressive, the choir being one of the finest in Warsaw.

The other building of special interest in this area is the Loreto
chapel, a five-minute walk to the north in ul. Ratuszowa, just outside the zoo. Built in 1640-4 with funds given by King Władysław
IV, the architect was probably the Italian, Constantino Tencalla.
There are several Loreto chapels in Poland, commemorating the
house of the Virgin Mary which, when threatened with destruction
by the Turks, was, according to pious tradition, carried by angels
from Ephesus to Dalmatia and then ultimately to Loreto, in Italy.
The interior of the chapel is Baroque, but it has been remodelled
on several occasions and now wears a Neo-classical façade. Inside,
there is a fifteenth-century sculpture of the Madonna and Child
from Kamionek church in another part of Praga.

We can cross the river now, using the Śląsko-Dąbrowski Bridge,
because it is the nearest to the Old Town. Climbing up the escarpment to the left, at the Warsaw end of the bridge, is the pretty little
quarter of Mariensztat. At first glance it looks like an extension of
the Old Town, but it is actually of much later date, having been
founded as late as 1762. It was originally one of the so-called 'jurisdictions', i.e. suburbs laid out privately and governed by their
owners, who were either members of the nobility or the Church.
Nearly a score of these private towns were established between the
mid-sixteenth and mid-eighteenth centuries, but following the
municipal reorganization of 1791 they were all abolished and
joined administratively to the capital. Mariensztat, which is the
Polish spelling of the German Marienstadt, or Maria's City, takes it
name from one of the original owners of the district, Maria
Potocka.

Straight ahead of us, al. Świerczewskiego disappears into a
tunnel constructed under the Old Town in 1947-9 as part of the
Trasa Wschód-Zachód, or East-West Thoroughfare. (The initials
W-Z have been adopted as the name of a delicious and very rich
chocolate cake served with whipped cream, which is meant to be
available only in the vicinity of the Thoroughfare, although I
myself have eaten splendid *wuzetki* in other parts of Warsaw as
well.) We have a choice; we can use the pedestrian escalator inside

the tunnel, or we can climb the steps outside, cars being useless in the Old Town, which is a pedestrian precinct. Either way, we end up in Castle Square (plac Zamkowy), which was originally a courtyard of the Royal Castle but was cleared in 1644 to allow the construction of the Zygmunt III Column. The oldest monument in Warsaw, it carries a statue of the king who transferred the capital from Cracow to Warsaw and was erected by his son, Władysław IV. One of its designers was Constantino Tencalla, who was also probably responsible for the Loreto Chapel in Praga. Like most of the Old Town, the Column was blown up towards the end of the last war, though the statue itself was only damaged and has since been repaired.

On the east side of the square stands the Royal Castle, the largest single building in the Old Town, and both one of the youngest and one of the oldest. Youngest, because rebuilding was begun as recently as 1971. Oldest, because a royal residence has stood on this site since the end of the thirteenth century, when Prince Bolesław II of Mazovia erected a wooden castle here and founded a settlement (the present Old Town) immediately to the north. Over the centuries, the castle underwent numerous reconstructions and transformations, at the same time witnessing many historic events. For example, the protracted parliamentary deliberations that ultimately led to the Union of Lublin, uniting Poland and Lithuania, took place here. This was also the scene, in the sixteenth and seventeenth centuries, of four acts of homage by the Hohenzollern electors of Brandenburg, who then held East Prussia as a Polish fief, a fact which seems bitterly ironic now, considering the events of subsequent centuries. No less ironic is the fact that in 1611, in the Senators' Hall at the north-west end of the castle, the Hetman (Commander-in-Chief) Stanisław Żółkiewski presented to King Zygmunt III and his court a number of important captives brought from Moscow, including Tsar Vasili Shuiski and his brothers.

Later, however, Poland — and the castle — fell on harder times. In the first years after partition, the Prussians, who then held Warsaw, painted the silver eagles in Stanisław August's throne-room black, a sign of the dismembered nation's grievous state. Then, in 1831, when the Russians regained the capital following the defeat of the November Insurrection, the castle treasures were plundered, part going to the tsar himself, part to his marshal Ivan Paskiewicz, and the remainder to the latter's underlings. The final tragedy came at the end of the 1944 Uprising, when the castle was almost completely destroyed.

Projects for rebuilding the castle had been considered by successive governments ever since the war, but because of the enormous cost involved, nothing was ever done about it. However, the issue was put in a different perspective by the events of December 1970, when the former Communist party boss Władysław Gomułka, who had led Poland since 1956, was replaced by Edward Gierek following serious rioting in many cities over food-price rises. A month later, the new government, sensing the popular support that the idea would have, at last gave the go-ahead, and reconstruction was begun shortly afterwards. But, because of the immense cost involved (estimated at 30 million dollars), it was to be financed entirely by voluntary contributions, although state credits, which have already been repaid, were also made available.

The Poles responded generously, giving both money and valuable objects to decorate the castle. People of Polish origin abroad made large donations as well, which were particularly useful for the purchase of the many materials and furnishings which could only be obtained in the West, for since the Polish *złoty* is a soft currency, i.e. not directly convertible against gold or the dollar, it is valueless abroad. (Thus, Polish firms wishing to buy goods in the West must either pay in a convertible foreign currency or resort to barter, exchanging their own merchandise for the desired Western goods.) As a result of countless donations, the reconstruction of the exterior has now been completed, giving it a largely Baroque appearance, with some Gothic elements, although a certain amount of interior work, particularly furnishing, remains to be done.

At the left, or north-west end of the castle we come to the most attractive approach to the heart of the Old Town, ul. Świętojańska (St. John's Street), which takes its name from the Catholic cathedral, one of the first buildings on our right. (In fact, the cathedral bears the somewhat bizarre dedication of the 'Decapitation of St. John the Baptist', but like the Warsovians themselves, we shall call it simply St. John's.) Erected at the turn of the thirteenth and fourteenth centuries, it is the oldest church in Warsaw, although it did not become a cathedral until 1797. Since 1946, it has been the chief seat of the Polish Primate (still, at the time of writing, the famous Cardinal Wyszyński), although his official title remains 'Archbishop of Warsaw and Gniezno', the latter being the ancient primatial see, in Great Poland.

Because of its considerable size and proximity to the Royal Castle, St. John's was often used — even before the transfer of the capital to Warsaw — for important state occasions, such as the opening of the Sejm, and royal coronations. Like the castle, it has been rebuilt frequently, acquiring perhaps its most bizarre accretion in the 1830s, when its high-gabled west front was covered in English neo-Gothic, with tracery, pinnacles and turrets reminiscent of Fonthill Abbey. The cathedral was damaged by the bombing of 1939, and during the Uprising the front line between the Nazis and the insurgents passed through it on more than one occasion. Following the defeat of the Uprising, it was burned and dynamited, only two chapels escaping complete destruction.

Post-war reconstruction has made it Gothic once again, and it is now a red-brick, three-aisled hall church (i.e., with nave and two side aisles, all of the same height), of a type which we shall see throughout northern and western Poland. Wartime destruction has deprived it of most of its former furnishings, giving it a somewhat stark appearance. Even so, it still contains several monuments of interest to the visitor. We have already mentioned one earlier in this chapter, the tombstone in the south aisle to Stanisław and Janusz, the last princes of Mazovia, who died in 1524 and 1526 respectively. The curious pose of the two princes, lying at roughly a 45° angle to the wall, is a typically Polish feature which we shall encounter repeatedly during our travels through the country. Further along the aisle is the enormous monument to Stanisław Małachowski, Marshal (i.e. President) of the reforming Four-Year Sejm (1788–92), erected according to the designs of the famous Danish Neo-classical sculptor, Bertl Thorvaldsen. Surmounted by a life-size statue of the great statesman, it is guarded at its base by the equally large figures of a Roman soldier and an American Indian warrior, personifying valour, ancient and modern. In the Baryczka family chapel — one of the two to come through the war reasonably intact — there is a late-Gothic miracle-working crucifix which was formerly considered to be Spanish but is now held to be of Wrocław workmanship. According to legend, the figure's head used to grow real hair, which was cut annually by a local virgin. Rather less extraordinary is the fact that Henryk Sienkiewicz (1846–1916), the Nobel Prize winner and author of *Quo Vadis*, is buried in the crypt, along with a number of archbishops and other churchmen, politicians and members of the extinct Mazovian ruling house.

Now we have a choice. Our next major site is the Old Town Market Square, but there are two ways of getting there. One route takes us back out into ul. Świętojańska, where, immediately adjacent to the cathedral on the north side, stands the late-Renaissance Jesuit church of St. Mary's. (In Poland, churches belonging to a religious order are usually referred to by the name of the order, rather than the patron. Thus, a church like St. Mary's is more likely to be referred to by the Poles, and particularly their guide-books, as the Jesuit Church, than as St. Mary's.) It is a pretty, almost entirely white structure, and worth entering if only to view the tall, graceful dome at its east end. Its west gable, with its rows of niches, finials and pilasters typical of the 'Lublin Renaissance' style which we shall encounter so frequently in the south-east of the country, provides a sharp contrast to the equally steep, but much more severe 'organ-pipe' gable of the cathedral next-door.

A few steps further along ul. Świętojańska and we are in the Old Town Market Square. But, if we had taken the second, more attractive route to the square, we would have left the cathedral by its south door, entering narrow ul. Dziekania (Dean's Street), with its covered overhead passage which formerly linked the cathedral with the castle. Ul. Dziekania leads in turn to the Kanonia (Canonry), one of the prettiest spots in the whole of Warsaw. It is a triangular-shaped 'square' and used to be a cemetery, until it was paved over in 1780. So it has always been something of a quiet backwater. The picturesque three-storey houses, rendered in pastel shades of yellow, tan, salmon, orange and pink, used to be the residences of the cathedral canons, hence the name 'Kanonia'. They now wear Renaissance and Baroque façades, but most of them are even older, dating from the turn of the fifteenth and sixteenth centuries. (They have, of course, been reconstructed, following near-total destruction in 1944.) From Kanonia our route leads through the slightly later ul. Jezuicka (Jesuit Street) into the Old Town Market Square.

This is not merely the nucleus of the Old Town, but probably the best known (to Pole and non-Pole alike) example of post-war reconstruction in the entire country. It was certainly one of the earliest, begun within a few weeks of liberation and completed by 1953. It was also one of the most ambitious, for this is one of the largest market squares in Europe, measuring 73 by 90 metres, and containing a wealth of decorative features. Whatever survived the war was, of course, used in the rebuilding of the square, but most of the ornamentation, as indeed the large majority of the houses themselves, had to be constructed anew. It was all done with great love and care, for this was the heart of the Warsovians' martyred city, and the result is an extremely attractive ensemble, particularly at night, when the street lamps lining the square heighten the dramatic impact of the area. In fact, after having lived within a stone's throw of the square for nearly a year, and seeing it literally hundreds of times, I would strongly suggest viewing it at night *only* after one has seen it by day, because to do the reverse is bound to lead to a certain feeling of anti-climax.

Houses began to be built around the Market Square in the early 1300s, and a century later a town hall was erected in the centre, although it was demolished in 1817. In the late Middle Ages these were the residences of prosperous merchants, many of whom were either German or Italian, underlining the fact that prior to the nineteenth century the bulk of the country's middle class was of foreign origin, the Poles themselves being by and large either too proud (the nobility) or too humble (the peasantry) to engage in trade. The area suffered five major fires between 1431 and 1749, and by the beginning of the present century it had become run-down, inhabited largely by poor artisans and tradesmen, their stalls and stands filling the Market Square. It was restored after 1912 and, of course, largely rebuilt following the last war. What we see now are four- and five-storey houses of basically sixteenth-century shape, but with exteriors of later periods, covered, like the rest of the Old Town, in plaster of various colours, and usually crowned with steep attics (the 'Warsaw lanterns') serving as sky-lights.

The four sides of the square—Dekert, Barss, Zakrzewski and Kołłątaj—bear the names of important figures in eighteenth-century Warsaw, the last, with its wealth of decoration, being on the whole the most interesting and attractive from an architectural point of view. No. 21 houses, in its Gothic vaults, one of Warsaw's best restaurants, the 'Krokodyl'. Further along, No. 27, with its handsome Neo-classical wall-paintings, contains one of the city's best wine shops, originally belonging to the Fukier family, who traditionally traced their descent to the Fuggers of Ausburg, the richest and most powerful bankers in the whole of mediaeval Europe. No. 31, on the corner, known traditionally (but in-correctly) as the House of the Dukes of Mazovia, contains a superb early-Baroque doorway and, in a first-floor niche overlooking ul. Wąski Dunaj, a sixteenth-century statue of St. Anne holding the Virgin, who is in turn holding the Christ Child. (Known as 'Anna Samotrzecia', this is a popular old-Polish motif.)

The houses on the north, or Dekert, side have been turned into the Historical Museum of the City of Warsaw (entrance from No. 42), with exhibits portraying the history of the town down to the present day. Every visitor ought to make a point of attending the 20-minute film shown there, covering the destruction of Warsaw and its post-war rebuilding (there is an English version). Perhaps the finest façade on this side is No. 36, which was also the first house on the square to be reconstructed after the war. It was originally built for Mayor Jakub Dzianotti (i.e. Gianotti) in the early seventeenth century and contains another fine Baroque doorway and some interesting green and ochre sgraffiti, i.e., designs formed by scratching a plaster surface to reveal a contrasting colour underneath. The exotic moor's head above the doorway is a sign that Dzianotti was engaged in the import business.

The south side, Zakrzewski, is architecturally the least interesting of the four, but the east side, Barss, offers some special attractions to the visitor. Not the least of these is No. 26, the Kamienne Schodki (Stone Steps) café, named after the steps immediately adjacent, which lead down hill in the direction of the Vistula. Small, intimate and attractively decorated (the brass wall sconces are particularly pretty), this is one of Warsaw's most charming cafés, and in the evening almost invariably filled to capacity. It serves only one hot dish — duck with half a baked apple and fried bread — which I can recommend very highly. The cream cakes, particularly the *wuzetki*, are delicious. Immediately next door, at No. 24, is one of the best bookshops in Warsaw, while No. 10 has been turned into one of the 'Cepelia' (i.e. Centre for Folk and Artistic Products) shops found in most large Polish towns. The ceilings have been painted by artists from the village of Zalipie, a well-known centre of folk art in Tarnów province, in the south of the country.

There are many other sights in the Old Town to tempt the visitor, who will probably want to spend the greater part of a morning or afternoon strolling through the area, wandering down its narrow streets and into picturesque courtyards, or popping into some of its shops, restaurants and cafés. But now our route lies northwards along ul. Nowomiejska (New Town Street) into the New Town itself. The street is intersected by a double row of defence walls — remains of the Old Town's mediaeval fortifications — and a sixteenth-century Barbican gate. All have been restored since the last war and provide a convenient location for Warsaw's lesser known artists to display their works, particularly in summer.

Just beyond the Barbican, ul. Nowomiejska becomes ul. Freta, taking its name from a mediaeval Latin word meaning 'suburb', which is what the New Town was when it was founded at the end of the fourteenth century. Maria Skłodowska, better known to the world as Marie Curie, the discoverer of radium and polonium and twice a Nobel Prize winner, was born in this street, at No. 16, and the house has been turned into a museum devoted to her. Further along, at No. 5, the Samson House, lived the German romantic writer E. T. A. Hoffmann, who served as a Prussian official here shortly after the Third Partition, at the beginning of the last century. A few minutes' walk to the north-east, on the New Town Market Square, stands the church of St. Casimir (the Nuns of the Holy Sacrament). Begun in 1688 on the initiative of Queen Marie Casimire, the French wife of King Jan Sobieski, as a votive offering for the latter's victory over the Turks at Vienna five years earlier, it was originally intended as the Sobieski family burial chapel. (The royal couple were ultimately interred in Wawel Cathedral, in Cracow.) Built in the form of a Greek cross, with a visually very satisfying dome, it is a small white jewel of a church, the work of Tylman van Gameren (1632–1706). Dutch by birth, he arrived in Poland in 1666 and began working for the King six years later, eventually becoming perhaps the finest architect of his day in the entire country.

Churches are fairly thick on the ground in the New Town, and there are at least half a dozen in the area. Of the others, perhaps the most interesting is St. Mary's, at the corner of ul. Przyrynek and ul. Kościelna, slightly to the north of St. Casimir's. Founded in 1411, it is the oldest church in the not-so New Town and possesses, apart from a simple basically Gothic interior, a distinctive — and very late (1581) — Gothic belfry. A few steps to the east, at the end of ul. Kościelna, the visitor has an excellent view of the Vistula and the Praga quarter.

Besides churches, the New Town and the adjacent area contain a number of imposing residences of the formerly very powerful nobility, although now of course they are the property of the state and for the most part house various educational, cultural and governmental institutions. One of these is the Krasiński Palace, standing between a square and a garden each of which is also named after the ancient Krasiński family. It is generally considered the most beautiful Baroque residence in the capital and is the work of several architects, including Tylman van Gameren. Begun in 1677 for Jan Dobrogost Krasiński, Governor of Płock, it was purchased a century later by the State Treasury to house the administrative offices of the country, which is why it is also sometimes called the Palace of the Republic. A grandiloquent exercise in the north-Italian style, and all of 19 bays long, the building is surmounted on both front and back by monumental classical pediments by the sculptor Andreas Schlüter of Gdańsk depicting episodes from the life of the legendary founder of the Krasiński family, the Roman Marcus Valerius Corvinus. Now under restoration, the palace ordinarily houses the special collections of the National Library and is well worth a visit.

From plac Krasińskich we turn south into ul. Miodowa (Honey Street), known as Napoleon Street between 1807 and 1814. Lined with churches and palaces, including Tylman van Gameren's fine Pac Palace at No. 15 (now the Ministry of Health and Social Welfare), Deibel's Branicki Palace at No. 6, and the former Warsaw residence of the bishops of Cracow at No. 5, ul. Miodowa runs into ul. Krakowskie Przedmieście (Cracow Suburb), so-called because it was — and is — on the main road connecting the Royal Castle with the old capital. It is also the first section of the 'Royal Route', which links the castle with Łazienki, King Stanisław August's summer residence in the south of the city. Krakowskie Przedmieście is the capital's most attractive thoroughfare and a favourite place for promenades. It is not difficult to see why. The whole street is tree-lined, providing plenty of cool shade during the warm summer months, and it also contains a number of interesting folk-art shops and bookshops. The Księgarnia im. Wojska Polskiego (Polish Army Bookshop) at No. 11 is well worth remembering because it usually has, on the first floor, a good selection of Polish art books in foreign languages, which, unlike most Polish bookshops, it will actually ship home for you, and fairly cheaply too. There is also a very pleasant café at No. 27, the 'Telimena', named after one of the characters in Adam Mickiewicz's long poem, *Pan Tadeusz* (Mr. Thaddeus), one of the masterpieces of Polish literature. But, of course, it is the beautiful buildings lining the street that constitute its main attraction. There are far too many to list them all, but of the churches, no visitor will want to miss St. Anne's (near the Castle Square), with its vastly impressive Neo-classical façade and detached belfry, and fine eighteenth-century inlay work in the sacristy. (Ask one of the priests for permission to view it.) Opposite ul. Królewska is the pretty little church of St. Joseph (the Nuns of the Visitation), one of the few in Warsaw to come through the last war virtually untouched. It is also one of the capital's best late-Baroque churches, two of its chief glories being its handsome front and the charming boat pulpit of *circa* 1760. Of the secular buildings, one of the handsomest is the Baroque Czartoryski (later Potocki) Palace, which now houses, appropriately enough, the Ministry of Culture and Art. The charming Rococo guardhouse which stands between its two fine neo-Baroque gates now accommodates an art gallery, the 'Kordegarda' with temporary exhibitions of works by modern Polish and foreign painters and sculptors. Directly opposite it — and immediately adjacent to the old Bristol Hotel, once owned by the great pianist Ignacy Jan Paderewski — stands the Koniecpolski (later Radziwiłł) Palace, originally a seventeenth-century structure, but now bearing a cool Neo-classical façade of 1818–19 by Chrystian Piotr Aigner, one of the best Polish architects of his day. After his remodelling, the palace became the residence of the tsarist viceroy, and it is now the official seat of the president of the Council of Ministers. The treaty which created the Warsaw Pact was signed here in 1955, as was the document establishing diplomatic relations between Poland and West Germany.

The large equestrian statue in front of the palace requires some explanation. It portrays Prince Józef Poniatowski, a nephew of the last king of Poland and commander-in-chief of the Polish forces under Napoleon. His great patriotism made him immensely popular in nineteenth-century Poland, and it was said that his heroic death at the battle of Leipzig in 1813 wiped the blot off the Poniatowski escutcheon left by his royal uncle, who had presided over the total dismemberment of the country. The monument, like the Małachowski tomb in the cathedral and the Copernicus Monument in front of the Staszic Palace at the south end of Krakowskie Przedmieście, is by Bertel Thorvaldsen. The outbreak and defeat of the 1830 Insurrection prevented its erection on its present site, as had originally been intended, and it ultimately found its way to Homel in deepest Byelorussia, where General Paskiewicz, the tsarist general who captured Warsaw in 1831, had his residence. In its place a monument was erected to Paskiewicz himself. The Poniatowski monument was finally returned to the capital in 1923 and stood in the plac Zwycięstwa (Victory Square), just behind Krakowskie Przedmieście, until 1944, when it was blown up by the Nazis following the defeat of the Warsaw Uprising. After the war the city of Copenhagen gave the capital a new casting of the monument, which was then placed outside the Orangery at Łazienki. It was only in 1965 that the monument was finally erected on its present site.

Krakowskie Przedmieście is very closely linked with one of Poland's greatest sons, Frederic (in Polish, Fryderyk) Chopin. Born in Żelazowa Wola west of Warsaw in 1810, he and his family soon moved to the capital, where his father obtained a post teaching

French at a local *lycée*. As a child, Chopin used to play the organ at the Church of the Nuns of the Visitation, and for a time the family lived in an outbuilding of the former Czapski Palace (now the Academy of Fine Arts) at Krakowskie Przedmieście 5, where their reconstructed drawing-room is open to the public. It was from here in 1830 that Chopin left for Paris where, following his early death in 1849, he was buried in the cemetery of Père Lachaise. His heart, however, rests in Warsaw — and, more specifically, in the central pillar of the left aisle of the Church of the Discovery of the Cross, at the southern end of Krakowskie Przedmieście. Not far away, at ul. Tamka 41, Tylman van Gameren's masterpiece the Ostrogski Palace now houses the Frederic Chopin Society and Museum, containing a wealth of interesting memorabilia connected with the great composer and pianist. Before the war it was the Warsaw School of Music, which numbered Paderewski amongst its students and the composer Stanisław Moniuszko amongst its professors. According to legend, its deep cellars contain buried treasure watched over by a golden duck, but considering the fact that the palace was extensively remodelled on several occasions and burnt in 1944, it seems very unlikely that either he or the treasure is still on the site.

Beyond the Church of the Discovery of the Cross, the 'Royal Route' continues southward as ul. Nowy Świat (New World), which takes its name from the earliest of the Warsaw 'jurisdictions', dating from 1539. One of the capital's busiest streets, it is lined with low, rather characterless buildings reconstructed after the war in a flat Neo-classical style, and will be of interest to the traveller largely because of the shops, delicatessens and snack-bars that it contains. (Some of the best privately owned clothing shops — and in a Polish context that means some of the best shops — in Warsaw can be found just off Nowy Świat in ul. Rutkowskiego, and also in the pavillion immediately behind, and paralleling, Nowy Świat to the east, near ul. Foksal.) For us, Nowy Świat will be little more than a means of taking us to the treasures that await us in the south of the city. But while crossing al. Jerozolimskie (Jerusalem Avenue), Warsaw's main east-west thoroughfare, and at this point one of the widest, most soul-less boulevards anywhere in Europe, it would be a good idea to note the whereabouts of the National Museum (al. Jerozolimskie 3). It is not one of the world's great museums. In the first place, it never was, and in the second place, the Nazis looted it during the war, although much was hidden by the museum staff. For most visitors with an hour or two to spare, it will have three chief attractions. The first is its fine collection of Polish Gothic painting and sculpture. The second is its views of Warsaw by Bernardo Bellotto, whom the Poles somewhat confusingly give the additional surname of Canaletto, which is the name by which the West knows his equally famous uncle. The third attraction is its set of frescoes from the early Christian cathedral of Faras, in Nubia, in the present-day Sudan. The result of extensive excavations undertaken two decades ago under the general supervision of Kazimierz Michałowski, the *doyen* of Polish archaeologists, the Faras frescoes are a collection unique in Europe.

Continuing south along the 'Royal Route', we almost immediately pass through plac Trzech Krzyży (Three Crosses Square) with its church of St. Alexander (1818–25), reminiscent of the Pantheon in Rome. The architect was Aigner, who also remodelled the façade of the Radziwiłł, or Koniecpolski, Palace. The square marked the end of a Via Dolorosa (Calvary Road), laid out by King August II through the Ujazdów estate to the south. The two columns topped by crosses in front of the church still commemorate this route, and it is these crosses, together with the one on top of the church, which give the square its name.

South of the square, the 'Royal Route' continues as the al. Ujazdowskie, a broad avenue roughly a kilometre long lined with foreign embassies and the mansions of the rich and powerful of nineteenth-century Warsaw. During the last war, al. Ujazdowskie and the district immediately to the west were reserved for Germans and *Volksdeutsche* (Poles of German origin), while all the Polish residents were expelled. The history of Ujazdów goes back a long way, at least to the thirteenth century, when the Prince of Mazovia erected a wooden castle, of which nothing now remains, at Jazdów (the original name of the area). By the time King Stanisław August bought the estate in 1766 for his summer residence, it contained a second, much rebuilt castle, standing on the site of the present structure. To remodel it, he immediately called in Domenico Merlini, who had been a royal architect since 1761 and originally hailed from the region of Lake Lugano. Merlini, who typified the Stanislavian style of romantic Neo-classicism *par excellence*, soon found himself engaged on the work of a lifetime, for the king, a passionate amateur builder, was ultimately to turn the Ujazdów estate into a vast complex of architecture and landscape, one of the finest in eighteenth-century Europe.

In a sense, the remodelling of Ujazdów Castle itself was only a pretext, for by 1784 it had ceased to be a royal residence, becoming

instead a barracks for the Royal Foot Guards. This was burned out
in 1939 and demolished in 1954, but is now being rebuilt. Long
before 1784, however, the king had turned his attention southwards, to what is now known as Łazienki (Little Baths) Park,
where, by the end of his reign in 1795, he, Merlini and the latter's
successors had created some twenty-odd structures of various sizes,
shapes and functions, set in an 'English' landscape park happily
superimposed on a much more formal and symmetrical French
pattern. The earliest was the delicious timber-framed White
Cottage (Biały Domek) begun in 1774, with rich painted interiors
by Jan Bogumił Plersch, including much charming chinoiserie,
something comparatively rare in Poland. Next came the Myślewicki
Palace, which is closed to the public, being reserved for eminent
guests of the Polish government. Other important structures ordinarily open to the public include the Old Orangery (Stara
Pomarańczarnia), the east wing of which contains one of Europe's
few surviving eighteenth-century theatres. The walls of the latter
are decorated with *trompe-l'oeil* paintings, also by Plersch,
depicting an audience of the period, including an old-fashioned
Polish nobleman in traditional costume with a shaven head and
enormous moustache, and a Frenchified dandy in a powdered wig.
The acoustics are excellent, and period plays and chamber operas
are occasionally presented here in summer. A theatre of a very
different sort is located on the long, narrow canal running through
the centre of the park. Here, in 1790, Johann Christian Kamsetzer
built the king a large stone amphitheatre, derived from the one at
Herculaneum and capable of accommodating 1500 spectators. The
most original feature of the theatre is its stage, which is situated on
an islet. The permanent backdrop consists of ruined columns based
on the Temple of Jupiter at Baalbek, in addition to trees and
statuary representing classical and modern dramatists. Like the Old
Orangery, the amphitheatre is used for stage performances in the
summer season.

But probably our chief reason for coming to Łazienki lies a
hundred metres or so north along the canal — the famous Palace on
the Island (Pałac na Wyspie). Here, in 1683–90 Tylman van
Gameren built a bathing pavilion for the Grand Marshal of Poland,
Stanisław Herakliusz Lubomirski, where the latter could come with
his friends to escape the worries of state. Ninety years later, its new
owner, King Stanisław August, used to stay here while inspecting
work in the White Cottage and the Myślewicki Palace. Finally, he
decided that this, after all, would be the ideal location for his

summer residence, whereupon Merlini set to work remodelling and enlarging it, at the same time adding a top storey, a belvedere and side pavilions. The first three rooms that the visitor sees preserve elements of Baroque decoration, but by and large this is a quintessentially Neo-classical building, and indeed one of the best examples of that style in the entire country. Perhaps the most stunning of all the rooms is the Ballroom, with its two large chimney-pieces, beautifully restored ceiling and crystal chandeliers, and broad expanse of parquet floor. Guests and members of the king's retinue lived in outbuildings, the exceptions being his English valet, Ryx, who occupied three rooms on the first floor, and his librarian.

It was here that the king gave his famous 'Thursday Dinners', where he entertained the best writers, poets, scholars and artists of his day. Whatever his faults as a statesman and politician, Stanisław August was undoubtedly the greatest patron of the arts that his country has ever known, a fact which was lost on the Nazis, who, in December 1944 soaked the palace interior with petrol and set it alight. They then drilled hundreds of holes in the walls in preparation for dynamiting it, but before they had an opportunity to carry out their plans, Warsaw was liberated. As throughout the city, it is hard to believe that the beautifully decorated rooms which we have just viewed are in fact the result of post-war reconstruction and restoration, but such is indeed the case, as the visitor will see from the small exhibition dealing with the recent history of the palace, in the former royal loggia outside the chapel.

After we have climbed back up to al. Ujazdowskie—much of Łazienki Park lies on a slope—two objects catch our attention. The first is the Chopin Monument, redolent of romantic agony, both the composer and the tempest-tossed willow above him looking as if they are about to be swept away by the sheer force of emotion. Vaguely *art nouveau*, it must have seemed rather daring when it emerged from the hands of its sculptor, Wacław Szymanowski, in the first years of this century, but by the time it was finally erected in 1926 it had begun to look more than a bit dated. In any case, the Nazis, appreciating the patriotic force of Chopin's music, cut the monument to pieces and smelted down its bronze, but in 1958 an exact copy was re-erected, and on Sundays in the summertime recitals of the great composer's music are presented at its base.

A few minutes' walk to the south, and we come to the Belvedere Palace, originally a timber residence built for Krzysztof Pac, Chancellor of Lithuania, in 1662, which derived its name from its beautiful views over the Vistula. A century later, it was acquired by Stanisław August, who eventually established a porcelain workshop (Belvedere ware) in its north annex. Later, in 1818–22, Jakub Kubicki rebuilt it in the Neo-classical style for the brother of Tsar Alexander I, the Grand Duke Constantine, who had contracted a morganatic marriage with a Polish noblewoman. It is now the official residence of the Chairman of the Council of State and is closed to the public, but a superb view of it may be had from below in Łazienki Park.

From Belvedere Palace, the 'Royal Route' — ul. Belwederska, ul. Jana Sobieskiego and al. Wilanowska — leads us straight to Wilanów Palace, which must be, by any reckoning, one of the major events in our tour of Poland. But either *en route* or on the way back, I would strongly suggest making two short detours. The first is to the small Bernardine church of St. Anthony of Padua, which is often, and somewhat confusingly, known as St. Boniface's, from the name of the parish in which it is located. On ul. Czerniakowska, which parallels ul. Jana Sobieskiego to the east, it was a gift of the same Lubomirski who built the original Palace on the Island, and was designed by Tylman van Gameren, which is reason enough for making a detour. Erected in 1687–9 and largely spared by the war, it has the form of a Greek cross surmounted by a dome, and contains interesting Baroque stucco work and frescoes, as well as a fine early sixteenth-century triptych from Quentin Massys' studio. Entrance is by a door at the end of the courtyard south of the church. In the passage leading to the church itself, be sure to note, on the right, an amusing eighteenth-century primitive painting of the Dance of Death. True to the prejudices of his day, the artist, no doubt a simple priest or local dauber, consigns to perdition every category of person — Protestants, Jews, Muslims, richly dressed women etc. — except his own.

My other detour would be westward to the Królikarnia (Rabbit Warren) in Arkadia Park, in ul. Puławska. Built in 1782–6 to Domenico Merlini's designs, it was the property of one Karol de Valery Thomatis, who was manager of the King's theatres, and also something of a gambler and adventurer. A handsome Neo-classical structure perched on the very edge of the Vistula escarpment, it takes its name from the fact that rabbits were bred here and hunted from the house. Burned out during the last war, it has been restored and now houses some hundred-odd pieces by the outstanding Polish sculptor, Xawery Dunikowski (1875–1964). His work, some of which is vaguely reminiscent of Rodin, is full of symbolism and metaphor and deserves to be far better known in the West.

Eleven kilometres south of the centre of Warsaw, at the end of the 'Royal Route', Wilanów awaits us. It was originally a small village and manor house named Milanów when Jan Sobieski chose it as his country residence, but as Polish kings at that time were forbidden to own landed property, it was acquired, in 1677, through the intermediary of the Crown Treasurer, Marek Matczyński, in whose name the deed was drawn up. The new residence which the King had built there was usually referred to as 'Villa Nova', which eventually fused with 'Milanów' to produce 'Wilanów'.

Tylman van Gameren may have had a hand in the original rebuilding, but by and large it is the work of a Polish architect of Italian descent called Augustyn Locci, who was also the King's secretary and chief art adviser. After the King's death, Wilanów passed to his son Konstanty, and after his death to a succession of owners which reads like a *Who's Who* of the Polish nobility: Sieniawska, Czartoryski, King August II, Lubomirska, Potocki, Branicki. The palace has undergone a number of remodellings, particularly in the 1720s, when long wings were added to the north and south, creating a courtyard on the entrance side. But what the visitor sees on arrival is still essentially Baroque in style, particularly the sunny, cream-coloured exterior with its rich carving, elaborate window and door recesses, highly ornamental corner towers and wealth of statuary. The interiors are of various periods, but here too, the Baroque predominates. A high proportion of the work was done by what was virtually the first generation of fine Polish artists and craftsmen, for King Jan organized a royal studio at Wilanów, with the double purpose of decorating the palace and at the same time creating a nucleus of native artistic talent. The results are very impressive, particularly after the skilful restoration work carried out following the last war. Of special interest are the painted ceilings in the Antechambers and Bedchambers of the King and Queen. Depicting allegories of the four seasons, they are the work of Jerzy Eleuter Szymonowicz-Siemiginowski, whose tongue-twisting name did not prevent him from becoming one of Poland's earliest painters of note. There is much fine stucco and fresco work throughout the palace, including an interesting set of wall paintings depicting scenes from the legend of Apollo, recently discovered under the plaster of the Queen's Study. Less dazzling than the grand ground-floor rooms, but not less interesting, is the upper half-storey, much of which now houses a gallery of Polish painting. The visitor will probably be particularly fascinated by the first room, with its numerous 'coffin portraits' from the seventeenth and eighteenth centuries. Generally depicting members of the gentry or lesser nobility, and often by fairly naive local artists, they were usually attached to the end of the coffin (hence their shape) before the funeral service, and then removed prior to burial and hung in the parish or estate church.

The palace stands in the middle of a large park, the oldest part being the formal Italian-Baroque gardens to the east. The park contains a number of outbuildings, the most interesting of which are probably the Chinese summer-house with its restored frescoes (1806), a few minutes' walk north of the gardens, and the former riding school, now housing the world's first poster museum (Muzeum Plakatu), to the right of the entrance to the palace.

The only fly in the ointment is the fact that Wilanów is one of the most popular tourist attractions in Poland, not merely in the summer, but even as late as September, when it is a favourite resort of school parties. Many hundreds of vistiors are 'processed' each day — one is obliged, alas, to join a guided tour — but, even so, the supply of tickets is limited. So the traveller might do well to join one of the English-language tours of Wilanów and Łazienki organized by ORBIS (the Polish National Tourist Office). Places may be booked directly at one of the Warsaw branches of ORBIS, or through the major hotels.

If I have given the impression that the beauties of Warsaw are to be found almost exclusively in the Old and New Towns and along the 'Royal Route', this has been intentional, for the actual heart of the city, though it contains many hotels, restaurants and shops useful to the visitor, is not of much interest to him as a sightseer. Largely a nineteenth-century creation, central Warsaw was heavily damaged during the last war and has largely been rebuilt. But the heavy hand of Stalinism in the first post-war decade, stifling virtually all creativity, coupled with a chronic shortage of money, materials and skilled manpower, produced much work of extremely mediocre design, though there are a few fine new buildings, such as the ultra-modern Central Station (Dworzec Centralny) on al. Jerozolimskie. Unforutnately, the one building which, more than any other, dominates the city, is also one of the most banal, the gigantic — 234 metres to the tip of its television mast — Palace of Culture and Science. In fact, because it is so tall, and the Warsaw area so flat, it is almost invariably the first structure the visitor glimpses, whether he or she arrives by land or by air. Strongly reminiscent of the colossal Moscow University skyscraper, one of

whose architects, Lev V. Rudniev, also designed the Palace, it was a
gift of the Soviet Union to the city of Warsaw and was erected in
1952-5. In fact, it is so large that, together with the surrounding
plac Defilad (Parade Square), it covers the site of several pre-war
city blocks. (The former street intersections are marked out in the
pavement.) It is easy to be rude about the Palace. It is heavy and
massive, particularly its ugly, sprawling base, with its two dozen
pretentious Corinthian porticos. The base, main structure and
corner towers are surmounted by ridiculous pseudo-Renaissance
finials reminiscent of the parapets of such noted Polish buildings as
the Cracow Cloth Hall and Baranów Castle. This bizarre attempt at
adding a quasi-national flavour to an otherwise characterless pile
has earned the Palace the nickname, amongst architectural critics,
of 'Stalinist wedding cake'. Witty Poles describe it as *'maƚy ale
gustowny'* ('small but tasteful'). All the same, the Palace serves two
useful, albeit very different functions. First, it provides Warsaw
with a focal point, however banal, the Royal Castle and Old Town
being too far away from the city centre to fulfil that role. Second, its
38 storeys and 3,300 rooms and halls house a vast number of
scientific and cultural institutions, including the Polish Academy of
Sciences, several departments of Warsaw University, the Polish
UNESCO Committee and the Polish PEN Club, as well as four
theatres, the same number of cinemas, a vast Congress hall seating
3,000 people, Museums of Technology and Zoology, three
restaurants, numerous sports and athletic halls and a swimming
pool. Specifically for the tourist, there is an observation terrace on
the thirtieth floor, which offers a spectacular view of Warsaw.

Of the other buildings in central Warsaw worthy of comment,
one is, to be exact, an entire architectural ensemble, Antonio
Corazzi's Bank Square, now called plac Dzierżyńskiego (Dzierżyński
Square), north-west of the pretty Ogród Saski (Saxon Gardens). An
interesting and successful example of town planning in the Neo-
classical style, it was erected in the 1820s at about the same time as
Corazzi's massive Teatr Wielki (Grand Theatre), one of the largest
opera houses in Europe, at the eastern end of the gardens. But
perhaps the finest single building in the city centre, and one of the
best of its period anywhere in Poland, is Szymon Bogumiƚ Zug's
Lutheran church of 1777-81. A Neo-classical cylinder surmounted
by a dome and lantern turret, austere and grey on the outside,
white and gold inside, its pure geometric shapes offer an extremely
satisfying contrast — one might almost say an antidote — to too much
Baroque. Still a place of worship on Sunday mornings, it has superb

acoustics and is often used for choral concerts.

A car is useful in Warsaw for reaching outlying sights, such as Wilanów, but in the city centre — and this applies to most Polish towns — it can be almost a liability, because of the growing number of one-way streets and the shortage of parking places. Visitors with cars might well prefer to leave them at their hotels and do their explorations on foot. Moreover, Warsaw and most other Polish towns are covered by a thick bus (and usually tram) network, which is indicated on most town plans on sale in bookshops. Both buses and trams can be unbelievably crowded and uncomfortable at rush hours, but they are also extremely cheap. Bus tickets (*bilety autobusowe*) are the same price everywhere and must be pre-purchased at the thousands of '*Ruch*' ('Movement') kiosks found on most major streets throughout Poland. The same applies to tram tickets (*bilety tramwajowe*), which are even cheaper than bus tickets. Few buses and trams have conductors, so immediately after boarding passengers are expected to cancel their tickets themselves in the small, box-like machines provided for this purpose, and then to retain them until the end of their journey. On express buses, which are designated by letters rather than numbers, cancel two tickets instead of one. If you appear to be one of the few passengers cancelling a ticket, this is because most regular travellers have season tickets. In any case, it is inadvisable to travel without a ticket, as spot checks are occasionally made by plain-clothed inspectors, and ticketless passengers are fined heavily.

A taxi (*taksówka*) will ordinarily pick up passengers only at a taxi stand (*postój taksówek*), although some do occasionally stop if flagged down, particularly at night. Fares are rather cheaper than in either London or New York.

It is tempting to linger in Warsaw, but we do, after all, have the entire country ahead of us. As for sightseeing in the immediate vicinity of the capital, our choice is fairly limited. Mazovia, the ancient province of which Warsaw is the centre, is extremely flat and featureless, and one does not visit it for its landscape. Poland has beautiful landscapes, but they lie elsewhere. Furthermore, because the soil of Mazovia is poor, the province itself was poor, at least until the rise of Warsaw, so its architectural treasures are fairly limited in number. Finally as the land was so flat, it almost invited invasion, so what little there originally was has often been damaged, if not destroyed.

Even so, there are at least one or two excursions which may tempt us to leave the capital. One is hardly an excursion at all, involving merely a short drive or bus or tram ride to the northern outskirts of Warsaw. Here, in the middle of the Bielany Woods overlooking the Vistula, stands one of the capital's finest seventeenth-century churches, the former Camaldolite church, now the parish church of the Immaculate Conception. The Camaldolites, an order of hermits originally deriving from Camaldoli in Italy, enjoyed considerable popularity and even royal patronage in seventeenth-century Poland, during which time they established a number of monasteries, such as the huge church at Wigry, in the extreme north-east of the country, and also one outside Cracow, the latter being the sole house of the order now functioning in Poland. The monks were called *Bielanie*, or White Friars, from the colour of their habit, and the name, in slightly altered form, was later given to this whole district of Warsaw. The interior of the church is full of Rococo stucco, while the chancel contains interesting Baroque portraits of the royal patrons of the order — Władysław IV, Jan Kazimierz and Michał Korybut Wiśniowiecki. Behind the church are the hermitages where the monks used to live. In front of it is the grave of Stanisław Staszic (1755–1826), the 'Polish Benjamin Franklin', a prominent scientist, politician and man of letters of the Enlightenment period. Incidentally, the two emblems on the front gable of the church will be a recurrent motif throughout our travels. They are the coats of arms of Poland (the white eagle) and Lithuania (the knight and charger).

Chopin country

A longer excursion, requiring a whole day, takes us due west of Warsaw, into Chopin country. There are two possible routes: via Leszno and via Błonie. The shortest journey takes us out by the first route and back by the second. The scenery is relatively uneventful in both cases, although the Leszno road goes through outlying stretches of the vast Kampinos forest. Fifty-three kilometres west of Warsaw we come to Żelazowa Wola. Here, in a small manor house on what used to be the estate of the Skarbek family, for whom Nicolas Chopin served as tutor, his famous son Frederic was born on 22 February 1810. To be sure, the family left for Warsaw when Frederic was only a year old, but he returned here frequently during his youth, and one may suppose it was here, in the depths of the Mazovian countryside, that the young composer first heard the folk tunes which he eventually turned into the most exquisitely refined music. The house was in a fairly dilapidated state prior to its reconstruction in 1931. Then, it was heavily damaged during the last war, and many of its contents destroyed. So, it was reconstructed again after 1945, and then filled with period furniture and whatever Chopin relics had survived the war, along with copies of what had been destroyed.

The manor is surrounded by a large park, intersected by the River Utrata which is here really more a stream, and composed of nearly 10,000 specimens of plants and trees donated by admirers of Chopin throughout the world. During the summer, free public recitals of Chopin's music are presented here on Sundays: the pianist, often world-famous, sits at the Steinway by an open window in the ground-floor music room, and the audience sits outside on the garden terrace. Needless to say, the atmsophere is perfect, and visitors without cars may wish to join the special excursions to Żelazowa Wola organized by ORBIS on recital Sundays.

Some nine kilometres north-west of Żelazowa Wola, via the uninteresting little town of Chodaków, lies Brochów, a sleepy village on the River Bzura. The greatest battle of the September 1939 campaign was fought near here, but one can hardly imagine it today, what with the ducks splashing about below the church, and the overwhelming sensation of being hundreds of kilometres from nowhere. The church is the goal of our detour, partly because of its Chopin connections, for his parents were married here in 1806, and he himself was baptized here four years later. Both the marriage and birth certificates are preserved in the church. But we have come here for another reason as well; for the church, which was built *circa* 1550 only a few kilometres from the strategic junction of the Vistula and Bzura, and restored to its original form following destruction in World War I, possesses a system of fortifications unique in Polish ecclesiastical architecture. Directly attached to it are three sturdy round towers — two at the west end and one directly above the apse — all three connected by a wall passage. The church and its immediate precinct are protected by a defence wall with corner bastions, the whole originally surrounded by a moat. (A dry moat still exists on the side facing the river.) Note the numerous loop-holes in both the defence wall and the church itself.

Our next stop is Łowicz, which we reach via Chodaków — a certain amount of backtracking will be unavoidable on this excursion — and Sochaczew (note, in passing, the ruins of an ancient castle of the Princes of Mazovia on a hill overlooking the Bzura). Łowicz was the property of the Archbishops of Gniezno from 1136 to 1795, so it comes as no surprise that the large collegiate church in the pl. Kościuszki contains a number of fine Renaissance and

Baroque memorials to various church dignitaries in its aisle chapels. Like so many other Polish churches, this is a splendid hodge-podge of styles. Originally Gothic, it was given late-Renaissance towers in 1624, rebuilt in Baroque a generation later, and embellished with a Rococo high altar a century after that.

Łowicz is located in one of Poland's main areas of folk culture, and if we are fortunate enough to be here on a Sunday or important religious holiday we shall see peasants in traditional costume on their way to church, the brightly striped aprons of the women, some of whom still wear the tall head-dress of the region, particularly attracting our attention. The greatest show is in the summer on Corpus Christi (a movable feast, normally the Thursday after Trinity Sunday), when hundreds of visitors from Warsaw and other parts of Poland gather to watch the peasants proceeding solemnly through the centre of town, bearing bright-coloured, gossamer-thin religious banners. Interesting collections of folk art and crafts of the region may also be viewed in the Łowicz Museum housed in Tylman van Gameren's former college of the Missionary Fathers opposite the church on the east side of pl. Kościuszki. The garden of the museum contains a number of typical peasant cottages from the surrounding area. Really keen enthusiasts of folk culture may wish to see similar cottages *in situ* and still inhabited, in which case I would suggest the following detour. We leave Łowicz by the Kutno road, travelling west for 12 kilometres, as far as Zduny, where we take a side road north for about six kilometres, to the village of Zlaków Kościelny. (The road is fairly well marked, though extra care has to be taken when driving anywhere in the Polish country-side, owing to the comparatively large number of horse-drawn vehicles.) Famous, like Łowicz, for its Corpus Christi processions, Zlaków Kościelny is full of typical peasant cottages, thatched and often blue-washed. However, having come this far we will probably want to turn right at the church and carry on for another three kilometres until we reach Zlaków Borowy, one of Poland's main show-cases of peasant crafts organized by 'Cepelia', the Centre for Folk and Artistic Products, which has retail outlets throughout the country and abroad. The cottages at Zlaków Borowy, some of which are open to the public, are full of traditional peasant decoration, including much brightly painted wooden furniture, as well as fantastically intricate paper cut-outs of animals and flowers mounted on white paper, which make superb Christmas cards and are sold in souvenir shops throughout Poland. Another attraction of the village is its crafts workshop, which has helped a great deal to keep folk traditions alive in this region.

Returning to Łowicz, we leave the town at its south-east end via the Skierniewice Road (ul. Obrońców Stalingradu). Four kilometres out of Łowicz we reach Arkadia, the romantic landscape park founded in 1778 by Helena Radziwiłł, owner of nearby Nieborów Palace. Designed by Szymon Bogumił Zug, the architect of the Lutheran Church in Warsaw, Arkadia is one of the best Polish examples of the 'English' landscape garden exemplified by Capability Brown—a style which began to be very popular in Poland at the beginning of the 1770s. Situated along the Skierniewka River, which here forms a small lake, the park contains a number of pavilions and romantic ruins scattered amongst tall trees and overgrown grass. Buildings include the High Priest's House, inset with interesting architectural features plundered from the collegiate church at Łowicz; the Gothic House, also known as the House of Misfortune and Melancholy, built above a Sybil's Cave; and the crenellated Margrave's House, with an adjoining, and somewhat incongruous, Greek arch. But surely the handsomest of all the pavilions in this magical spot is the classical Temple of Diana on the lake shore, with its charming ceiling ('Dawn'), now being restored by the French painter Jean Pierre Norblin, and its romantic quotation from Petrarch over the Ionic portico: *Dove pace trovai d'ogni mia guerra* ('Where I have found peace after my every struggle').

Six kilometres further along the Skierniewice road, we come to the Baroque palace of Nieborów, originally built by Tylman van Gameren for Cardinal Michał Stefan Radziejowski in 1690–6. It ultimately passed to the Radziwiłłs, who owned it from 1774 to 1945. The first Radziwiłł owner, Michal Hieronim, whose wife, Helena (*née* Przeździecka) established Arkadia, was a great art-collector and began the famous Nieborów library. Two generations later, Zygmunt Radziwiłł, a notorious spendthrift, sold Arkadia, at the same time disposing of the contents of the library at a Paris auction in 1866. It has been replenished with later acquisitions and remains one of the most attractive rooms in the house. The next owner, Michał Piotr, bought back Arkadia and, in 1881, taking advantage of the deposits of high-quality clay near the house, established a majolica factory in Nieborów, which produced plates, vases, stove tiles etc. over the next two decades. During the last war Nieborów was taken over by German officers, becoming, on liberation, part of the National Museum in Warsaw. The restoration of the house was completed in 1970. Furnished largely in the Rococo and Neo-classical style, the house is particularly memorable for its main staircase, the walls and ceiling of which are lined with Dutch blue and white tiles. Another interesting feature of Nieborów is the fact that one enters by means of a carriage drive passing through the centre of the house at ground-floor level. After seeing the house, the visitor may wish to inspect its extensive grounds consisting of two parks: the formal, geometrical one designed by Tylman van Gameren directly behind the house, and, on the other side of the L-shaped water course, a later landscape park laid out by Zug.

Our excursion completed, the best route back to Warsaw is via the side road running north from Nieborów to a kilometre or two beyond the village of Bednary, where we rejoin the main road to Sochaczew and (via Błonie) continue on to the capital. Back in Warsaw, there is one more excursion to tempt us, but as it lies in the direction of Lublin, we shall do as Sheherazade might have done, and save it for the next chapter.

3 LUBLIN AND THE SOUTH-EAST

The Lublin region has always seemed to me one of the most 'Polish' parts of Poland, possibly because, prior to the post-war border changes, it lay in the very heart of the country, which made it all the more difficult for foreign influences to penetrate. It is interesting to note that one of the few truly Polish styles of architecture, the so-called 'Lublin Renaissance' (steeply pitched roofs, highly decorated gables and elaborate plaster-patterned vaulting), evolved precisely here. At the same time, this used to be one of the less developed parts of the country, though by no means as backward as the lost territories just across the Bug River to the east. To some extent this is still the case, though factories are beginning to spring up here and there, particularly on the outskirts of Lublin itself. Much more worrying are the possible effects on the region as a whole of the large-scale mining soon to begin in the hitherto exclusively agricultural region to the east and north-east of Lublin, where vast deposits of high-grade coal have recently been discovered. But for the time being, and one hopes for many years to come, this remains a basically unspoiled area of broad horizons spanning gently rolling uplands, lazy rivers, large forests and seemingly endless fields — not sensational scenery, to be sure, but all the same scenery with 'scale', perfect for leisurely motoring.

From Warsaw to Lublin

What is perhaps the most interesting route from Warsaw to Lublin takes us out of the capital in a southerly direction via Piaseczno to Góra Kalwaria and nearby Czersk. This area, of which Grójec to the south-west is its actual centre, is a prosperous agricultural region, and its peasants, who mainly supply Warsaw's private greengrocers and market stalls (which are in competition with, and largely superior to, the state-owned shops), are reputed to be amongst the richest men in Poland.

Thirty-four kilometres from Warsaw, the old pilgrimage town of Góra Kalwaria (Mount Calvary) on the Vistula attracts us today mainly because of its history, and if the traveller is in a rush he or she may, I suppose, pass right through it and make directly for Czersk. But it has an interesting history and merits a few words all the same. Founded in 1672 by its owner, Bishop Stefan Wierzbowski of Poznań, it was planned in the form of a cross, that being the contemporary idea of the lay-out of ancient Jerusalem. One arm of the cross was a Via Dolorosa, closed at either end by a church, the other being the Vistula road. It was called New Jerusalem, and to ensure the Christian character of the place no Jews were allowed to settle here. But in 1794 the Prussians seized it during the Kościuszko Uprising, and secularization and decay ensued. Today the two big churches on the market square — the one at the west end is by Jacopo Fontana, one of Poland's best Baroque architects — bear witness to the past glory of the town.

Three kilometres to the south lies Czersk. It is a small village now, but it was at one time the capital of Mazovia until the Vistula shifted its main course a kilometre or so eastward, leaving Czersk high and dry; whereupon the local princes transferred their residence to Warsaw in 1406. In 1656 the invading Swedes attacked the castle, leaving it a ruin, in which state, despite a certain amount of restoration, it basically remains to this day. It is certainly an impressive sight, standing on the very edge of the Vistula escarpment, its long red-brick perimeter wall, two tall round towers and square gate-tower dominating the sleepy valley below. Archaeological investigations, which are still being carried out within the castle precincts, have uncovered the foundations of residential buildings and a chapel. Another almost equally large ruined Mazovian castle dating from the turn of the fourteenth and fifteenth centuries — a sturdy rectangle with two massive round towers — can be seen at Ciechanów, 99 kilometres north of Warsaw; while at Liw (near Węgrów), 83 kilometres east of Warsaw, a chunky bastion is all that remains of a third Mazovian stronghold of the same date.

Travellers interested in the Polish contribution to the American War of Independence may want to continue another 21 kilometres southwards to Winiary, now part of the small town of Warka and birthplace, in 1747, of Kazimierz (or Casimir) Pułaski. A refugee following the defeat of the Confederation of Bar, he left for America and fell at the battle of Savannah in 1779. The manor house where he was born has been turned into a museum, with exhibits dealing with Pułaski's life and the whole subject of Polish emigration to the two Americas.

Crossing the Vistula at Góra Kalwaria, we head south along the river road, the river itself being visible only occasionally. Passing through the village of Maciejowice on the Okrzejka River, we are reminded that one of the most significant battles in Polish history took place five kilometres to the east when, on 10 October 1794, Tadeusz Kościuszko was wounded and taken prisoner by the Russians, resulting in the collapse of his insurrection and the third, and final, partition a year later.

Thirty-five kilometres further along the Vistula, roughly midway between the towns of Dęblin and Puławy, we come to the turn-off for Gołąb, a small village less than a kilometre from the main road. We are drawn here because of the massive red-brick church of 1626–36, with interesting late-Renaissance features and corridors built into the walls of the nave above the windows for defence purposes, and also because of the Loreto House of roughly the same date immediately to the south. We have already seen one of these structures in the Praga district of Warsaw. The one at Gołąb is an equally ambitious effort, with half-columns, broken pediments, putti and life-size bas-relief figures on either side of the doors. The six niches between the half-columns formerly contained large terra-cotta figures of Old Testament prophets, but when I was last in Gołąb, in 1976, the figures had been removed—to be restored, I was informed—so one hopes their displacement will only be temporary.

Puławy twelve kilometres away is our next stop, though the park-and-palace complex there is overshadowed, and hardly improved, by the construction in the 1960s of the vast Azoty nitrates combine, one of Europe's largest, on the outskirts of town. But despite the dust and the bustling population (up from 14,000 in 1961 to 50,000 today) at its gates, the park—somewhat overgrown, like most Polish parks—is still worth a visit and is described below. The house itself was begun in 1671 by Tylman van Gameren for Stanisław Herakliusz Lubomirski—by whom he was also employed to design the original bathing pavilion at Łazienki—and passed to the Czartoryskis, then the most powerful family in Poland, 60 years later. Under Prince Adam Kazimierz Czartoryski, his wife Izabela and eldest son Adam Jerzy, Puławy became, after Warsaw, the most important political and cultural centre in Poland, for the family were great patrons of the arts, surrounding themselves with the best writers, painters and architects of their day. For example, Chrystian Piotr Aigner, a native of Puławy and one of the best Polish Neo-classical architects, was trained in Rome at their expense. Equally important, King Stanisław August Poniatowski was their cousin. But whereas the King was dubious in his patriotism and shilly-shallied in his support of political reform, the Czartoryskis were strongly pro-Polish, even going so far as to back the Kościuszko Uprising, for which they were punished by Catherine the Great with the confiscation of their estates. They soon got them back, but only on condition that Prince Adam Kazimierz's sons be brought up in St. Petersburg, where a careful watch could be kept on them.

In the Russian capital the young Adam Jerzy made the acquaintance of the future Tsar Alexander I who, after he ascended the throne in 1801, made him Minister of Foreign Affairs of the Russian Empire. But Prince Adam Jerzy eventually fell out with the Tsar, and during the November Insurrection of 1830–1, it was he who led the provisional government. For this the new tsar, Alexander's brother Nicholas I, sentenced him to death *in absentia*, at the same time confiscating his estates. Most of the great Czartoryski collection was hidden, however, and eventually removed to France, where Prince Adam Jerzy had settled, becoming one of the most influential leaders of Poland's political exiles.

The vacant palace at Puławy was turned into a girls' school in 1842, and in 1862 it became an agricultural institute, which it remains to this day. It has been altered considerably over the last three centuries and is not tremendously interesting. What *is* interesting is the park, which is being restored following war losses and, with its several hundred different species, still contains a more varied flora than almost any other park in the country. It began as a late seventeenth-century ordered and symmetrical Baroque affair, but by the late 1790s Princess Izabela had set to work turning it into a romantic landscape park, a grander version of what we have seen at Arkadia. A number of foreign gardeners, including the Englishman James Savage, were called in to advise on the planting. Then in 1798, Aigner, the Czartoryski family architect, began to design the half-dozen pavilions which constitute the main charm and attraction of the park.

In fact, he had worked at Puławy earlier in the decade, when he designed the so-called 'Marynka' (a diminutive for Maria) Palace for Princess Izabela's daughter, Maria Wirtemberg, author of the first Polish sentimental novel, *Malvina, or the Perspicacity of the Heart*. The palace, a charming yellow and white porticoed structure at the south-east edge of the park, is the quintessence of the romantic Neo-classical style in Poland.

Following the loss of Polish independence, Princess Izabela was determined that her fellow Poles should preserve their sense of national identity. To this end—being a keen collector, like her husband—she began amassing all manner of souvenirs and memorabilia connected with Poland's glorious past, and in 1798 she commissioned Aigner to build a Temple of Memory, now known as the Temple of the Sybil, at the end of a long avenue of limes stretching in a south-easterly direction from the courtyard of the house. Modelled on a classical temple at Tivoli, outside Rome, it is a colonnaded cylinder, guarded on either side of a flight of steps by two of the most bashful looking lions I have ever seen. The inscription over the portico—'*Przeszłość-Przyszłości*' ('The past to the future') indicates the role which the collections contained within the temple were meant to play. However, the collections soon outgrew the temple, so in 1800 Princess Izabela commissioned Aigner to convert a nearby Baroque garden pavilion into a 'Gothic' House, the walls of which are embedded with bits and pieces of ancient buildings and tombs. Today it contains a varied collection of uniforms, banners, prints, tiles and other objects, most of which are in one way or another connected with the history of the Puławy region.

The park includes several other pavilions, among them a small Chinese summer house, a number of statues, and even a man-made limestone cave, the abode of a hermit in Princess Izabela's time, so it is said. But perhaps the most interesting building yet to be seen is the former palace chapel, now the parish church, to the north of the park, in ul. Zwycięstwa. Built in 1803 by Aigner—one might have guessed—it was modelled on the Pantheon in Rome, and its interior contains a gallery supported by a dozen Ionic columns.

From Puławy we continue south along the Vistula, but now the scenery is changing. The river is still there, but its bed is narrower now, and the land on both sides, but particularly to the east, has begun to rise. We are entering the Vistula Gate, the point where the Lublin Plateau—extensive uplands of limestone and loess stretching many kilometres to the south-east, deep into the Ukraine—meets the Vistula. Indeed, by the time we approach Kazimierz Dolny, 13 kilometres south of Puławy, the river valley has become a narrow terrace, dominated by the steep escarpment to our left.

Kazimierz Dolny (Lower Kazimierz, to distinguish it from an up-river Kazimierz, now part of Cracow) is famous throughout Poland for its superb Renaissance architecture, as well as for its delightful location at the foot of the escarpment in a narrow valley formed by the Grodarz stream, which flows into the Vistula here.

Strategically, it made great sense to have a settlement commanding the Vistula at this point, and Kazimierz developed early. According to tradition supported by the fifteenth-century historian Jan Długosz, the town was founded by Kazimierz the Great, the last of the Piasts, who ruled between 1333 and 1370, hence its name. Tradition also maintains that King Kazimierz settled his beautiful Jewish mistress, Esterka, in a small castle (now ruined) at Bochotnica, three kilometres to the north, at the same time connecting the castle to the town by an underground passage, so that he could visit the lady unobserved. But this is pure legend: there was an Esterka, to be sure, but the castle at Bochotnica had nothing to do with either her or the King. In fact, Kazimierz the Great seems merely to have confirmed the charter of an earlier, twelfth-century settlement named after a Cracovian prince, Kazimierz the Just — which would explain the confusion over the origin of the name.

Kazimierz soon began to grow, aided by the fact that it lay at the point where two trade routes crossed the Vistula. Timber, cattle, wine and grain all brought in big money, as did the brewing of beer. But disaster struck in 1561, when fire broke out in one of the breweries and destroyed the largely timber-built town. However, this proved to be a blessing in disguise, for although the King soon forbade the townspeople to brew any more beer, he gave them in exchange the right to deal, free of taxes, in the all-important commodity of salt. They also began to concentrate on trading in grain, shipping it down the Vistula to Gdańsk on fleets of rafts in exchange for salted herring, then a staple food of the poor. Salt and grain together made Kazimierz a thriving commercial centre, and traders of many nationalities settled here, including a number of Englishmen and Scots. By the end of the sixteenth century, Kazimierz boasted 45 granaries, of which several survive, including the two late-Renaissance examples just outside town on the Puławy road. The rich burghers of the town erected splendid mansions, a number of which also survive, and the parish church, which we shall soon visit, was converted into one of the finest examples of the 'Lublin Renaissance' style.

During the following centuries, Kazimierz, like Poland itself, went into a gradual decline, as the Swedish wars of conquest, plague, drought and torrential rains all took their toll. But towards the end of the last century the town began to revive, partly because it had been 'discovered' by holiday-makers, including a number of painters and writers, who built villas there. In the final stages of World War II the town suffered heavy damage, finding itself on the front line for several months prior to the Soviet Army's final push across the Vistula. Since the war Kazimierz has been rebuilt and is once again a favourite destination for holiday-makers and day-trippers, particularly as it is less than a three hours' drive from Warsaw by direct route.

Even so, the town is wonderfully unspoilt and looks likely to remain so, although this has not always been the case. Several years ago a 'development' plan was drawn up, according to which a main road was to be laid out along the Vistula, and a huge rest centre built for workers from the Puławy fertilizer combine. The plan was passed, even though it would have completely destroyed the unique character of the town. Word got out, and the friends of Kazimierz — the painters, architects, writers and journalists who used the town as a holiday centre — prepared for battle. Articles began to appear in newspapers and journals, and eventually a committee of enquiry was set up, and the plan was shelved. It was also decided that no hotels or rest homes would be built in the town, that such necessary tourist services as restaurants, souvenir shops etc. would be accommodated in existing buildings, and that any new housing for residents would have to be built according to traditional styles, and in materials characteristic of the area.

Standing in the Market Square, we immediately appreciate the wisdom of this decision. To the south-east are two of the most remarkable structures in Poland, the houses of the Przybyła brothers, both dating from *circa* 1615. Rich merchants, the two brothers embellished their houses with more or less life-size bas-relief figures of their patron saints — Nicholas for Mikołaj, and Christopher, leaning on an entire tree, instead of a mere staff, and with crayfish at his feet, for Krzysztof — but they did not stop there. In fact, virtually every centimetre of the façades is covered either with pictorial representations or with architectural features in a Renaissance style which has gone over the top and become exuberantly Mannerist. Nearby, across the stream, in ul. Senatorska, stands an equally Mannerist structure, the house of the Celejs, another rich merchant family, erected *circa* 1635. The highly ornamented windows, fine portal and remarkable attic storey, with its handsome scallop-shell niches topped by a fantastic array of saints, dragons and other imaginary creatures are enough to make it well worth a visit; but it also houses the new Kazimierz Dolny Museum, its two floors containing a number of charming pictures of the town and surrounding countryside painted during the last 100 years, as well as some interesting exhibits connected with the ancient Jewish colony, which dated back to the time of King Kazimierz and Esterka and was totally annihilated during the last war.

Also in this part of town is the monastery of the Reformed Franciscans, which is of interest partly for the steep covered passage leading up to it, and partly for the fine view from the monastery courtyard. The visitor looking for unusual souvenirs might do well to step into the tiny bakery at the foot of the hill, which sells delicious bread in the shape of roosters, crayfish and other animals.

The best view of Kazimierz is to be had from the hill a short distance away on the north side of the Market Square. On our way we make a brief detour eastward into ul. Lubelska to see the former synagogue with its wooden-tiled roof, typical of many buildings in Kazimierz. First erected in the eighteenth century and destroyed by the Nazis, it has been rebuilt and is now a cinema.

A short way up the hill lies the parish church, one of the chief attractions of the town. Originally Gothic, it was heavily damaged in the great fire of 1561, but the Reformed faith was so strong in this area that reconstruction was not begun until 1586, nor completed before 1630. The main work of rebuilding took place in 1610–13 under the Italian Jacopo Balin, who employed the 'Lublin Renaissance' style, the elaborate plaster-patterned vaulting being a particularly fine feature of the church. Of considerable interest too, are the interior furnishings, including the Renaissance stalls and pulpit, the canopy of the latter being surmounted by carved figures representing the Four Evangelists; the highly ornate Rococo confessionals at the back of the church; the side altars with their fronts of coloured and embossed Cordovan leather; the extraordinary nave chandelier, formed from a stag's antlers; and, last but not least, the magnificent organ of 1620, one of the oldest and finest in the country, and often used for recitals.

Higher up the hill are the ruins of a castle built around the middle of the fourteenth century by, it is said, Kazimierz the Great. Nearby are the three crosses which give the hill its name, Góra Trzech Krzyży (Three Crosses' Hill). Erected in 1708, they commemorate the victims of the first of three plagues that decimated the population of Kazimierz in the early years of the eighteenth century. There is a superb view from this spot, but a still better view can be had by climbing to the top of an even earlier tower higher up the hill. Standing 20 metres high with walls four metres thick at the base, it dates to some time between the twelfth and fourteenth centuries and is probably the sole remnant of a castle built to guard the river-crossing and collect tolls from passing merchants.

Kazimierz offers a number of interesting marked trails, some of which pass through the numerous gorges of the region, containing rare and protected plant species. Three to six kilometres long, they all originate in the Market Square near the 'Esterka' restaurant. Another attractive excursion takes us a few hundred metres upstream from Kazimierz, where we catch the ferry across the Vistula to the ruined sixteenth-century castle of Janowiec, the former residence of the Firlejs and then the Tarłos, two of the most powerful families of Renaissance Poland. The ruins are supposed to be haunted by the ghost of a young woman whose father, a rich magnate, furious with her for falling in love with a fisherman, walled her up in one of the towers. Finally, visitors who are unencumbered by a car and have the time to spare, may wish to take one of the pleasure boats that ply the 13 kilometres between Kazimierz and Puławy during the summer season. The Kazimierz ticket office is on the river-front in the ul. Kazimierza Wielkiego; in Puławy, the ticket office is to the north of the bridge at ul. 1 Maja 74.

The journey to Kazimierz makes one of the most delightful excursions from Warsaw, and even with stop-overs in Czersk, Gołąb and Puławy, it can all be done in a day. But instead of returning to the capital, we shall continue on to Lublin, taking the route through Nałęczów, a popular holiday resort and spa celebrated for its mild climate and luxuriant vegetation, and also because, over the last century or so, many of Poland's best writers have stayed here. But, since, alas, few of these writers are known in the West, and as Poland has prettier spas, we shall give Nałęczów a miss and push on to Lublin.

Here I must declare an interest: Lublin is one of my favourite Polish towns, though I would be hard-put to say exactly why. Perhaps it is because Lublin was less damaged in the last war than Warsaw, for example, and has thus preserved more of the patina of age, giving a sense of authenticity which not even the most skilful reconstruction can reproduce. My fondness for the city may also have something to do with its picturesque location, for it lies stretched out along a ridge between the river Bystrzyca and Czechówka, its main thoroughfare, the Krakowskie Przedmieście, terminating at its eastern end in the Old Town, which sits perched on a hill, separated by a small valley from another hill on which the old castle stands.

A town was bound to develop on this spot, for Lublin lay at the intersection of two main trade routes, one of which ran from Kiev to the Baltic, and the other, from Lithuania to Cracow, the Czech lands and Austria. The town received its charter as early (by Polish standards) as 1317, but there had been a castle here even earlier, as can be seen from the thirteenth-century foundations of the massive round tower of the present castle. Kazimierz the Great added to it in the fourteenth century, and early in the following century King Władysław Jagiełło commissioned Master Andrzej to adorn the remarkable Holy Trinity chapel (two storeys supported by a single central pillar) at the end of the castle courtyard with a magnificent set of murals in the Russo-Byzantine style. Completed in 1418, the latter are amongst the finest examples of mediaeval wall painting in Poland and are, in themselves, sufficient reason for visiting Lublin. Alas, the same cannot be said of the castle itself, which after lying in ruins for well over a century was rebuilt as a prison by Ignacy Stompf in 1823–6 in a grotesque style which he doubtless considered to be neo-Gothic, but which in fact gives the building the appearance of an outpost of the French Foreign Legion. History repeated itself during the last war, when the castle was again used as a prison, some 400,000 people passing through it, many on their way to summary execution by the Nazis.

Pausing for a minute on the castle terrace to admire the superb view of Lublin, we descend into the valley via ul. Zamkowa (Castle Street) and then enter the Old Town by the Grodzka (Town) Gate. The Old Town here is roughly the size of Warsaw's and centres on the Rynek, or Market Square. In the middle of the latter stands the Old Town Hall, which was originally erected in 1389, becoming in 1579 the seat of the Crown Tribunal, the highest law court in Małopolska (Little Poland). It was given its present Neo-classical façade two centuries later by Domenico Merlini of Łazienki fame, but whereas in Warsaw his efforts were crowned with success, here they were hampered by the need to economize, and the Town Hall is, frankly, uninspired. Much more attractive are the old houses lining the square, including No. 2, the Klonowicz House, a fourteenth-century structure with a Neo-classical exterior, named after Sebastian Klonowicz, a well-known Polish poet, who lived here at the end of the sixteenth century; No. 8, the Lubomelski House, also of mediaeval origin, containing a wine cellar with Renaissance murals depicting contemporary social customs; and No. 12, known variously as the Sobieski or Żółkiewski House, with its rich Renaissance ornamentation.

A short walk down to the east down ul. Złota brings us to one of the two finest churches in Lublin, the Dominican basilica of St. Stanisław. Originally a fourteenth-century Gothic 'hall' church, it was remodelled in the Renaissance style at the beginning of the 1600s and then, towards the end of the following century, given a Baroque interior, which has recently been restored. Its glory is the magnificent domed and stuccoed Firlej family burial chapel at the east end of the south aisle, perhaps the finest example of late-Renaissance architecture in the province. Just to the north, beyond the chancel, is the early-Baroque Tyszkiewicz chapel, its oval dome covered with a powerful fresco portraying the Last Judgement and, by implication, the triumph of the Counter-Reformation. (Protestantism had been strong in the Lublin region.) Of considerable interest, too, is the series of eighteenth-century paintings in the south-aisle chapels, depicting the various miracles (such as halting the spread of plague, checking a great fire that threatened to engulf the town, etc.) wrought by a fragment of the True Cross that was formerly paraded through Lublin during times of calamity.

Leaving the basilica, we turn left into ul. Klonowicza, round the corner into ul. Trybunalska and pass through the Trynitarska Gate, emerging in front of the cathedral. Erected in 1586–1603 as a Jesuit church, its monastery was ultimately dismantled following the suppression of the Order in the 1770s, creating the square that now exists in front of the cathedral. Around 1821, Antonio Corazzi, who was soon to begin work on Warsaw's Bank (now Dzierżyński) Square, gave the cathedral its present Neo-classical front. The interior, however, is a beautiful warm late-Baroque, largely the work of the Moravian painter Józef Majer, who decorated it in the years 1756–7. The marbling (i.e. wood painted to look like marble) is particularly fine. The sacristy at the south-east end is well worth a visit, both for the strange 'whispering gallery' accoustics of the first room, and, in the second, for Majer's extraordinary *trompe-l'oeil* ceiling, the figures on which appear to change position as one moves from one end of the room to the other.

A few steps away to the west is the third, and by far the most picturesque and authentic, of the three Old Town gates, the crenellated Gothic Krakowska (Cracow) Gate with its tall clock tower, which marks the beginning of the main thoroughfare of modern Lublin, the Krakowskie Przedmieście, so called because, like the street of the same name in Warsaw, it forms part of the main road to the former capital. The best restaurants and hotels of the town lie in this direction, as does the Catholic University of

Lublin, the main academic institution of the Polish Church, and the only one of its kind in the whole of Eastern Europe. Founded in 1918, and the first university to re-open following World War II, it has several thousand students (their degrees are recognized by the State) and pursues an active and distinguished research and publishing programme.

Our interests, however, lie closer at hand. There are several interesting old churches within ten minutes' walk of the Cracow Gate, including, to the north of the Krakowskie Przedmieście in ul. Sawickiej, the Discalced Carmelites' church of St. Joseph, with its high-pitched roof, picturesque stumpy bell-tower and highly ornamented, typically 'Lublin Renaissance' gable. The interior, however, is not particularly interesting. On the other side of the Krakowskie Przedmieście, in ul. Narutowicza, stands one of the oldest strctures in Lublin, the church of the Brigittines, founded by King Władysław Jagiełło as a votive offering following his victory over the Teutonic Knights at Grunwald in 1410. It is remarkable for its 'Lublin Renaissance' plaster-patterned vaults, as is the somewhat later Bernardine church one street away in ul. Podgrodzie, just off pl. Wolności. Midway along the Krakowskie Przedmieście we come to the plac Litweski, lined with former mansions of the nobility, including the Czartoryskis and Radziwiłłs. The old palace in the north-west corner of the square now houses the administration of the Maria Skłodowska-Curie University, Lublin's other (state-run) institution of higher education. The obelisk in the middle of the square commemorates the Union of Lublin (1569), by which Poland and Lithuania were merged to form a single state.

A memorial of a very different kind lies three kilometres south-east of the town centre via ul. Buczka and ul. Armii Czerwonej. Here, in the suburb of Majdanek, in 1941, the Nazis constructed an extermination camp through which passed some half a million people of 26 nationalities, Polish citizens predominating. The final death count has never been precisely determined, but the Poles estimate that the figure exceeds 360,000. Following liberation in 1944, a number of the camp buildings, including barracks and crematoria, were preserved as a museum. Near the road, the massive monument to the victims of Majdanek creates a powerful impression, which is reinforced by the guard towers and many hundreds of metres of formerly electrified barbed wire stretching endlessly, so it seems, across the empty fields.

Of all the possible excursions from Lublin, by far the most

1 The Old Town market square, Warsaw

2 The Grand Theatre and Opera House, Warsaw

3 The modern city centre, Warsaw

4 Wilanów, King Jan Sobieski's palace outside Warsaw

5 The Przybyła houses, Kazimierz Dolny

6 Baranów castle

7 The towers of Wawel cathedral, Cracow

8 St. Mary's church, Cracow

9 The Cloth Hall and Town Hall tower, Cracow market square

10 Jasna Góra monastery, Częstochowa

11 Pieskowa Skała castle seen from the road below

12 Pieskowa Skała courtyard

13 Folk festival at Nowy Sącz

14 Mount Giewont in the Tatra range

15 Hill-farming in southern Poland

16 Wrocław University

17 Lądek Zdrój in the Kłodzka Valley

18 Old market square and Town hall, Poznań

19 Country inn, Poznań province

20 Hunting at Biały Bór, Koszalin province

21 The beach at Cetniewo

22 The Artus mansion, Gdańsk

23 Malbork castle

24 Bison, Białowieża forest

25 Lake Białe, near Augustów

26 Pre-Christian stone statue from Barciany, now in the courtyard of Olsztyn castle

interesting is the one to Zamość, 86 kilometres south-east of the city by the Majdanek road. Our route is not particularly eventful, but it is far from unpleasant, the landscapes of this region reminding one of the vast fields and broad horizons of northern France, perhaps Champagne. Just beyond Krasnystaw, an unremarkable small town 52 kilometres from Lublin, we enter present-day Zamość province, an area scheduled by the Nazis for German colonization during the last war. As a result, in 1942–3, a total of 297 of the 696 villages and towns in this region were emptied of their Polish inhabitants, those who had not fled to the neighbouring forests to join the partisans being sent to a transit camp in Zamość, where hundreds died of hunger and disease, or as the result of execution. Those who survived were transported to forced labour or concentration camps. All told, over 110,000 Poles were deported from the region, and a large proportion never returned. In one of the more bizarre aspects of the operation, towards the end of 1943 the Germans began to divide the very youngest children into two categories: those who were blonde and blue-eyed, and thus represented the Nazis' 'Nordic' ideal; and the rest. The latter largely perished, but the former, some 4,500 in all, were shipped off to Germany to be adopted and Germanized, and even now one hears stories of parents from this region who have travelled to Germany to try to find their lost children, usually with no success.

Zamość comes as something of a surprise, for here, in the middle of the Lublin Plateau, is a Renaissance planned town in the Italian style. In fact, it is the creation of the architect and engineer, Bernardo Morando of Padua, who was engaged in 1578 by Jan Zamoyski, King Stefan Batory's brilliant Chancellor and commander-in-chief, to turn his ancestral village into a town designed on a grand scale, as befitted his new power and prestige. Morando was also commissioned to construct a large palace for the Zamoyski family, as well as a complete system of fortifications. The latter served the town well, for Zamość was one of the very few towns to withstand the Swedish 'Flood' in the 1650s, and it was also the last fortress to capitulate to the Russians during the so-called November Insurrection of 1830–1.

By the end of the last war, Zamość had become extremely dilapidated, its architectural beauties effaced by wear, tear and the elements, and hidden under centuries of grime. Even so, the town has long been recognized as a superb example of Renaissance town planning, Unesco classifying it as a 'Group Zero' historical monument, a category reserved for buildings and architectural ensembles of international importance, like Wilanów and Łazienki. Not surprisingly, therefore, in the 1960s a gradual, but thoroughgoing programme of renovation was launched, during which, over the next 30 years, the services of the town will be completely modernized, and its buildings restored to their original Renaissance character, all unsympathetic later accretions being removed. At the same time, a New Town is being laid out to the east to accommodate Zamość's rapidly growing population, which was 39,000 in 1978 and is expected to increase to 60,000 by 1985, while the old Renaissance town was originally designed to house a mere 6,000. To harmonize the new with the old, certain basic design principles have been adopted: the New Town blocks will be of the same size as those on the Old Town grid, and there will be the same interplay of streets and open spaces, with numerous arcaded passages, a typical feature of the Old Town. There will also be a limitation on the height of the new buildings, varying from three storeys near the Old Town to eight storeys in districts furthest away.

Now is a good time to visit Zamość, while restoration is still going on, and one can compare the 'before' and 'after'. A good place to start is the market square, known as the pl. Mickiewicza, where much work has already been completed, particularly on the restoration of the great town hall of 1591–1600, with its huge double flight of steps and tall tower, both features of a later date and in the Baroque style, and also on the pastel-coloured arcaded houses lining the square, the former residences of rich merchants of the town. The side which has best kept its original Renaissance features is the north side, ul. Ormiańska (Armenian Street), named after the many merchants of that nationality who lived and traded throughout south-eastern Poland. To the south of the square, Morando, the overall architect of the town and its mayor after 1584, built a house for himself in 1599, a year before his death.

Behind the town hall, to the west of the Salt Market (Rynek Solny), lies the massive block — now Neo-classical, but originally Renaissance and later Baroque — which formerly housed the Zamość Academy, founded in 1594 by Jan Zamoyski and for two centuries one of Poland's main centres of learning. It is now a branch of the Maria Skłodowska-Curie University of Lublin. The original Renaissance character of Morando's system of fortifications, which included three gates and seven bastions, has been largely altered, particularly by the Russians in the 1820s. Probably the most interesting feature is the Old Lublin Gate (just behind the Academy), which Zamoyski had permanently walled up in 1588 to commemorate the passage through it of the Austrian Archduke Maximilian, a claimant to the Polish throne, whom the former had captured that year at the battle of Byczyna, in Silesia. To the south, the Zamoyski palace, which the family left over a century and a half ago, has been remodelled so often as to be of little interest to the visitor. Two of the churches, the Hospitalers' and the Franciscans', were converted in the last century to secular use and await restoration. Of the remainder, one, the collegiate church, near the Szczebrzeszyn Gate in the south-west part of town, is of very considerable interest. Originally Morando's work, it lost its Mannerist façade and acquired its present Neo-classical one during the remodelling of 1824–6. Jan Zamoyski is buried in the south-east, or Zamoyski, chapel, while the four paintings in the chancel have been attributed to Domenico Robusti, Tintoretto's son. All in all, with its fine proportions, plaster-patterned 'Lublin Renaissance' vaults and early-Baroque stucco decoration by Giovanni Battista Falconi, an Italian who did a lot of work in this district, this is one of the most attractive churches of its date anywhere in Poland.

From Lublin to Cracow

To reach Cracow, which is our next major sight, and arguably the supreme architectural and artistic event of our tour, we have a choice of several routes. The shortest, and one of the most rewarding, takes us directly from Lublin (110 kilometres), or cross-country from Zamość (144 kilometres), to Sandomierz, one of the oldest cities in Poland. Settled as early as the eighth century, it became a fortified stronghold in the tenth century, and the capital of a principality in 1138. Lying high above the Vistula at the crossing of a major trade route linking Russia with Western Europe, Sandomierz was for centuries an important commercial centre, dealing chiefly in grain and timber. The numerous storage cellars and passages constructed between the sixteenth and eighteenth centuries in the soft loess soil on which Sandomierz rests have become a serious liability in recent years; and to prevent the town, which had come through the war unscathed but had begun to look down-at-heel, from slipping into the Vistula, a thoroughgoing programme of restoration and underpinning was launched in 1964.

As might be expected of a town of such antiquity, Sandomierz offers architectural styles of every period from the Romanesque to the present. One of its most interesting buildings is the earliest surviving one, the red-brick church of St. James, on a hill south-west of town, the original site of Sandomierz prior to its destruction by the

Tatars in 1259. The death of the Dominican monks who lost their lives during that invasion is depicted in the Baroque chapel of the Sandomierz Martyrs in the north aisle. The interior of the church — which contains a number of interesting tombs, the oldest of which dates to the thirteenth century — is of various periods, but the exterior was restored in 1907–9 to its original late-Romanesque form. (Note the remarkable north portal.) The detached Gothic bell-tower contains two of Poland's oldest bells, cast in 1314 and 1389. Of the other churches in town, the most noteworthy is the cathedral, originally a collegiate church, to the north-east of the oft-rebuilt, and as a result fairly characterless, castle. Founded, like the castle, by King Kazimierz the Great, it was given a mediocre Baroque façade in 1670, but this should not put the visitor off, for the interior has much to offer, including fine Gothic cross-ribbed vaulting and richly carved capitals, and, in the chancel, Russo-Byzantine frescoes from the beginning of the fifteenth century, i.e., roughly the same date as those in Lublin. Immediately to the east, at ul. Długosza 9, the Diocesan Museum now occupies the house built for the great Polish mediaeval historian, Jan Długosz, in 1476, four years before his death. From behind the house, which stands on the very edge of the Vistula escarpment, there is a fine view of the river valley below.

Of the secular buildings, by far the most impressive is the brick Town Hall, which fills the middle of the Market Square. It is a picturesque combination of Gothic in the lower storeys and late Renaissance in the attick storey, with its blind arcading and spiky skyline. There is a large Renaissance sun-dial to the left of the first-floor window on the south side. To the north of the square, at the end of ul. Skopenki, stands the town's single surviving gate, the enormously tall Brama Opatowska, built in the middle of the fourteenth century of the same warm, subtle reddish-brown brick as the Town Hall. Its Renaissance top storey, added two centuries later, offers a superb view of the town and the surrounding countryside.

Leaving Sandomierz, we re-cross the Vistula and continue southward through Tarnobrzeg, 14 kilometres away. Formerly a sleepy riverside town, it is now a thriving industrial centre, thanks to the discovery nearby, in 1953, of some of the richest sulphur deposits in the world. A fortunate consequence has been the restoration by the sulphur industry of Baranów (sometimes known as Baranów Sandomierski), one of the greatest of all Polish Renaissance castles, 12 kilometres south of Tarnobrzeg. In fact, Baranów was one of the first projects of this kind, and it all makes a great deal of sense, for now that the powerful magnate families of the past have left their great houses, someone has to prevent structures like Baranów from falling into ruin; and in Poland, apart from the state itself, only the state-owned industrial giants have the financial resources with which to take over this role. In the case of Baranów, the castle has been converted into a Museum of the Sulphur Industry, at the same time providing facilities for special company receptions as well as holiday accommodation for employees. What will most interest us, however, is the splendid architecture of the building, which was erected for the Leszczyńskis in 1591–1606, possibly by the Italian Santi Gucci. On the outside, it is a cream-coloured oblong rectangle, with a bright red-tiled roof, corner towers, and the decorated gables and (on the main façade) the spiky attic outline so favoured in Renaissance Poland. One of the shorter sides is arcaded, leading directly on to a pretty formal garden. The interior courtyard is even more picturesque, with its two storeys of arcading and massive double staircase superimposed above the entrance. Note, at knee-level, the curious Renaissance stone masks on the arcade plinths.

South of Baranów we leave the Upper Vistula basin and enter gently hilly country, the northernmost foothills of the Carpathians. We are now in Galicia, formerly the Austrian Partition. This has always been one of the poorer areas of the country, providing a high proportion of the millions of Polish emigrants to the New World; and it still looks fairly backward today, with its winding lanes, duck ponds and picturesque blue-washed thatched cottages.

The last reasonably sized town before Cracow is Tarnów, 94 kilometres south of Baranów. It is now a growing industrial centre, with several large chemical, electrical and metallurgical plants, and it also boasts one of the country's best known modern churches, to the north of the town, in ul. Nowodąbrowska. The Old Town, however, still retains much of the atmosphere of a pleasant Austro-Hungarian backwater, and it is here we shall concentrate our attention.

A settlement existed here at least as early as the beginning of the twelfth century, for the town lay at the intersection of two important trade routes, connecting Poland with Hungary (north-south) and Kievan Russia with Cracow and Western Europe (east-west). By 1330 it had become the property of Spicymir of Melsztyn, a close friend of King Władysław Little-Ell and direct ancestor of the powerful Tarnowski family. The latter were to make the town an important centre of Renaissance culture, even establishing a branch of Cracow University here. That is gone now, but Tarnów is still rich in examples of Renaissance architecture, particularly the houses around the Rynek (Market Square), and in the streets and lanes nearby. In the middle of the square stands the Town Hall, originally a fourteenth-century structure, as can still be seen from its tall Gothic tower, but later adorned with an attic storey complete with the blind arcading and spiky skyline so favoured by Polish Renaissance architects. The building is now the Town Museum, with a good collection of armoury, painting (both Polish and foreign), glass and ceramics. An even more fascinating museum lies five minutes to the north-west, at pl. Katedralny 6. Here, opposite the west end of the cathedral, in the Mikołajowski House, one of a series of late-Gothic and early-Renaissance houses built directly into the old city walls, is the Diocesan Museum, one of the most important of its kind anywhere in Poland. It is largely devoted to sacred art and houses a rich treasury of Gothic carvings, paintings and triptychs, most of which have come from country churches of the region. It also contains, on the upper floor, much fascinating folk art, including what must be Poland's largest collection of paintings on glass, mostly depicting saints and biblical scenes, and full of enormous naive charm.

As the result of insensitive restoration at the end of the last century, the cathedral, which dates from *circa* 1400, lacks character on the outside, but its interior contains a number of features which make it well worth a visit, including two sets of fifteenth-century stalls (under the choir loft), highly carved Gothic portals, and, in the Scapular chapel (entrance from the former Holy Cross chapel at the south-east corner of the nave), the remains of frescoes of 1514–26 depicting scenes from the life of the Virgin and the Passion. In a small chapel off the north nave there is an extremely moving late-Gothic wood carving of the *Chrystus Frasobliwy* (Sorrowful Christ), showing the Saviour wearing the Crown of Thorns and seated on a rock, his right elbow resting on his knee as he pushes the hair out of his eyes with the fingers of his right hand. This has been a favourite Polish religious motif since the Middle Ages, and versions of it appear throughout Poland, particularly in the countless wayside shrines that dot the countryside.

But the cathedral is famous above all for the four magnificent Renaissance tombs in the chancel, of which the greatest — on the north wall — is that of the last two Tarnowskis, Hetman (i.e., Commander-in-Chief) Jan Tarnowski, who died in 1561, and his son, Jan Krzysztof, who died without a male heir six years later. Nearly 13 metres high, it is the largest tomb of its period anywhere in Poland. The work of Giovanni Maria Mosca, known in Poland as the 'Padovano', it is made of sandstone, coloured marble and alabaster, and is a virtual catalogue of Renaissance architectural forms, full of pilasters, friezes and, at the top, a sequence of cornices culminating in a figure of the resurrected Christ. Much more prominent, however, in this highly secular monument are the figures of the great Hetman (between the two Tuscan columns), surrounded by bas-reliefs depicting his most important military successes, and (below) his son. To the right, adjoining the Tarnowski monument, is the tomb of Zofia Ostrogska, who died in 1570. Hetman Tarnowski's daughter, she married Wasyl Konstanty Ostrogski, to whom Tarnów passed on the death of her brother. Although her monument forms a structural whole with that of her father and brother, it is probably the work, not of Padovano himself, but of his Polish assistant, Wojciech Kuszczyc. Directly opposite the Tarnowski monument, and only a few centimetres lower, is the late-Renaissance tomb of Prince Janusz Ostrogski and his Hungarian-born wife Zuzanna, the son and daughter-in-law of Wasyl Konstanty. Executed in red and black marble and yellow alabaster, the tomb is the work of the Wrocław sculptor, Jan Pfister, who completed it in 1620. Janusz was the first Catholic Ostrogski in an Orthodox family, and his enthusiasm for his new faith is reflected in the deeply religious spirit of the monument. The central subject is Christ on the Cross, surrounded by the prince and princess in prayer and adoration. Below are two figures personifying Faith and Hope, while above is a relief depicting Christ's Resurrection. But in fact the entire monument is covered with religious figures (prophets, angels' heads etc.) and images of death, such as skulls and crossbones, as well as a skeleton bearing an hourglass and a sickle. The last of the four important chancel monuments is also the earliest and was erected, probably in 1520, by the great Hetman in honour of his mother, Barbara of Rożnów, who had died three years earlier. The Renaissance was then only beginning to reach Poland, and the artist's technique — he was almost certainly a local man — indicates that he had not yet fully grasped the full implications of the new style and was still thinking, to some extent, in Gothic terms. The reclining figure of the deceased is, in fact, a Gothic figure of the grieving Virgin of the Crucifixion, turned on her side.

Tarnów has a number of other interesting attractions, including, a short drive across the river in the south of the town, two of the oldest wooden churches in Poland, one dating from *circa* 1450, and the other from 1562. But it is above all the cathedral, Diocesan Museum, Town hall and Market Square which make Tarnów one of the artistic and architectural 'musts' of southern Poland. It is also, from a practical point of view, a useful food, fuelling and leg-stretching stop before continuing on to Gracow, 82 kilometres away.

Side-trips to the south-east

The Lublin-Cracow itinerary which we have just traced should be particularly useful for a first visit to Poland, as it offers a higher proportion of interesting sights per kilometre travelled than any other route I know of in the south-eastern part of the country. However, for visitors wishing to go further afield there are a number of other possibilities, most of which take us along the middle and upper reaches of the San River. Music lovers will be particularly attracted by the fortified seventeenth-century Bernardine monastery of Leżajsk. The beautiful Baroque organ here is renowned throughout Poland, and virtuoso performances are given on it during the summer months.

Further upstream is the ancient town of Jarosław, which was probably founded by the Kievan prince Jarosław the Wise in 1031, becoming Polish three centuries later. Owing to its position at the intersection of the San River and the main trade route linking Kiev and Western Europe, and also thanks to a law of 1443, according to which any merchant travelling in the area had to pass through Jarosław, the town became one of the richest in mediaeval Poland, with an annual fair that ranked amongst the largest in Europe. Numerous foreign merchants settled here, including many Armenians and Italians, and it was a family of the latter, the Orsettis, who in 1570 built the largest house in town, at the corner of the Market Square and ul. Trybunalska. One of the most famous Renaissance structures in the entire country, it is a vast block with big arcades, an ornate, typically Polish attic storey and a huge Great Hall with a decorated ceiling and the remains of old frescoes. It now houses the Regional Museum. An unusual feature of Jarosław are the deep, multi-storey cellars, some of which are open to the public, under the great merchants' houses. Reaching a maximum depth of 15 metres, their complicated system of underground passages was used both for storage and as hiding places during the frequent raids by the Swedes, Hungarians and Cossacks, which, together with fires and plague, led to the decline of the town in the seventeenth and eighteenth centuries.

Further upstream, and only 14 kilometres from the Soviet border, is the even more ancient city of Przemyśl. According to the Mediaeval historian Jan Długosz, it was founded by Prince Przemysław, a semi-legendary ancestor of Mieszko I. In any case, it was already an important fortress when Prince Vladimir of Kiev seized it in 981. During the next three and a half centuries it passed back and forth between Russia, Hungary and Poland, remaining in Polish hands more or less permanently after 1344. Like Jarosław an important mediaeval trading centre, it too went into a decline in the seventeenth century as the result of continual foreign invasions. The decline was reversed, however, in 1873, when the Austrians, the local partitioning power, constructed an important fortress here; but this proved to be a mixed blessing, for during World War I it attracted the unwanted attention of the Allies, who besieged the town, destroying much of it. A great deal still remains, though, including a number of old monastic churches, mostly Baroque. The most interesting is the cathedral (south-west of the Market Square), originally built in the Gothic style in the late fifteenth century on earlier, Romanesque foundations, although it too, is now largely Baroque. Of secular structures, by far the most interesting is the old castle, on a hill further to the south-west. This was the original centre of Przemyśl, and it has been rebuilt on several occasions over the centuries. In addition to the surviving walls and bastions, post-war excavations have uncovered the remains of an eleventh-century princely residence, cottages, an early cemetery and the foundations of a twelfth-century Orthodox church, which was 'cannibalized' in the Gothic period to provide building material for the town cathedral. The castle is now used by the 'Fredreum' theatre, an amateur dramatic society founded in 1878 and named after the greatest Polish comic dramatist, Count Aleksander Fredro (1793–1876), whose family hailed from these parts. Their burial chapel is one of the main attractions of Przemyśl Cathedral.

Only ten kilometres to the west of Przemyśl, nestled in a valley amongst wooded hills near the San, stands Krasiczyn, one of the grandest of Polish houses, and also one of the finest examples of late-Renaissance architecture anywhere in the country. Built for the powerful Krasicki family in 1592–1614 by Galeazzo Appiani, who also helped with the reconstruction of Przemyśl castle, Krasiczyn is a huge quadrangle, with round towers at three corners and a domed chapel at the fourth, a large, arcaded inner courtyard and the highly decorative attic-storey skyline so typical of Polish Renaissance structures. Like Baranów, Krasiczyn has been taken under the patronage of a large industrial concern — in this case, the Warsaw Automobile Factory — and much progress has already been made in restoring it to its former glory.

The largest town in this region is Rzeszów, on southern Poland's main east-west road, which connects Cracow with Przemyśl and the Soviet frontier. A small provincial town before the war, its population has since trebled to over 85,000, and along the way it has acquired considerable industry. Its Market Square, or Rynek, contains a number of antique houses and a much-rebuilt eighteenth-century Town Hall, and north-east of the square in ul. Bóżnicza there are two old former synagogues, one dating from the beginning of the seventeenth century. Tylman van Gameren worked here — both the old castle and the Piarist church were remodelled according to his plans — but for many visitors probably the most interesting building in town will be the late-Renaissance (1624-9) Bernardine church to the north-west of the Market Square, in ul. 1 Maja. Its most remarkable feature are the tombs of the Ligęza family, the founders of the church and one-time owners of Rzeszów, whose life-size alabaster effigies surround the high altar. The alabaster bas-relief in the high altar itself is by Jan Pfister, the sculptor of the great Ostrogski tomb in Tarnów cathedral.

Rzeszów is a useful night-stop for visitors intending to visit the Potocki mansion at Łańcut, 17 kilometres to the east. A second-category hotel has been set up in a wing of the house itself, but it is small — only two dozen rooms — so travellers attracted by the romance of sleeping in Łańcut would do well to book early.

Abroad, Łańcut is probably the best known of all the great Polish country houses, owing largely to the publication (in English) of the memoirs of its last private owner, the late Count Alfred Potocki, *Master of Lancut*. But Łańcut was famous as long ago as the end of the sixteenth century, before the present house was built, when the town was the seat of the notorious Stanisław Stadnicki, the 'Devil of Łańcut', a powerful robber baron who terrorized the neighbourhood. The property eventually passed to the Lubomirskis, a much more law-abiding lot, and it was Stanisław Lubomirski who, in 1629, commissioned the Italian Matteo Trapola to construct a three-storey Renaissance residence surrounded by fortifications in the form of a five-pointed star, the latter being the latest Dutch and Italian fashion. Since then, the fortifications have largely disappeared, while the house itself has been remodelled on several occasions. Tylman van Gameren is said to have been responsible for the pretty onion domes, while Aigner redecorated much of the interior in the Neo-classical style, particularly the dining room and the great salon. An especially charming feature of the house is its white and gold theatre of 1792. Aigner also erected the fine orangery to our right as we approach the house, the semi-circular gloriette to our left and, behind the house to the north-east, the romantic neo-Gothic *zameczek* (little castle). But perhaps the most interesting of the outbuildings is the old coach house, a short walk through the pretty garden behind the orangery. One of the largest museums of its kind in Europe, and the only one in Poland, it contains over 50 old vehicles, some dating back to the early nineteenth century, and ranging from ordinary traps to the grandest carriages.

The house itself is, on the outside, one of the prettiest and most romantic in Poland, a combination of salmon and off-white, with a thick growth of ivy covering the entire north-west tower and parts of the façade. The interior has been turned into a museum of paintings, sculptures, furniture and other works of art collected by the Potocki family, who, from the beginning of the last century until 1944, when this part of Poland was liberated by Soviet and Polish troops, lived here in the greatest style. For example, lackeys used to sleep outside guests' doors, and when a morning bath was required, one clapped one's hands, and a steaming tub was rolled in. Before the Germans left, however, arrangements were made for Alfred Potocki to remove 11 goods wagons full of art objects to neutral Switzerland. One room has been left unrestored in order to show the gaping bits of plaster where pictures were ripped out of the walls. How one views Potocki's actions probably depends to some extent on one's politics: were the contents of Łańcut simply his own personal property, to be dispensed with as he chose, or were they the cultural heritage of the whole nation, and thus not his to remove? In any case, most of the very best things are gone, but more than enough remains to give a good idea of the pre-war grandeur of the house.

The towns and cities of the south-east are only part of its attraction, for it contains some of Poland's finest scenery as well, particularly in the Carpathian mountain region, stretching from the main Cracow-Przemyśl road, which runs just to the north of the foothills of the chain, all the way to the Czechoslovak border. The whole area is one vast beautiful landscape: green hills and mountains, well forested and watered by countless streams and rivers, including several fairly major ones, such as the San, Poprad, Dunajec, Raba and the almost identical-sounding Wisłok and Wisłoka. Many of the houses are still in the picturesque old style, with thatched or wood-shingled roofs, while many of the churches in this timber-rich region are also made of wood, with high-pitched roofs to cope with the huge snowfalls that winter almost invariably brings.

Mountain passes and rivers divide this part of the Carpathians into a number of smaller chains, including the Tatras, Pieniny and Beskids, the latter being further divided into the High, Low, Island, Żywiec and Silesian Beskids. (Some of these we shall visit in the next chapter, from Cracow.) Perhaps the most unusual, and certainly the most untypical, region is that of the Bieszczady, a wildly beautiful, almost wholly undeveloped section of the Car-pathians in the extreme south-eastern corner of the country, in Krosno province. This is a fascinating area for a number of reasons, not least because of its recent history. Before the war it was an extremely backward sheep-raising area largely inhabited by Or-thodox Ukrainians, known as Łemkos and Bojkos, whose ancestors had lived there for centuries. After the war, during the population transfers, large numbers of them were moved eastward into the Soviet Ukraine, while at the same time bands of right-wing Ukrainian nationalists began to operate in the area, giving the new left-wing government in Warsaw a very hard time indeed. In March 1947, they even went as far as to attack a military convoy, killing General Karol Świerczewski, the commander of the Polish Second Army and deputy minister of national defence. But by the end of 1947 the region was finally pacified, and the remaining Łemkos and Bojkos were deported to the previously German areas of northern and western Poland.

Despite the construction of an 137-kilometre-long circular road called the *Pętla Bieszczadzka* (Bieszczady Loop) through the heart of the Bieszczady, the region is basically as unspoilt as it was when the Łemkos and Bojkos left it. The mountains, which reach a maximum elevation of 1,346 metres (Mount Tarnica), are densely wooded, largely with oak and spruce, to a level of 1,100–1,200 metres, and crowned with beautiful steppe-like pastures, called *połoniny*, covered with a lush carpet of field grass often over a metre high. The whole region is extremely rich in wildlife, in-cluding brown bears, wolves, lynxes, wildcats, wild boars and several kinds of deer — not to mention adders, which seem to like the Bieszczady too. An unusual feature of the area are the *żubry*, the sole surviving European bison, a small herd of which were moved here after the war from their original home in the Białowieża Forest, on Poland's north-eastern border with the Soviet Union. Another curious feature is the fact that each year many thousands of sheep are transported here by train for pasturing from the Tatra mountains, 160 kilometres — as the crow flies — to the west.

When the Ukrainians left this area, they also left behind their pretty Orthodox churches, most of them wooden and full of superb icons. Many of the best of these icons are now on display in the Historical Museum which has been set up in the fifteenth century castle of Sanok, 73 kilometres south of Rzeszów, on the edge of the Bieszczady. The collection, which contains icons as old as the fourteenth century, is the largest of its kind in Poland, and said to be the second largest in the world, after the Tretiakov Gallery in Moscow. Another unusual attraction of Sanok lies just across the San River in the suburb of Olechowiec, where a *skansen* (outdoor museum of folk architecture) has been set up. One of many such museums in Poland, this one was established in 1959 to represent the extreme south-east of the country and contains a number of typical buildings from all over the area, including a small Orthodox church, a windmill, a watermill, an oilmill (the Krosno region to the west has been the centre of the Polish petroleum industry since the middle of the last century) and several houses and cottages, including one dating to 1630 and reputed to be the oldest peasant dwelling in Poland.

The Bieszczady have to some extent been 'discovered' by the Poles in recent years, and tourist facilities are gradually being developed, though the intention is to restrict them to certain spots, preserving most of the region as a primeval wilderness. This is, of course, an ideal area for camping, though limited hotel and hostel accommodation exists in three or four centres, particularly in the small town of Lesko (15 kilometres south-east of Sanok), the starting-point of the 'Bieszczady Loop' and thus the gateway to the whole region. While in Lesko, the traveller should make a visit to the late-Renaissance synagogue, which the Nazis burned down during the last war, and which has been rebuilt to house the local museum. The main point of interest are the magnificent tombstones, some dating back to the fourteenth century. They are tall and richly carved, full of Hebrew lettering and ancient symbolism: hands with outspread fingers for the Cohens, or descendants of priestly families; bowls and jugs for Levites; bunches of grapes for women who have borne children; palm fronds for dead maidens; and countless animals — eagles, lions, leopards etc. — representing particular families and individuals.

Before the last war the whole eastern half of Poland — and, indeed, all of Eastern Europe — was full of small towns and villages with a largely, and in some cases almost entirely, Jewish population. But today, as a result of Hitler's persecutions, there can hardly be more than a handful of Jews within 100 kilometres of this spot; while their culture — portrayed so effectively in the works of the Polish-born Nobel Prize winner Isaac Bashevis Singer — has been completely destroyed, leaving only such tangible memorials as the lonely tombstones of the deserted cemetery at Lesko.

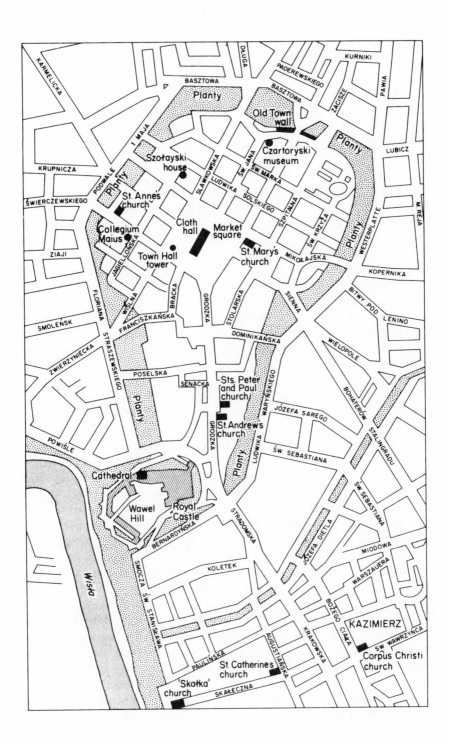

4 CRACOW AND ENVIRONS

Lying at the foot of the historic Wawel Hill, in the heart of the upper Vistula basin, Cracow (in Polish, Kraków) is the most beautiful city in Poland. This is no mere opinion, but a statement of fact, and one confirmed by virtually every foreign visitor whom I have met, not to mention the proud Cracovians themselves, who wax indefatigably lyrical on the subject! Cracow is also, together with Prague, the best preserved large town in east-central Europe, having miraculously escaped destruction towards the end of the last war, for the retreating Nazis had every intention of turning Cracow, like Warsaw, into fields of rubble. But in January 1945 the Red Army under Marshal Konev suddenly outflanked the Germans, obliging them to flee before they could blow the city up. Thank God they did, for the destruction of Cracow would have been as great a loss to humanity, in terms of art and architecture, as the massive damage wrought by the saturation bombing of Dresden only a month later.

The Cracovians have every reason to be proud of their city, which is, after all, the former capital of the country and, with a population which has recently passed the 700,000 mark, its third largest centre, after Warsaw and Łódź. Cracow is a very old city, and traces of early man have been found here that date back 100,000 years. It is not definitely known who founded the city or why, but, as usual, legend has something to say on the matter. Once upon a time, a fierce dragon was terrifying the neighbourhood, his favourite prey being pretty maidens, whom he used to drag back to devour in his cave at the base of Wawel Hill. But one day a local shoemaker's apprentice, a giant named Krak (or Krakus), hit upon a clever idea. He threw the dragon a sheep soaked in burning pitch, whereupon the former ate it and expired in a mass of smoke and flames. Krak went on to found Kraków, becoming its first prince. Whether or not he actually existed, he is commemorated by a great eighth- or ninth-century mound, the Kopiec Krakusa, across the Vistula in the south of the city. The dragon himself has recently been immortalized by a local sculptor, Bronisław Chromy, whose tall bronze effigy of him has been placed outside his cave on the banks of the Vistula, where it belches forth fire every couple of minutes.

Cracow was one of the main towns of the powerful Wiślanie tribe as early as the eighth century, and two centuries later it had developed into a prosperous commercial centre, the meeting-point of five important international trade routes. A bishopric was established in Cracow in 1000, and by Bolesław Wry-Mouth's statute of succession of 1138 it became the residence of the senior Polish prince. However, as we have seen, the 'musical chairs' formula of succession seriously weakened the country, rendering it a fairly easy prey to invaders, and in 1241 the Tatars attacked Cracow, which was then largely based on and around the Wawel, burning the almost entirely wooden city to the ground. They returned in the following year, but by 1257 the Cracovians were already laying out a new town based on a grid system some distance to the north, and this pattern has been preserved down to the present day.

In 1320 Cracow was confirmed as the capital by the coronation in Wawel Cathedral of Władysław Little-Ell, the first king of a united Poland, and for almost three centuries the town was to enjoy a Golden Age of commerce and culture. The strongest stimulus to economic and cultural expansion was provided by Władysław's successor, Kazimierz the Great (1333–70), who especially encouraged foreigners with much needed skills to settle in Poland. As a result, many Germans and, to a lesser extent, Italians, Armenians and others, arrived in Cracow, and with the passage of time they and their descendants gradually became assimilated and began to think of themselves as Poles. One group which found it much harder to assimilate was the Jews, large numbers of whom were by the end of the century already well established south-east of the Wawel in the Kazimierz suburb, which the great king himself had founded between two channels of the Vistula in 1335. The Jewish community here became one of the most famous in the whole of Europe, its rabbis acquiring the kind of reputation for solving complicated problems which Philadelphia lawyers enjoy in America. Indeed, there was an old saying which began: 'It doesn't take a Cracow rabbi to. . . .'

In the cultural sphere, King Kazimierz's greatest achievement was undoubtedly the establishment in Cracow in 1364 of the second oldest university — after Prague's — in central Europe. It was later named the Jagiellonian University following rich endowments from members of Poland's next dynasty, Kazimierz being, of course, the last Piast king. Copernicus, perhaps its most famous alumnus, studied here from 1491 to 1494.

The three centuries that preceded the transfer of the capital to Warsaw in 1596–1611 saw the erection of most of Cracow's greatest architectural beauties — churches, monastic buildings and proud town houses. To be sure, a number of its finest structures were erected in the decades following the transfer, but even so the city was clearly on the decline, a process accelerated by Swedish sieges in 1655 (the so-called 'Flood') and 1677 and further raids in 1702 at the beginning of the Great Northern War.

During the 1700s Cracow's fortunes plummeted, as did its population, which was no more than 10,000 by the end of the century. The Third Partition gave Cracow to Austria, but according to the terms of the Congress of Vienna (1815), the city was made a republic under the supervision of all three partitioning powers, lying, as it did, at their sole point of intersection. In February 1846, however, the Cracovians rebelled and succeeded in expelling the Austrian troops who were then in the city. The rebellion was put down within a fortnight, and Cracow was finally incorporated into Austria but, as events were to prove, the situation could have been worse. Habsburg rule was never as oppressive as that of the Russians and Prussians, and as the century progressed the Poles of Galicia (i.e. the Austrian Partition) acquired substantial cultural freedom and political autonomy. Two factors played a particularly large part in this process. First, the Austrian censorship was much more easygoing than, for example, the Russian. Second, the Austrian Germans were obliged to be conciliatory towards the Poles, whose delegates' support they required for their majority over the other nationalities — Czechs, Ukrainians, South Slavs, Italians etc. — in the Viennese parliament. As a result, large numbers of artists, writers and other creative people moved to Cracow, which soon became the cultural capital of the dismembered nation, a position it maintained until at least the beginning of World War I.

As we have seen, Cracow is one of the few Polish cities to have come through the last war virtually intact. Its dozens of churches and scores of historic secular buildings might, by their number alone, daunt or at least confuse even the most indefatigable sightseer, so it may prove helpful to consider the town section by section — the Wawel, the Old Town, Kazimierz, and outlying districts — which is in fact, the approach which we shall follow here.

It is appropriate that we should begin our tour on the Wawel, for it is here that Cracow itself began, many centuries ago. In fact, the hill was occupied long before the rotunda of SS. Felix and Adauctus, perhaps the earliest surviving Polish stone building, was erected on its summit sometime during the second half of the tenth century. (The rotunda, a small structure with four apses, lies beneath the south-west, or kitchen, wing of the royal castle and has been incorporated into an extremely well arranged archeological exhibition, about which more later.) The hill, which dominates the town, stands 238 metres above sea level, and its summit, which lies nearly 30 metres above the surrounding terrain, is encircled by a number of buildings, of which the cathedral and the royal palace are by far the most interesting. Indeed, the latter constitute what is arguably the most important complex of buildings in the entire country, occupying a place in Polish history comparable to that of Westminster Abbey and Windsor Castle in the history of England.

Viewed from below, the Wawel is an almost fairy-tale assembly of towers, spires and fortifications, and once one has reached the summit, whether by the main entrance to the north, passing an equestrian statue of Tadeusz Kościuszko given by the people of Dresden to replace one destroyed by the Nazis, or by the south entrance, climbing up from plac Bernadyński, the magic still holds. The cathedral, which lies just inside the main entrance to the Wawel, was begun in the fourteenth century and is in fact the third cathedral to stand on this site. Nothing remains of the first, but of the second the Romanesque St. Leonard's crypt still survives. The visitor cannot fail to notice that the exceptionally short nave lies at a slight angle to the chancel, the reason being that during the fourteenth-century reconstruction the architects, who worked from east to west, beginning with the chancel and ending with the nave, followed a new orientation for the former but reverted to the old one for the latter. At the bend stands the tomb of St. Stanisław (i.e. Stanislaus) with its imposing baldacchino of 1626 by the Italian Giovanni Trevano. The saint's silver coffin is Gdańsk work and dates from 1671. St. Stanisław, an eleventh-century bishop of Cracow, was found guilty of treason in 1079 — whether justly or unjustly is open to dispute — and sentenced to the loss of his limbs, which naturally meant death. As the knights appointed to execute him wavered, the King, Bolesław the Bold, himself performed the dire deed. History, however, has given the last word to Stanisław, for the bishop, who is reputed to have performed a number of miracles, even bringing a dead man, Piotrowin, back to life, was

canonized in 1253, becoming the first Polish saint; whereas
Bolesław was soon driven out of the country by rebellious nobles
and died in Hungary in mysterious circumstances two years after
Stanisław's death.

Beginning with Władysław Little-Ell in 1320, the kings of
Poland were all crowned here, and most of them are buried here as
well, their tombs lining the aisles and several of the eighteen side
chapels. The royal tombs are, in fact, one of the glories of the
cathedral, the earliest being (in the north aisle) that of Władysław
Little-Ell himself, dating from the middle of the fourteenth century. Undoubtedly one of the finest tombs is the red marble figure
of Kazimierz IV (or 'the Jagiellonian'), begun in 1492, the year of
the king's death. Standing in the chapel of the Holy Cross, at the
south-west end of the cathedral, the tomb is the work of Veit Stoss,
the great Nuremberg sculptor, whom the Poles call Wit Stwosz.
The canopy above the tomb, a highly expressive structure with
richly carved capitals supporting an intricate pattern of arcading
and vaulting, is by Jörg Huber of Passau and is the earliest, and a
fairly rare, example in Poland of a decorative style of stonework
which flourished particularly in Austria and southern Germany.
Another notable feature of the chapel is its fifteenth-century
Russo-Byzantine frescoes, painted a generation or two after those of
Lublin and Sandomierz.

Amongst the other noteworthy features of the cathedral is the
crucifix of Queen Jadwiga, a large fourteenth-century work in the
north-west of the ambulatory (i.e. the space surrounding the
chancel). According to legend, the figure of Christ told the Queen
to marry Jagiełło, the Grand Duke of Lithuania, thereby bringing
his people to Christianity. To the right is the Lady Chapel, with
Santi Gucci's highly architectural monument to Stefan Batory.
Opposite, across the ambulatory, stands Francesco Placidi's
enormous pair of monuments erected in 1757 to King Michał
Korybut Wiśniowiecki and his more famous successor, King Jan
Sobieski. The latter monument is particularly dramatic, with busts
of the King and his French Queen raised in triumph above the
trophies of war, beneath which cower two Turkish prisoners. Just
around the corner of the ambulatory, to the left of Queen Jadwiga's
crucifix, is the entrance to the treasury, a rich repository of
coronation robes, royal insignia and cathedral vestments. Adjacent,
with entrance from the sacristy, is the Sigismund Tower. Besides
offering a magnificent view of the surrounding city, it also houses
the largest bell in Poland, the Sigismund bell, which measures

nearly two and a half metres in diameter and was cast from captured enemy cannon in 1520, during the reign of Zygmunt (or Sigismund) the Old, hence its name.

Off the south aisle is the greatest architectural glory of the cathedral, the Sigismund chapel, which the same Zygmunt the Old commissioned from the Florentine Bartolomeo Berrecci to serve as a mausoleum for himself and his children, his son and successor Zygmunt August and his daughter Anna Jagiellonka, Stefan Batory's queen. It took Berrecci 14 years (1519–33) to complete the project, the result being an extremely satisfying, and quintessentially Renaissance, composition of mathematical forms: a cube surmounted by a drum, cylindrical on the inside and octagonal on the outside, the whole crowned by a dome. The pure mathematics of the chapel is softened by a wealth of ornamentation such as statues, busts, angels, dynastic symbols, garlands, beasts, mythological creatures etc., while the dome is pierced with an elegant lantern topped by a gilded crown. The superb red marble effigies of the two kings (father on top, son below) are most likely by Padovano, while that of Queen Anna is definitely the work of Santi Gucci. The Kaplica Zygmuntowska — to give the chapel its Polish name — is generally acknowledged to be the supreme achievement of Renaissance architecture in Poland, and one of the finest mausolea of its period anywhere in Europe.

The Vasa chapel, which lies a few steps to the west, was begun in 1605 and is a handsome affair, though not of the outstanding architectural merit of the Sigismund chapel. Of the other attractions of the cathedral, the crypt contains interesting Romanesque vaulting, as well as the tombs of a number of Polish heroes, including the Romantic poets Adam Mickiewicz and Juliusz Słowacki and the twentieth-century soldier and politician Marshal Józef Piłsudski, not to mention the actual coffins of many of the 'royals' commemorated upstairs.

Leaving the cathedral by the west entrance and turning left, we come to a broad lawn containing the foundations of two ancient churches now demolished, St. Michael's and St. George's. The lawn is bounded in part by ancient fortifications, and in part by visually uninteresting barracks erected by the Austrians, of which there has been some talk of pulling down recently, as they rather obscure the view of the royal castle from below.

It is from this side that the cathedral appears to best advantage, its spires, towers, gables and domes — including those of the Vasa and Sigismund chapels, which appear almost identical on the outside, except that the latter dome is gilded — forming an extremely picturesque ensemble. Passing along the south side of the cathedral, we enter a large gateway, at the end of which lies the castle courtyard. The originally eleventh-century princely residence had been enlarged and remodelled on a number of occasions, not least by Władysław Little-Ell and Kazimierz the Great, but a serious fire in 1499 necessitated near-total reconstruction. To this end, Zygmunt the Old employed a Florentine architect named Francesco, and when the latter died in 1516, Berrecci took over, to be assisted in later years by the Pole, Benedykt of Sandomierz. Further rebuilding took place during subsequent reigns, even after the transfer of the capital to Warsaw.

The results are pretty impressive. The huge courtyard is surrounded on two and a half sides by two storeys of fine Ionic arcading topped by an upper storey of double height, its slender, elegant colonnades supporting a massive projecting roof. The double height, an unusual feature in Poland or indeed anywhere else, has sometimes been explained as a means of admitting extra light to upper-storey rooms on dark winter days. The walls carry the remains of brightly coloured sixteenth-century frescoes. Nowadays open-air concerts are given in the courtyard, replacing the tournaments and pageants of an earlier day.

The entrance to the royal apartments (*Komnaty*) is at the southeast corner. The Austrians converted the castle into a barracks, but independence brought restoration, and the interiors are now once again Renaissance or, in the case of Zygmunt III's chambers, Baroque. The richly carved stone doorways are an exception, revealing distinct Gothic elements. Probably the most unusual room is the Ambassadors', or Audience, Hall (*Sala Poselska*), the coffered ceiling of which originally contained 194 wooden heads. Thirty survive, including one obviously very garrulous woman with a broad bandage across her mouth. The frescoes in this room were painted by Hans Dürer in 1535 and depict a humanist allegory of human life. The richest rooms are Zygmunt III's and include his handsome study, the walls of which are literally covered with paintings, and the Bird Room (*Sala pod Ptakami*), so called because the king, who was a keen alchemist by the way, had toy birds suspended on wires from the ceiling. The splendour of Zygmunt's apartments is augmented by a great deal of gilding, and also by the highly wrought Spanish leather that covers so many of the walls.

For many visitors the most impressive feature of the castle, and doubtless its most valuable, will be the mangificent collection of tapestries, largely formed by Zygmunt August, the last Jagiellonian king. From the Flemish artist Michiel van Coxien, who had been strongly influenced by Raphael, he specially commissioned 150 tapestries largely based on animal and biblical themes such as the Garden of Eden, the Tower of Babel, the Flood etc., and on his death he left a total of 356, of which 136 survive. They were taken to Canada for safe-keeping during the last war and were returned to Poland, following lengthy diplomatic negotiations, in 1959. They are reputed to be the largest collection of their kind in Europe.

Another treasure of the castle is its collection of Turkish tents captured by Jan Sobieski's troops at the battle of Vienna in 1683. They are decorated with appliqué work, that is to say, the flowers, mathematical designs and other embellishments have been sewn onto canvas. They are also extremely rare, for whereas the Turks at home went on using their tents, gradually wearing them out in the process, the Poles preserved what they had captured as mementoes, and it is even said that Turkish scholars travel to Cracow especially to see them. They are very effectively displayed, along with a number of beautiful carpets and other Oriental objects, in several climate-controlled upper-storey rooms. Unfortunately, the breath of too many visitors threatens to destroy them, so they are open to the general public only infrequently now, and mention of them has disappeared from recent travel brochures, although specialists are naturally given access.

At the north-east corner of the courtyard is the entrance to the crown treasury (*skarbiec koronny*), which is housed in vaulted rooms surviving from the fourteenth-century Gothic residence of Kazimierz the Great and his immedite successors. Much of the collection was plundered by the Prussians, who occupied Cracow in 1794–6, but many interesting pieces remain, often with royal connections, like the fourteenth-century silver-gilt and enamel chalice from the chantry of Kazimierz the Great, the sword of Zygmunt the Old, the exquisite gilded and bejewelled Italian chain that once belonged to Zygmunt III and the handsome silver Polish eagle commissioned from Heinrich Männlich of Augsburg by Jan Kazimierz. Undoubtedly the most famous exhibit is the thirteenth-century '*Szczerbiec*', meaning 'Jagged Sword', so called because an early Polish king is reputed to have notched its blade on the great gate of Kiev. It was used at all Polish coronations, beginning with that of Władysław Little-Ell in 1320.

Adjacent to the treasury is the castle armoury, which, like the treasury, has frequently been plundered, but still contains much of interest, including some unbelievably dashing suits of winged armour, complete with winged helmets and leopard-skin capes, formerly worn by seventeenth-century Polish hussars.

Passing back out through the gateway into the grassy forecourt, the visitor would be well advised to turn left into the old castle kitchen block, where a permanent exhibition showing the history of the Wawel has recently been assembled. A tour of the archaeological section dealing with the so-called 'Underground Wawel' is an exciting experience, as the visitor follows a ramp suspended in mid-air amidst the remains of the tenth-century rotunda of SS. Felix and Adauctus (mentioned above) and numerous showcases containing architectural bits and pieces as well as models of previous Wawel buildings. Back upstairs in the ground-floor section there are fascinating displays of early tools, utensils, tiles, jewellery etc., some as old as the paleolithic period.

Leaving the Wawel, we have a choice of two — actually one and a half — routes to take us back to the Main Market Square (*Rynek Główny*), the heart of the Old Town. One follows ul. Kanonicza, architecturally one of Cracow's most interesting streets. Its name derives from the fact that it was once the residence of the canons of Wawel cathedral. Most of the houses were originally Gothic but have undergone a certain amount of remodelling, much of it fortunate, as in the case of their handsome Renaissance portals, those at Nos. 18 and 21 being especially fine. The latter house, the Deanery, is the best building in the street, with a beautiful Renaissance courtyard by Santi Gucci. Jan Długosz, the mediaeval historian, lived on the corner at No. 25, across the road from the Wawel. At the moment, this part of Cracow is being restored, so the houses in ul. Kanonicza have been stripped of their plaster, which renders them less picturesque perhaps, but provides, as compensation, an unequalled opportunity to study their original 'naked' architectural style, as well as later additions.

Ul. Kanonicza terminates at ul. Senacka, which will take us into ul. Grodzka and thence to the Market Square. Or we could just as easily have taken ul. Grodzka directly from the foot of the Wawel. My advice would be to backtrack a bit and cover both routes, each of which is fairly short, as it would be a pity to miss either street. Ul. Grodzka is particularly rich in churches, amongst the most important being St. Andrew's (św. Andrzeja). One of Cracow's oldest, it was erected towards the end of the eleventh century and was the only church in the city to withstand the massive Tatar invasion of

1241. The church is constructed largely of stone, a far commoner building material in hilly Little Poland than in the flatter north, where brick is almost universal. In striking contrast to the severe exterior, the inside of the church is a warm pastel Baroque, full of exquisite stucco work and a delightful boat pulpit, both by Baldassare Fontana, a member of a family which, like Merlini, hailed from the Lake Lugano region and provided eighteenth-century Poland with numerous first-rate builders and craftsmen.

Literally only a few metres to the north lies one of the city's finest churches, SS. Peter and Paul (św. Piotra i Pawła). Begun by Zygmunt III for the Jesuits in 1596, it was the first Baroque church in Cracow, and one of the earliest in the entire country. Standing back from the street, its tall, broad façade, which was modelled on that of II Gesù, the Jesuits' mother church in Rome, is one of the most impressive in Cracow. The screen of railings and pillars that once divided it from the street was, unfortunately, largely dismantled in the sixties, and the statues of saints that formerly stood on the pillars have been relegated to the adjoining yard, to await, one hopes, restoration. The interior of the church is fairly sober, apart from some fine stucco work by Giovanni Battista Falconi in the vaulting of the chancel and chapels. The lay-out of SS. Peter and Paul is characteristic of the so-called 'Jesuit' style, with its large dome, single broad nave for preaching to large congregations — the Order has always been famous for its oratory — and numerous side altars, typifying the Counter-Reformation ideal of making religion more accessible to the people.

A few minutes' walk further north, partly along galleried pavements, brings us to a busy tram crossing, formerly the site of an ancient market place and now consisting of two squares, plac Dominikański (to the east of ul. Grodzka) and plac Wiosny Ludów (to the west). At the west end of the latter, almost adjoining the huge Wielopolski Palace, now the City Hall, stands the Franciscan church, which was completed *circa* 1270 and has been rebuilt on several occasions since. In Poland, the church is mainly celebrated for its *Art Nouveau* stained glass windows and murals of 1895 by Stanisław Wyspiański, which some visitors will like, and others find fairly mawkish. What is undeniably interesting is the Gothic cloister to the south of the church, with its fifteenth-century frescoes and valuable collection of old portraits of the bishops of Cracow.

The plac Dominikański takes its name from the big monastic church erected at its east end in the latter part of the thirteenth century to replace an earlier structure burnt by the Tatars in 1241.

The collapse of the roof in 1850 and subsequent restoration has effaced a great deal of the church's character, but it still retains a number of very fine chapels, particularly that of St. Jacek (up the steps from the north aisle), with more first-rate stucco work by Baldassare Fontana. Like most of the old buildings of Cracow, the Dominican church lies below the surrounding ground level. This is particularly noticeable at the main entrance, the richly carved fourteenth-century western portal. The reason for this is somewhat more complicated than might at first be imagined. Obviously, there has been a certain amount of settlement over the centuries, as is only to be expected in the case of massive structures, such as churches and palaces. But there is a second factor, too. In olden days, Cracow was largely surrounded by marshes, most of which have since been drained. When carts arrived in the city, they inevitably carried mud on their wheels, and gradually, over the centuries, this mud raised the level of Cracow's streets.

Five minutes to the north lies the Rynek Główny, one of the great market squares of Europe, measuring over 200 metres on each side. The centre of the square is filled by the arcaded *Sukiennice* (Cloth Hall), which was originally Gothic but, following a serious fire in 1555, was rebuilt by our old friends Padovano and Santi Gucci, the latter providing its highly ornate, and typically Polish Renaissance, attic. Note the masks on the parapet, which are reminiscent of those in the courtyard at Baranów, also — probably — by Santi Gucci. The shops lining the vaulted hall that runs the length of the *Sukiennice* are colourful and picturesque, but I think it doubtful that any visitor who goes to the trouble of reading this guide-book will find much of interest there. (The same, alas, applies to many, if not indeed most, of the 'souvenirs' on sale in the country.) The first floor is much more interesting, with its large collection of Polish paintings of the eighteenth and nineteenth centuries.

Of the other two structures standing in the Market Square, the larger is the Town Hall tower (*Wieża Ratuszowa*), all that remains of a fourteenth-century structure demolished by the Austrians in 1820. It now houses a branch of the Cracow Historical Museum, while the dungeon underneath has been turned into a café renowned for its *miód* (mead, i.e. honey wine). Opposite the tower, at the entrance to ul. Grodzka, stands the Romanesque church of St. Adalbert (św. Wojciecha), a tiny copper-domed cube partly concealed by trees. Its crypt contains a fascinating archaeological exhibition dealing with the history of the Market Square.

The sides of the square are lined with beautiful houses and

mansions of various periods, most originally dating to the fifteenth to seventeenth centuries. Amongst the most interesting are No. 8, the 'Kamienica pod Jaszczurami' ('House of the Salamanders'), and No. 17, the 'Kamienica Hetmańska' ('Hetman's House'), each with superb Gothic vaulting in their ground-floor rooms; No. 27, the 'Pałac pod Baranami' ('Palace of the Rams'), housing a popular cabaret in its Gothic vaults (open Saturdays and Sundays, late evenings only); and No. 35, the Krzysztofory Mansion, also with Gothic vaults (now containing an art gallery) as well as, on the first floor, more fine stucco work by the ubiquitous Baldassare Fontana. By the way, the bookshops around the square have the best selection in Cracow of travel guides, art books and postcards, and there is a fine music shop on the south side. Also on the south side, at No. 16, is the ancient Wierzynek restaurant, reputed to be the best in Poland, while the 'Antyczna' cafe at No. 38 is one of the most old-fashioned, and consequently one of the pleasantest, in the city.

The most important of the buildings lining the square is not, however, a house or mansion, but a church, and undoubtedly the most famous church in all Poland, the *Kościół Mariacki*, or St. Mary's. A church has stood on this site since at least as early as the 1220s. In 1241, a watchman stationed in the church tower caught sight of the invading Tatars and sounded the alarm on his trumpet, rousing his fellow Cracovians to the defence of their city. A Tatar arrow pierced the trumpeter's throat in mid-tune, making him immortal, for every hour on the hour a modern trumpeter repeats his performance, stopping abruptly at the point where, according to tradition, the arrow silenced his ancient predecessor. What is more, the trumpeter's haunting melody, known as the 'Hejnał', is broadcast, Big Ben-like, every day at noon, on Polish Radio.

The church has changed beyond recognition since the time of the first trumpeter. In the fourteenth century, the original brick hall of pre-Tatar days began to be rebuilt as a tall, narrow basilica. Two square western towers were added towards the end of the century, although the more northern of the two had to wait another hundred years before receiving its octagonal top surmounted by a gilded crown. The latter signifies the fact that this is the church of the Blessed Virgin, Queen of Poland. It is from this tower that the present-day trumpeter sounds his truncated call.

The interior of the church is dominated by one of the greatest works of art in the entire country, the magnificent Mariacki Altar, created by the Nuremberg sculptor Veit Stoss and his Cracovian studio specifically for the church in the years between 1477 and

1489. One of the largest Gothic triptychs ever, it remained here undisturbed until 1939, when the Nazis carried it off to Nuremberg. After its return to Poland in 1946, it was subjected to many thousands of man-hours of painstaking renovation, during which the wood was restored and several layers of over-painting removed.

Closed, the altar displays a dozen painted bas-relief panels of the life of Christ. The triptych is opened regularly at noon, and the visitor would do well to arrive a quarter of an hour beforehand to be certain of a seat on one of the benches in the chancel. Great drama accompanies the opening: the organ begins to play, whereupon a nun steps forward, speaks a few words to the inevitable large crowd and then, armed with a long hooked pole, proceeds to pull back the wings of the triptych. The effect is overwhelming. This is Gothic, but of a highly expressionistic, even mannered sort. The colours are bright, there is much gilding, and the scale is very large: the figures in the centre panel, the Dormition of the Virgin, are in fact larger than life. The six side panels, which portray scenes from the life of the Virgin, are smaller, but just as vivid. Note the delicately delineated expressions, the extraordinarily three-dimensional rendering of the draperies and the numerous details from everyday life, like the kettle warming over the burning logs in the panel depicting the Birth of the Virgin.

High above the altar are three windows of ancient (*circa* 1370–1400) stained glass, extremely rare objects in a country which has experienced so many destructive invasions. The panels, which represent Bible stories, are probably too small for even the keenest-sighted worshipper to make out at such a distance and were probably intended purely as decoration. On a smaller scale, but of the very highest quality, is the superb stone crucifix of 1491, also by Stoss, above the baroque altar at the end of the south nave aisle. The larger rainbow-beam crucifix hanging in the chancel arch dates to 1473 and is also thought to be Stoss' work.

The little fourteenth-century church directly behind St. Mary's is St. Barbara's, originally a chapel for the cemetery which lay between the two churches. The front of St. Barbara's contains a rare Gethsemane group dating to the last part of the fifteenth century. In the Middle Ages, St. Mary's was the church of the large and prosperous German community, and it was the latter who commissioned Stoss' altar, while St. Barbara's served the Poles. However, with the growth of Polonization the demography of the town altered, and the two nationalities eventually exchanged buildings.

The streets off the square contain seemingly countless architectural pleasures — too many, at least, for us to attempt to deal with any but the most important here. However, any visit to Cracow should include the old university quarter, lying to the west and south-west of the square. The oldest structure here is the *Collegium Maius* (ul. Św. Anny 8/10), one of the earliest surviving university buildings in Europe, dating from 1492-7. Its charming courtyard is surrounded by vaulted arcades, while the building itself now houses the Historical Museum of the university. One of its greatest treasures is a globe of 1510, the first ever to show the newly discovered continent of America. In the same street stands Tylman van Gameren's magnificent university church of St. Anne's (1689-1703), somewhat reminiscent of SS. Peter and Paul in its adherence to the Jesuit architectural ideal. It has recently been restored, and its superb stucco, the work, not surprisingly, of Baldassare Fontana, is by common consent the best in Poland. Many visitors eventually become saturated with churches in a city as rich in fine ecclesiastical buildings as Cracow, but St. Anne's is truly one of the most beautiful in the entire country, and definitely not to be missed.

The same applies to the Dom Szołayskich (Szołayski House), now a branch of the National Museum, a short walk to the north on pl. Szczepański. This is one of the great treasure-houses of mediaeval Polish painting and sculpture, and most of the collection comes from country churches in the surrounding province of Little Poland, although some of the best works are from Cracow itself. Undoubtedly the most famous piece is the exquisite carving of the Virgin and Child from the parish church of Krużlowa, which formed part of the Polish exhibition at the Royal Academy in London in 1970. The graceful, rhythmic curve of the Virgin (in Poland the style is known as 'curved Gothic'), her tender expression and the delicate harmony of the two figures reveal a close kinship with other examples of the so-called 'Beautiful Madonna' style current in central Europe around 1400. From the hand of an unknown sculptor, the 'Madonna of Krużlowa' is undoubtedly the finest surviving Polish work of art of its period.

Just to the north of pl. Szczepański, in ul. Reformacka, lies one of Cracow's comparatively unknown curiosities. Here in the crypt of the Reformed Franciscans — the church itself is not particularly interesting — lie a large number of coffins, each containing a mummified body. No special embalming process has been used. Instead, as in St. Michan's church in Dublin special micro-climatic conditions in the crypt, which is very dry, preserve the bodies naturally. The monks' favourite show-pieces include that of an extremely tall (over two metres) eighteenth-century mayor of Cracow, a Napoleonic soldier in uniform, and an unfortunate bride who died on her wedding day and was buried in the same dress in which she had been married. The crypt is not generally open to the public, so if one is going to trouble the overworked monks to have a peek at the mummies, it might be advisable to look apologetic and foreign (the Poles are often willing to do favours for visitors which they would not ordinarily do for each other) and to leave a few dollars or a couple of pounds as a donation for the church. Foreign currency is always welcome in Poland.

Around the corner and a few minutes along ul. Pijarska lies one of Cracow's best late-Baroque churches, that of the Piarists, built between 1718 and 1759 to designs by Kacper Bażanka (or Barzanka) and Francesco Placidi, the latter having previously worked on the court church in Dresden.

Immediately adjacent is the permanent home of the Czartoryski Museum. In 1876, the family's rich collections were brought to Cracow from France, whither they had been taken following the defeat of the 1830–1 Insurrection and the confiscation of their estates in Russian-occupied Poland. To house the collections the Cracow town council provided the former Piarist monastery buildings, and here they remained until 1939, when the Nazis removed the best pieces. Most, though by no means all, were recovered and returned to the museum after the war, and here they remained until a few years ago, when restoration was begun on the building itself. The *chefs-d'oeuvre* are for the time being exhibited in the former seventeenth-century Arsenal next-door, and here the visitor can view, amongst other superb works, two of Poland's finest paintings, Rembrandt's 'Landscape with the Good Samaritan' (also known as the 'Landscape before a Storm') and Leonardo's 'Lady with an Ermine'.

The Arsenal abuts onto the remains of Cracow's mediaeval town walls. The latter originally encircled the town and contained seven gates and 33 bastions, each defended by a different guild. They gradually fell into ruin and were almost completely dismantled in the second decade of the last century, to be replaced by a green belt (the 'Planty') four kilometres long, which encircles the Old Town. Only the most beautiful section was left standing: St. Florian's Gate (including the Furriers' Bastion), erected *circa* 1300, as well as the Carpenters', Joiners' and Trimming-makers' Bastions. The huge, squat Barbican facing the gate is, along with Warsaw's, one of the very few remaining in Central Europe and dates from 1498–9.

Further along the Planty we come to pl. Św. Ducha (Holy Ghost Square), much of which is occupied by the competent, but architecturally uninspired Słowacki Theatre, built in 1893 to plans obviously influenced by the Paris Opéra. What we have come here for is, above all, the church of the Holy Cross (św. Krzyża), a fourteenth-century structure, its fine vaulted nave of 1528 supported by a single column, from which 16 stone ribs spread upwards palm-like. The church is not always open, so it may be necessary to request admission from the priests in the presbytery to the south of the church. Here also, an apologetic, foreign look, and a subsequent donation, is highly recommended. Once inside, note too the fine Gothic and Renaissance frescoes. Outside, at the east end of the church, a life-size figure of Christ stooped beneath his cross emerges somewhat unexpectedly from a window at ground level.

On the whole, this is the least remarkable part of the Old Town, so we shall backtrack a bit and head south along ul. Floriańska, the most interesting street north of the Market Square. For some, the most rewarding stop will be at No. 45, the *'Jama Michalikowa'* (Michalik's Cave') café, formerly the location of a famous literary cabaret, the *'Zielony Balonik'* ('Little Green Balloon'), founded in 1907. The ice cream is excellent here, particularly the peach melba, but basically the reason we are here is to admire the delightful *art nouveau* decoration of the back room (sensibly reserved for non-smokers). The beautiful polished wood, the bits of stained glass, the waitresses' charming long dresses and the fascinating period mementos make it difficult — as I know only too well — to prevent an hour's stop here from turning into an entire afternoon or evening.

Visitors interested in large, heavily romantic historical canvases will want to visit ul. Floriańska 41, the house of Jan Matejko (1838–95), one of Poland's most popular and renowned painters, where a number of his canvases are displayed, along with some of the old costumes and weaponry depicted in them. But now our route takes us south of the Old Town proper to the ancient suburb of Kazimierz, formerly an island between two branches of the Vistula, until the Old Vistula was filled in during the last century and replaced by a ring of boulevards. Substantial remains of the wall that used to encircle Kazimierz can still be seen in the gardens of the Paulite church on Skałka rise, in the extreme west of the suburb, near the river. The church itself, which was built in

1734–51, is not particularly remarkable, although it has an attractive location, and the crypt contains the tombs of a number of
eminent Poles, including the historian Jan Długosz (1415–80) and
the eminent composer Karol Szymanowski (1882–1937). No, what
draws us here is the quiet, usually fairly overgrown monastery
garden with its fish-pond dominated by a figure of St. Stanislaw,
whose remains were, according to tradition, thrown into it.

The heart of Kazimierz is dominated by two truly monumental
Gothic basilicas: the Lateran Canons' Corpus Christi (*Bożego
Ciała*), originally founded by Kazimierz the Great in 1340, and the
Augustinian church of St. Catherine (*św. Katarzyny*) of slightly
later date. Both churches have typically late-Gothic high naves, St.
Catherine's particularly so, and both also have cloisters. Corpus
Christi has some extremely rare fifteenth-century stained glass
windows in the chancel, while St. Catherine's is remarkable for its
magnificent seventeenth-century high altar, and for the Gothic
wall paintings of its cloister, some as old as the fourteenth century.
The latter church — on balance, the more interesting of the two — is
often closed, so it may be necessary to hunt for a priest in the church
chancellery (entrance in ul. Augustiańska and then up the stairs).

Many visitors will want to investigate the folk art and costumes
and the authentic rooms from peasant cottages on display in the
Ethnographic Museum, housed in the former sixteenth-century
Kazimierz town hall on pl. Wolnica, roughly midway between the
two churches. But we shall make our way north-eastward to the
former Ghetto, centred on ul. Szeroka (Broad Street), the old
Jewish market place. Somehow most of the old synagogues in the
area survived Hitler, and although few of them now function as
places of worship — for example, two of them have been turned into
art or restoration workshops — one or two are active, especially the
old Remu'h synagogue, established over 400 years ago. It is
surrounded by an ancient Jewish cemetery, one of the oldest surviving in Europe, and full of richly carved Renaissance and
Baroque tombstones. Chief amongst them (directly behind the
synagogue) is that of Remu'h himself, a wise and famous Cracow
rabbi, the top of whose tomb is always covered with stones (a
traditional Jewish sign of respect) and Hebrew messages left largely,
or so the caretaker once informed me, by visiting American Jews.
Even more ancient than the Remu'h synagogue is the Stara (Old)
synagogue at the south end of ul. Szeroka. The oldest Jewish
religious structure in Poland, dating back probably to the end of
the fifteenth or the beginning of the sixteenth century, it was

destroyed by the Nazis and has been reconstructed to serve as a museum of Jewish culture.

Excursions from Cracow

The suburbs of Cracow contain one or two buildings good enough to lure us outside the city. By far the grandest is the Camaldolite church of Bielany, in the south-west corner of the Wolski Woods, some five kilometres to the west of Cracow. Begun in 1605 to the plans of Andrea Spezza, it is a massive structure, easily visible from several kilometres away across the Vistula to the south. Unlike its counterpart outside Warsaw, the Camaldolites still occupy this church, and as they are an eremitical order, no women are allowed inside. What *male* visitors are allowed to see is the rich Baroque interior, the gardens where the monks — strict vegetarians — till the soil in total silence, the tiny hermit cells where they live and the sober crypt where they are finally interred.

On the opposite (south) bank of the Vistula lies the ancient Benedictine abbey of Tyniec, founded in 1044. The original Romanesque structure has been altered frequently over the centuries, and the church is now largely Baroque, although substantial remains of the early fortifications have survived. Post-war archaeological excavations have uncovered many interesting objects, some of which are on display in the church cloisters, although one of the most valuable, an eleventh-century travelling chalice, is now amongst the prize possessions of the Wawel Crown Treasury. The greatest attraction of the abbey is, however, its charming position on a great rock high above the Vistula, and its wonderful atmosphere of peace, the loudest sound being the mooing of the cattle grazing in the meadows below. Here, too, as in Brochów near Warsaw, the visitor might well imagine that he is a hundred kilometres from nowhere, though in fact the automobile tachometer has registered a mere nine from Cracow!

A journey of about the same length to the east of the city brings us to Nowa Huta (New Foundry), the newest district of Cracow, conceived shortly after the last war to serve a twofold purpose. The first was to create a great steel-making complex, and in this the project has been successful: Nowa Huta is now the largest foundry in Poland, its huge work force of 35,000 producing some seven million tonnes of steel annually. But the project also contained a strong element of social engineering. Cracow is and always has been the most traditional, the most Catholic and — dare one say it? — the most bourgeois city in Poland. So, the idea was that by building

Nowa Huta to the east of the city, and with the old industrial centre
of Upper Silesia only an hour's drive to the west, Cracow would be
surrounded by healthy, working-class ideals (remember, this was
during the height of Stalinism) and would quickly lose its bourgeois
character. It should be added that the location of Nowa Huta made
little economic sense, as it was on the wrong side of Cracow from the
point of view of transport and raw materials. Also, the prevailing
winds blow Nowa Huta's pollution westward, damaging Cracow's
beautiful ancient architecture, a problem which has only recently
begun to be discussed, though it has long been recognized. The
social engineering has been less than a complete success, however,
for the workers of Nowa Huta have been largely drawn from the
peasantry, the most conservative and religious layer of Polish
society. No church was built for them — the construction of new
churches has always been a thorny issue in Church-state relations in
post-war Poland — so every Sunday for a quarter of a century a high
proportion of the total population of some 200,000 poured into
Cracow to attend Mass. Finally after years of negotiations, approval
was given to erect a church, and in 1976 the huge, whale-shaped
ultra-modern structure was consecrated by the local archbishop,
Cardinal Karol Wojtyła, now known to the world by a different
name and title. As for social engineering, there has naturally been
considerable interplay between Cracow and Nowa Huta, but on the
whole the residents of the latter are not noticeably different from
other Poles, having acquired all the so-called bourgeois aspir-
ations — colour televisions, automobiles, bigger flats, holidays
abroad etc. — that characterize most Europeans and Americans,
whatever their political philosophy. So much for social engineering.

A fascinating and virtually unique excursion to a very different
type of industrial centre takes us 13 kilometres south-east of Cracow
to the ancient salt-mining town of Wieliczka. The mine here has
been worked since at least the thirteenth century, its product
formerly being transported across the Carpathians to Hungary and
adjacent countries in exchange for wine and other southern
commodities. Its legendary founder was St. Kinga, a thirteenth-
century princess, the daughter of King Béla IV of Hungary.
Betrothed to Prince Bolesław Wstydliwy (the Bashful) of Cracow
and Sandomierz, she wanted, according to legend, to bring her
new subjects a gift which would please them all. Having heard
that her husband's land, though rich, lacked salt, she informed her
father, who thereupon endowed her with a salt well in the
Hungarian provinces, into which, for no apparent reason, she

tossed her engagement ring. Later, on her way to Cracow to join her new husband, she stopped at Wieliczka, then a small village, and — again for no apparent reason — ordered a deep shaft to be dug there, whereupon her ring was found embedded in a lump of rock salt. The shaft, so the legend maintains, was the origin of the present-day mine.

Over the last couple of centuries Wieliczka has been visited by countless travellers, Goethe and Balzac being only two of the most famous. It is still being worked today on nine levels, reaching a maximum depth of over 300 metres, and the total length of its galleries exceeds 150 kilometres. Tourists descend some 60 metres underground for the start of the tour, which lasts about an hour and a half and covers a three-kilometre route. The main attractions are probably the chapels, which the miners themselves have carved over the centuries, the grandest being the vast St. Kinga's Chapel, which is 54 metres long, 17 metres wide and 12 metres high. Note the detailed niches and doorways, the altar rails, and the magnificent chandeliers, all carved out of rock salt. Another chamber, that of the Great Legend, depicts the discovery of St. Kinga's ring, while yet another houses a tennis court for the miners. Several others contain underground lakes. During the last war the Nazis coverted the huge (36-metres high) Staszic chamber into an aircraft spare parts factory. A much better use has been found for another chamber which, because of the special micro-climate of the mine, now serves as an underground sanatorium for asthmatics. The mine also contains a fascinating museum dealing in non-technical terms with the geology and history of the mine, and also displaying ancient and modern mining equipment.

Visitors to Cracow in search of beautiful scenery are in luck, for some of the grandest views in Poland, if not indeed the whole of Europe, lie within a couple of hours' drive from the city. Above all there are the Tatras, the highest mountains in the country, towering above the popular resort of Zakopane, a mere 104 kilometres due south of Cracow by the wide, scenic main road. (If one is using public transport, the bus journey, which follows this road, is much shorter than the slow, winding rail route, and visually just as rewarding.)

Originally a small mountain village, Zakopane was 'discovered' towards the end of the last century, and it now copes with two and a half million visitors a year. The 'season' lasts the year round, although Zakopane is particularly popular in the winter, when it has the reputation of being 'the second capital of Poland'. Yet,

Zakopane as a town is not particularly fascinating, though it does possess an interesting little museum (ul. Krupówki 10) dealing with the flora, fauna and folklore of the Tatra region, and one can visit the Villa 'Atma', where the composer Karol Szymanowski lived and worked. There are also numerous examples of the picturesque 'Zakopane style' of architecture — vaguely reminiscent of the Swiss chalet but based on local traditions — which Stanisław Witkiewicz, father of the famous (in Poland, at least) dramatist of the same name, founded at the turn of the century. But for the most part people go to Zakopane because, with its numerous hotels, guest houses and eating-places (its home-made ice-cream ranks amongst the very best in Poland), it provides an ideal base for excursions into the mangificent unspoiled countryside.

A first-time visitor would do well to walk or drive to the north-west end of ul. Krupówki, just across the Zakopianka river. There a funicular awaits to carry him up to the summit of Mount Gubałówka (1,123-metres high), which offers, besides a very good restaurant, a truly breathtaking panorama of the whole Zakopane valley and the great Tatras beyond, stretching all the way to the Czechoslovak border. Geologists divide the Tatras in two. To the east lie the High Tatras (the highest point is Mount Rysy, at 2,499 metres), whose granite peaks show the marks of intense glaciation. A special feature of this area is its more than a hundred lakes, the largest and most beautiful of which is the crag-rimmed Morskie Oko, lying at a height of 1,393 metres. According to legend, it is connected by a tunnel with the Adriatic Sea, which would explain its rich emerald-green colour. In addition to the High Tatras, there are the Western Tatras, which are formed of limestone. They are also somewhat lower — Mount Bystra (2,250 metres) is the highest point — and their contours are gentler, too. This is an area of lush mountain valleys and pastures, full of rare plants and wild flowers, and also caves, particularly in the Kościeliska valley, the most beautiful in the Western Tatras.

Zakopane is a haven for the sportsman, particularly in the winter, when the Tatras offer some of the finest skiing in Poland. The winter season ordinarily begins around the middle of November and lasts into April, while the summits and higher slopes are covered with snow for fully eight months of the year. For visitors who prefer to take their snow sitting down, as it were, the *kulig*, or horse-drawn sledge cavalcade, is just the thing. You board your sledge, snuggle into the furs or blankets wisely provided by the driver, and, bells jangling and torches glowing, you will be swept across vast snow fields and into the mountains, to a forest clearing or cabin, where steaming plates of traditional Polish food, and lots of equally traditional Polish *wódka*, await. (Enquire about departures at your hotel reception desk or at the local ORBIS office, ul. Krupówki 22.)

The Tatras are a centre of folk culture, and the colourful costumes of the mountaineers (*górale*) — the women in their bright, floral-patterned skirts and bodices, and the men in their low, broad-brimmed hats, embroidered white felt trousers, white shirts and black waistcoats, often topped with embroidered sheepskin jackets or white felt capes — are a common sight throughout the region, even in Zakopane. Indeed, their highly carved walking sticks and pungent ewe's-milk cheese, made in moulds covered in geometrical patterns and sold in shapes vaguely reminiscent of two cocktail shakers joined at the rim, are two of the most popular holiday souvenirs of the area.

Some of the most interesting excursions from Zakopane lead to centres of folk culture. Seventeen kilometres to the north-west lies the picturesque village of Chochołów, whose shingle-roofed cottages, their high gables facing the road, are amongst the finest to be seen anywhere in the Polish mountains. Chochołów is also an active centre of wood-carving, embroidery and pottery-making. Another 37 kilometres further to the north-west lies Zubrzyca Górna, the site of one of Poland's most famous *skansens* (ethnographic parks). This one deals with the surrounding Orawa region, a frontier area displaying considerable Slovak cultural influence, and contains a number of cottages with traditional interiors, as well as barns, wells, mills and peasant workshops.

Sixteen kilometres north-east of Zakopane lies Bukowina Tatrzańska, a large village famed throughout Poland for its folk arts and crafts, particularly its paintings on glass, modern counterparts of the examples we saw in the Diocesan Museum in Tarnów (see chapter 3). Further to the north-east lie the Pieniny, a small and extremely beautiful limestone range which, like the Tatras, has been declared a national park. What makes the Pieniny so special is the magnificent nine-kilometre-long Dunajec River gorge which pierces the range, its sides formed by rocky peaks towering as much as 300 metres above the level of the river. Throughout much of Poland's history the Dunajec formed part of the border with Hungary — Slovakia did not exist then — and the river was dominated by a number of castles. One of the most picturesque is that of Niedzica, once the stronghold of the powerful Hungarian family of Palóczi-Horváth. Begun in the early fourteenth century in the Gothic style, it was rebuilt during the Renaissance, and although the upper part of the castle is now only a ruin, the middle part houses an interesting museum devoted to the Spisz region, while the lower part is a holiday centre for art historians. Across the river to the north lie the romantic ruins of Czorsztyn, a castle erected by Kazimierz the Great in the fourteenth century. The climb up to it is rewarded by a superb view of the Pieniny and the distant Tatras. At the foot of the castle stands the boarding jetty for the highly recommended raft trip down the Dunajec River to the health resort of Szczawnica, 21 kilometres (three to four hours) away. The rafts, which are formed of hollow tree trunks tied together, with foliage stuck in the crevices to make them as water-tight as possible, are steered by a pair of mountaineers in colourful regional dress, and each raft seats about a dozen people. As well as some of the grandest mountain scenery in Poland, this journey offers the excitement of traversing the Dunajec rapids, which can be a rather wet affair, but perfectly safe, as the boatmen know the river just about as well as any river can be known. Once the rafts have arrived at Szczawnica, the tree trunks are untied and carted back to Czorsztyn for the next trip. The rafts ply the river from May to September, and here, too, the Zakopane ORBIS office can advise on bookings and departures.

Many of the wooden churches in southern Poland have richly painted interiors, but those between Zakopane and the Pieniny range are the most famous. Of these, the churches at Grywałd, Trybsz and Dębno (often called Dębno Podhalańskie to avoid confusion with another Dębno on the main Tarnów-Cracow road) are particularly interesting, the last being generally considered the most outstanding example of its kind anywhere in Poland. From the outside Dębno church, which dates to the fifteenth century, is remarkable enough, with its high-pitched shingle roof flared out at the bottom and swooping down almost to the ground at the tower end. Inside virtually every centimeter is covered in geometrical and floral patterns applied by means of leather stencils, as well as animal and hunting scenes — all by peasant artists working *circa* 1500. Also noteworthy are the charmingly naive figures on the rood screen overhead and the traditional Gothic-Renaissance triptych of the Virgin and Saints above the high altar.

We have really only touched on the highlights in describing this part of Malopolska (Little Poland). The hilly region south and south-east of Cracow is particularly rich in old ruined castles, most of them picturesquely perched on hill-tops. One of the most beautiful and architecturally important is the castle at Nowy (i.e. New) Wiśnicz, which began as a stronghold of the Kmita family in the fourteenth century and subsequently passed to the powerful Lubomirskis. Around 1620 the latter commissioned the Italian Matteo Trapola—who was later to work for them at Lancut—to transform Wiśnicz into a monumental early-Baroque magnate's residence surrounded by pentagon-shaped fortifications pierced by a highly ornate entrance gate. Ensuing centuries left it a ruin, though some of Giovanni Battista Falconi's superb stucco work has survived, especially in the domed chapel. It is all being restored now and will eventually serve as a museum.

Before leaving Little Poland, let us turn our attention westward. Thirty-three kilometres out of Cracow on the Cieszyn road lies the furniture-making town of Kalwaria Zebrzydowska, one of Poland's most popular pilgrimage centres, particularly in August, the month of the Virgin's Assumption. Founded by the Zebrzydowski family (hence its name) *circa* 1600, it centres round a large Bernardine monastery and huge Mannerist church with an impressive two-towered west façade facing a huge courtyard known as Plac Rajski (Paradise Square) from the practice of selling indulgences there in olden days. The interior is rich and largely Baroque, the high altar being dominated by a silver figure of the Virgin brought from Loreto in Italy in 1590. However, the most remarkable feature of Kalwaria Zebrzydowska are the 42 chapels covering the slopes of Mount Żar above the town and the River Cedron. Representing scenes from the Passion of Christ and the Sorrows of the Virgin ('Pilate's Hall', 'Gethsemane', 'the Crucifixion', 'the Heart of Our Lady' etc.), they are in various shapes and sizes, though essentially Mannerist or Baroque, and largely the work of Paul Baudarth of Antwerp, who also helped to design the church itself.

Fourteen kilometres further west lies the small town of Wadowice, which is mainly of interest as the birthplace of Pope John Paul II (Karol Wojtyła). Forty-six kilometres to the south-west, on the River Sola, lies the old brewing centre of Żywiec, its beer being one of the two finest in Poland. (The other comes from Okocim, just outside Brzesko on the Cracow-Tarnów road.) Żywiec offers a number of sights well worth a stop, if not exactly a long detour, such as its originally Gothic parish church with an unusual multi-storeyed Renaissance west tower topped with open arcading, and an oft-rebuilt old castle, also originally Gothic, with a fine arcaded Renaissance courtyard. But the town is chiefly important as a base for excursions into the surrounding Beskid mountains, which are full of pretty villages where folk culture is very strong, like Korbielów, 19 kilometres to the south-east, or — even closer — Jeleśnia, with a wooden inn dating to 1774 that serves regional food. Along the Sola upstream from Żywiec lies a string of mountain resorts beginning with Węgierska Górka, which means 'Hungarian Hill' and boasts of an important iron foundry whose name is found on seemingly every man-hole cover in the country.

To the west rise the Silesian Beskids (the highest point is Mount Skrzyczne — 1,257 metres), an attractive and popular holiday area which serves as the 'lungs' of heavily industrial Upper Silesia, some 80 kilometres away. Below its gently rounded summits, nestled amongst its steep, densely wooded slopes, lie the villages of Istebna, Brenna and Koniaków, famous for their lace-making, wood-carving and picturesque folk costumes. Here, too, a few kilometres south-east of a popular resort fittingly called Wisła, are the sources of the River Vistula (Wisła, in Polish).

We have left Małopolska (Little Poland) and are now in the former Austrian Silesia, i.e. that part of Silesia which Maria Theresa retained after she was obliged to cede the rest of that huge and prosperous province to Prussia in 1742. It was divided between the newly independent Poland and Czechoslovakia in 1920, following the Austro-Hungarian defeat in World War I. This region is unusual in being one of the two areas in Poland — the other is Masuria in the north-east — with a substantial Protestant population. The most populous town is Bielsko-Biała, the second-largest (after Łódź) textile centre in Poland, specializing in high-quality woollen fabrics, some of which are imported into England. However, the old cultural capital of the region is Cieszyn (Teschen, in German), an early Piast settlement on the River Olza, which here forms the border with Czechoslovakia. The historical centre of the town, which is very attractive, being full of parks and trees, lies on the Polish side. On the eastern slopes of Castle Hill, close to the Olza, lies a Neo-classical castle built for the Habsburgs in 1837. Three years later Liszt presented a number of concerts in the nearby orangery. Further up the hill lies the square Piast Tower, which offers a fine panorama of the town and river and is all that remains of a fourteenth-century castle erected by the local Piast princes. At the foot of the tower stands a fortified Romanesque chapel in the shape of a rotunda, with a semi-circular apse and walls over a metre thick. Dating from the middle of the eleventh century, it is one of the oldest stone structures in Poland.

Mid-way between Cracow and Cieszyn, at the confluence of the Sola and Vistula rivers, lies Oświęcim, once the capital of the former principality of Oświęcim-Zator, but much better known to non-Poles as the infamous Auschwitz, largest of all Hitler's death camps. (Actually, it was three camps: Auschwitz proper, Birkenau (Brzezinka) and the Konzentrationslager Au III at nearby Monowice.) To some extent our senses have grown benumbed by the volume of horror perpetrated here, and indeed by subsequent, post-war atrocities. For this reason a visit to the camp, which has been turned into a National Museum of Martyrology, may be necessary to re-awaken us to the ghastly reality of what happened at Auschwitz.

From the moment one enters the camp, with its bitterly ironic inscription '*Arbeit Macht Frei*' (roughly, 'Work Will Set You Free') over the gate, the horrors begin to mount: the cell blocks with their piles of prisoners' hair, false teeth, eye-glasses, shoes, orthopedic appliances and children's toys; Block 10, where sterilization experiments were carried out on helpless human 'guinea pigs'; the 'Death Wall', where some 20,000 prisoners were killed by a shot in the back of the head; and, of course, the infamous gas chambers and crematoria. This is not a journey to be undertaken lightly, and visitors are almost invariably deeply shaken by the experience. One can only regret that the fanatics and racists of this world never seem to make the journey.

To balance the horrors of Auschwitz, I would recommend a visit to Częstochowa, the greatest spiritual centre in Poland, lying some 110 kilometres north-west of Cracow along the 'Route of the Eagles' Nests'. This is one of the most picturesque routes in Poland, and highly recommended, unless the traveller's time is limited, in which case he should proceed to Częstochowa via Olkusz, Sławków and Siewierz, the second half of the journey being by motorway.

The 'Eagles' Nests' are actually castles, now mostly ruined, which crown the summits of the Cracow-Częstochowa Upland and were erected, many as early as the fourteenth-century reign of Kazimierz the Great, to guard the frontier between Poland and the minor principalities of Silesia, which were largely Bohemian fiefs. The Upland is formed of limestone pierced by streams flowing through deep gorges, like the Prądnik Valley, of which the upper reaches — the most beautiful part of the entire Upland — have been made into Ojców National Park, centred on the village of Ojców, only 22 kilometres from Cracow. Over the ages erosion has created a large number of caves and grottoes (Łokietek's Cave near Ojców and

Wierzchowska Grotto near Murownia are open to tourists) at the
same time forming the limestone into some pretty fantastic shapes,
like the enormous (18 metres tall) Hercules' Club, a short distance
below Pieskowa Skała, the best preserved castle in the region. It is
also one of the most picturesque, dominating the Prądnik Valley
from the summit of a forested limestone cliff. Erected by the Great
Kazimierz himself, it was remodelled as a Renaissance mansion in
the sixteenth century. Its owners, the Szafraniec family, were said to
have decorated it so richly that it rivalled the Wawel castle itself,
but it fell on hard times in the nineteenth century (a fire in 1849,
artillery bombardment during the 1863 Insurrection, the sale and
dispersal of its furnishings), and it has had to wait until the post-war
years to be restored to its former grandeur. Its arcaded inner
courtyard is its chief architectural glory, but it also houses a fine
collection of furniture, tapestries, pictures (including one each by
Hogarth and Lawrence) and *objets d'art* from the Wawel collection. There is also a good restaurant and charming roof-top café
with a superb view.

An hour and a half away, at the northern end of the 'Route of the
Eagles' Nests', lies Częstochowa, an ancient and rapidly expanding
iron-and-steel centre on the River Warta with a population of over
200,000. But we have not come here because of the industry, but
because this is Poland's chief pilgrimage centre, made famous by
the presence of the 'Black Madonna', or 'Mother of God of
Częstochowa', a miraculous picture, possibly of Byzantine origin,
hanging in the church of the Paulite Fathers on Jasna Góra (Bright
Hill) in the west of the city. The monastery was founded in 1382 by
Prince Władysław of Opole, who may also have deposited the
picture here. In any case, it was soon attracting pilgrims; and the
success of the monastery in withstanding the Swedish siege of 1655
(it had luckily been fortified in the 1620s) when almost the whole of
Poland succumbed to the invaders, was attributed to the presence
of the picture, which further increased its popularity as an object of
devotion.

The original fourteenth-century structure has been considerably
augmented by later additions, the most impressive being the
enormously tall (105 metres high) tower, which dominates the town
and can be seen from many kilometres away. The monastery
treasury contains a glittering array of church vestments and furnishings, as well as numerous gifts presented by generations of the
faithful — crowned heads and ordinary folk alike — and including an
extremely moving rosary fashioned by a concentration-camp in-

mate from bits of stale bread. There is also a richly decorated
library dating to the 1730s, containing a painted ceiling and a fine
collection of *incunabula* and early printings. (This is not open to
the general public; scholars and others interested in viewing it
should apply beforehand to the Reverend Prior.) But the chief goal
of the hundreds of thousands of pilgrims to Częstochowa each year
is the miraculous picture hanging above the altar in the north
chapel of the monastery church, its face still bearing the scars
reputed to have been inflicted by a Hussite soldier who was trying to
steal it. Unable to dislodge the picture, he slashed the face with his
sword, whereupon blood issued from the wounds. The picture,
which is ordinarily concealed by a golden door, is open for viewing
during the morning and for one hour (3.30–4.30) in the afternoon.
Regardless of one's religious beliefs, the opening and closing
ceremonies, which take place during Mass and are accompanied by
singing and a trumpet fanfare, are extremely moving; while the
piety of the crowds of pilgrims, including a high percentage of
young people, leaves no doubt as to the immense spiritual power of
the Catholic Church in Poland.

From Częstochowa it is only 217 kilometres to Warsaw. On the
way one may safely skip the textile-manufacturing centre of Łódź,
which, despite being the second-largest city in the country with a
population of over 800,000, has little to offer the tourist, apart
from a Museum of Art with a reasonably interesting collection of
nineteenth- and twentieth-century painting. Alternately, if the
traveller is returning to the capital from Cracow, there is scenery a-
plenty in the relatively 'undiscovered' Holy Cross Mountains (Góry
Świętokrzyskie), lying roughly midway between the two, and
centred on the town of Kielce. The latter, though picturesquely
situated, has little to offer, apart from a moderately interesting
cathedral and a rather more interesting early-Baroque bishop's
palace, but it is useful as a base for excursions. 'Mountains' is a
somewhat misleading description, for after ages of erosion the
highest point in the whole Holy Cross range reaches only 612 metres
above sea level (Mount Łysica). But what the range lacks in height,
it makes up for in beauty, with its largely fir-and-beech covered
slopes, stretching like a green band across the horizon. Some of the
summits are crowned with churches or monasteries, like the twelfth-
century Benedictine abbey of the Holy Cross atop Łysa Góra (Bald
Mountain), once the centre of an ancient pagan cult and, according to legend, a witches' rallying-point. Other notable attractions of the region include the ruins of Chęciny castle, its low

stone walls and three massive towers perched on a high limestone rock and all but dominating the Cracow-Kielce road, almost immediately below. There is also the originally Romanesque, though oft-rebuilt, Cistercian church at Wachock, with its fine chapter-house containing well-preserved Romanesque capitals and vaulting. But perhaps the most unusual piece of architecture in the whole area is the fortified castle of Krzyżtopór, at Ujazd, near Iwaniska, between Kielce and Sandomierz. Built for the proud Ossoliński family in a highly Manneristic style by the Swiss-Italian Lorenzo Muretto ('Wawrzyniec Senes' to the Poles) in 1631–44, it was so enormous that legend ascribed it a window for each day of the year, a room for each week, an audience chamber for each month and a tower for each season. But it was destroyed during the Swedish 'Flood' little more than a decade after its completion, and now it stands, its vast rooms as open to the sky as its huge courtyards, one of Poland's greatest ruins.

So far we have treated the south-eastern third of Poland, and it is this area that I would recommend to first-time visitors to the country. In fact, the route that we have taken, from Warsaw through the Lublin and Cracow regions and back to Warsaw, can be covered in about a fortnight, give or take a day or two, depending on one's mode of transportation and the number of side-trips one makes. This is by no means to imply that the other regions of Poland do not possess sights as interesting, or almost as interesting, as the very best that we have seen so far. It is just that the Warsaw-Lublin-Cracow triangle is particularly rich in first-rate sights in a good state of preservation and, in my opinion, offers more to the general traveller per kilometre travelled than any other part of the country.

There are two main reasons for this. First, much — though by no means all — of the northern third of Poland has always been heavily forested, thinly populated and, traditionally, relatively poor, so, whilst there is a great deal of fine scenery to be seen as compensation, the best architecture of the region is generally more scattered than in other, more prosperous, parts of the country. Second, of the regions that remain to be covered, Silesia, Pomerania and the former East Prussia (i.e. Warmia and Masuria), suffered heavy damage during the last war, as the Red Army, joined by Polish forces, pushed westward towards Berlin. The most important buildings have largely been repaired, but a number still await restoration, and of course there are some which can never be restored. So, for the remainder of this guide, rather than giving a suggested itinerary, as I have done thus far, I shall attempt instead to point out the unique general features of each region, such as might tempt the traveller to make a foray or two into areas which deserve to become far better known outside Poland.

5 SILESIA

Silesia has always been a rich province, long coveted by Poland's neighbours. Problems began at least as early as the fourteenth century, when Silesia, which had become fragmented into small principalities, remained outside Władysław Little-Ell's newly unified Polish state. To make matters worse, in 1327 eight of the Silesian Piast princelings swore allegiance to John of Luxembourg, King of Bohemia, to be joined later by several more of their cousins. Most of Silesia remained under Bohemian domination until 1526, when Bohemia itself, and with it Silesia, came under Habsburg rule. This lasted until 1741, when Frederick the Great cast a covetous glance southwards, marched in and seized the province. Prussian rule ultimately became German rule, which persisted until 1945, when Silesia once again became Polish, along with Pomerania, Warmia and Masuria. Those Germans who had not fled westward with the retreating German army were expelled by the Poles, to be replaced by their own people, including a large number from Poland's lost eastern territories. These Poles joined the more than 800,000 Silesians who, despite centuries of Germanization, still considered themselves to be Polish.

The wealth of Silesia lies both in and beneath her soil. Almost the whole of the broad, flat Upper Oder valley is covered with rich black earth, which holds the national record for grain (particularly wheat) yields per acre. It was the soil, at least initially, which enticed the steady stream of German immigrants who began to settle here in large numbers as early as the thirteenth century, following the massive destruction and depopulation wrought by the Tatar invasion of 1241. But Silesia also has great mineral wealth: copper, lead, zinc, lignite and, above all coal, and it is the last which, together with the iron ore of nearby Częstochowa, made the great steel-making district of Upper Silesia such a bone of bitter contention when the new Polish-German border was being drawn in the years immediately following World War I.

The Treaty of Versailles left most of what was then an ethnically very mixed region to Germany, a decision the Silesian Poles resisted fiercely. Three insurrections later, the plebiscite of 1921 awarded Poland a more generous slice, though not as much as the Poles thought fair. The Germans had rigged the voting, they claimed, which was no doubt partly true. Now, of course, the whole of Silesia belongs to Poland and is economically its richest region, with Upper Silesia alone contributing almost a quarter of the total industrial output of the country, and, above all, coal, of which Poland is the world's fourth largest producer, after the United States, the Soviet Union and China.

Katowice, the capital of the region, has been much modernized since the war, its dingy industrial tenements replaced by large housing estates. The town centre now contains an enormous sport and recreation hall that looks like a stray flying saucer and, next to it, a large modern memorial to the Silesian insurgents of 60 years ago. But there is little else to interest the traveller in this smoky, Ruhr-like district, so we shall pass it by and make instead for Wrocław (in German, Breslau), the historic capital of Lower Silesia, and indeed an ideal base from which to explore the whole of the province.

Wrocław has a great deal to offer the traveller. Picturesquely situated at a spot where the Oder divides into several branches and is itself joined by four other rivers, it is known as the 'city of bridges' — 85 at the last count. It is also a city of islands, which in the past provided refuge from invaders such as the Tatars, who burned down much of the town in 1241. However, the greatest destruction occurred during the final days of World War II. In January 1945 the Germans, anticipating the arrival of the Red Army, turned Wrocław into an armed fortress, which involved evacuating most of the civilian population (some 700,000 people), constructing a powerful ring of anti-tank defences around the city and razing to the ground much of the historic centre. Marshal Konev's army arrived a month later and surrounded the town, and by the time the Germans surrendered on 6 May 1945 over 200,000 persons, both civilian and military, had been killed or wounded, and 70 per cent of Wrocław lay in ruins.

After the war, the town was repopulated largely by settlers from Poland's lost eastern provinces, and particularly from the ancient city of Lwów, almost all the Polish inhabitants of which moved to Wrocław. It now has a population of over 600,000. Before the war, Lwów had been, alongside Warsaw and Cracow, one of the great centres of Polish cultural life, and modern Wrocław is clearly proud of its distinguished heritage. Besides possessing three theatres, an opera house and an operatic theatre, it also sponsors an annual oratorio and cantata festival, 'Vratislavia (i.e. Wrocław) Cantans', in September, as well as an international student jamboree, 'Jazz on the Oder', in early spring. Wrocław is also home to two of Poland's most unusual and, as a result of frequent tours abroad, world-famous dramatic ensembles. One is the Wrocław Pantomime Theatre (aleja Dębowa 16), all the performances of which are still personally designed and directed by the man who founded it in 1956, Henryk Tomaszewski. The second is Jerzy Grotowski's experimental and highly innovative Laboratory Theatre, or 'Theatre of Thirteen Rows' (from the small size of its auditorium), beside Wrocław's ancient Town Hall. For Grotowski, the actor's self-expression is at least as important as what the audience experiences. To this end, Grotowski usually re-works plays that he directs in order to make them more relevant to his actors, while the latter perform amongst the audience in a very physical, often writhingly cathartic, style. Needless to say, Grotowski's approach is extremely controversial: some critics like it and think he is on to something very significant, while others see it as a self-indulgent dead-end. In any case, tickets are extremely hard to come by; though here, as elsewhere in Poland, visitors are advised to pour on the charm and foreignness in the hope of obtaining a rare available ticket at the box office.

Wrocław is pre-eminently a city of imposing Gothic brick churches, and even after wartime destruction it contains more first-rate ecclesiastical architecture of this period than any other city in Poland. In fact, all the most important buildings have been, or are being, restored, though unlike Warsaw no attempt is being made to restore the entire historical heart of the city to its pre-war appearance. As a result, the chief sights are somewhat scattered, although virtually everything of interest to the general traveller lies between the old town moat (Fosa Miejska) and the Oder River (an area of roughly one and a half square kilometres), or on the islands immediately to the north-east.

The islands make a good place to begin our tour. By 'islands' I am thinking above all of the Sand Island (Piasek) and the Cathedral Island (Ostrów Tumski), which is actually no longer an island, following the filling in of one of the many channels of the Oder. This is one of the most charming spots in the whole of Wrocław, with its little streets, picturesque bridges, and an even greater concentration of fine churches (seven in all) than elsewhere in this church-studded city. The obvious 'star' is the cathedral of St.

John the Baptist with its two massive west towers (constructed of warm dark-red brick, like most of the structure) dominating the surrounding area and forming one of the best-known landmarks of Wrocław. The present cathedral, the fourth on this site since the establishment of the Wrocław bishopric in AD 1000, replaces a structure destroyed by the Tatars in 1241. Begun three years later, its chancel and low east towers are the earliest example in Poland of construction entirely in the Gothic style. The cathedral was largely completed by 1350, although various chapels and other embellishments continued to be added throughout subsequent centuries. All this work was undone during the final stages of the siege of 1945, when 70 per cent of the cathedral was destroyed. It has since been rebuilt (there are some fascinating 'before and after' photographs at the back of the cathedral), and pictures, stalls and other fine objects have been brought from other churches to augment the furnishings that survived the war.

The cathedral is usually fairly dark and (doubtless because of this) full of atmosphere. A visitor can easily spend the better part of an hour here, but I would suggest concentrating on the two splendid Baroque chapels to the north and south of the Lady Chapel at the east end. (They are usually closed, so one must make enquiries in the sacristy off the south aisle.) The south chapel, dedicated to St. Elizabeth of Hungary, was built by Cardinal Frederick of Hesse in the 1680s. A convert to Catholicism, he was obviously determined that his chapel should be a grand affirmation of his new faith, and to this end he employed a highly talented Italian, Giacomo Scianzi, as his architect, also commissioning him to paint the fine fresco of the 'Apotheosis of St. Elizabeth' in the oval dome. Other Italians were also brought in to help with the decoration, including Domenico Guidi, who carved the handsome kneeling statue of Cardinal Frederick facing the altar, while the bust of the Cardinal over the entrance to the chapel comes from the studio of the great Bernini himself.

Even more splendid than St. Elizabeth's Chapel is the Elector's Chapel, at the north-east corner of the cathedral. Founded in 1716 by Franz Ludwig Neuburg, Archbishop of Wrocław and Elector of Trier, it is the only work on Polish soil by Johann Bernhard Fischer von Erlach, the architect of Schönbrunn Palace and St. Charles' Church in Vienna and one of the greatest exponents of the Baroque style in the whole of Europe. Oval in form, like the St. Elizabeth Chapel, it is even more richly decorated, with delightful putti by one of the best sculptors of the period, Ferdinand Brokof of

Prague, and dome frescoes ('The Revolt of the Angels') by Carlo Carlone, who also painted the magnificent ceiling fresco glorifying Prince Eugene of Savoy in the Marble Hall of the Upper Belvedere in Vienna. This great profusion of international talent is partly explained by the fact that at this time, of course, Silesia still belonged to Austria, and when an important ecclesiastical prince of the Empire commissioned a chapel, he was able to draw on the architectural and artistic resources of the whole Habsburg dominions.

If the visitor is still in the mood for churches, there are six others within a five-minute walk of the cathedral. Just over the road to the north lies St. Giles (św. Idziego), the oldest church in Wrocław. It is basically late-Romanesque with a pretty brick arcade frieze around the outside. It is joined to an old Gothic chapter-house by an arch, through which lies the entrance to the Archdiocesan Museum, with a rich collection of Silesian church art from the fifteenth century to the present day. A few minutes' walk to the west brings us to a church with one of the highest spires (69 metres) in the whole of Silesia. It is in fact not one church but two, the upper storey being in the form of, and dedicated to, the Holy Cross, while the lower storey is known as St. Bartholomew's. The reason for this curious arrangement is still a subject of dispute amongst architectural historians. Founded in 1288 by the poet-prince Henryk IV Probus (Latin for 'Good' or 'Upright'), it has had a somewhat chequered history, with the lower church even serving as a stable for a time. Like most of Wrocław, it was seriously damaged during the last war, but it has since been restored; and, as in the case of the cathedral and indeed many of the rebuilt churches of Wrocław, a number of Gothic triptychs and other art objects have been brought from various Silesian churches to help refurnish it.

Of the other churches in this area, by far the most important is St. Mary's on Piasek Island. Even if our otherwise indefatigable traveller is beginning to tire of churches — which would be a pity, as these are the great treasure of Wrocław — he really must make an effort to see this magnificent building. What raises St. Mary's so far above the level of the average Gothic hall church is the quality of its interior, and above all its beautiful vaulting, which ranks amongst the finest in Poland. At the end of the last war, fire destroyed almost the whole of the interior, including the roof and vaulting, so it has all had to be reconstructed, and what a splendid job the restorers have made of it! The nave vaulting is in the form of eight-pointed stars, while that of the side aisles follows the so-called 'Piast' system of asymmetrical tripartite vaults, an unusually attractive way of co-ordinating one nave bay with two shorter window bays. It is unfortunate that St. Mary's, like so many Polish churches, is only partly open outside the hours of public worship. That is to say, the street doors will be open, but access to the main body of the church is prevented by glass doors or a screen. Sometimes this is only temporary, as for example when a church is being cleaned, and in any case kneelers are placed in front of the screen for worshippers, but it complicates matters for sightseers like ourselves. In the case of St. Mary's, the beautiful vaulting *can* be seen from the back of the church, and there is also a fine view of the bright red and yellow east window by Teresa Reklewska, which is unusually impressive for modern stained glass and goes very well with the red brick and white plaster of the interior. There is also, in the north-west corner, a large late-Gothic font surrounded by finely carved animals lolling round its base. And, if we are lucky and the whole church is open, we shall be able to see, in the south aisle, a superb Romanesque tympanum from the twelfth-century predecessor of the present church, which was founded by Maria, the wife of the governor of Wrocław, Piotr Włost, or Włostowic. It depicts Maria and her son offering the church to the Virgin and bears the inscription (in Latin): 'This sanctuary I offer Thee, Maria to Maria, Mother of Mercy, together with my son Świętosław.' At the end of the opposite, i.e. the north aisle, in a Baroque altar, is another Virgin, a miracle-working picture known as the Victorious Mother of God (*Matka Boska Zwycięska*). Like many such objects of pilgrimage scattered throughout Poland, it originally comes from Poland's lost eastern territories — in this case from Mariampole, in Soviet Lithuania — and was brought westward by post-war Polish repatriates.

In the centre of Wrocław there are several more extremely fine Gothic churches to tempt the tireless devotee of religious architecture, including (east of the Market Square) St. Mary Magdalen's, with its richly carved Romanesque south portal from the dismantled abbey of St. Vincent at Olbin, north-east of Wrocław; St. Elizabeth's (north-west of the Square), the tallest church in the city, burned out under suspicious circumstances in 1976 — several other important buildings in Poland were destroyed by fire at the same time — but now under reconstruction; the Ursuline church of St. Clara (in pl. Biskupa Nankiera, south of Piasek Island), rebuilt in the Baroque style and containing the Mausoleum of the Piasts of Wrocław; and, last but hardly least, St. Dorota's on ul. Świdnicka, in the south of the Old Town. A tall, imposing structure, it is also known as the Church of Reconciliation, after the meeting in Wrocław in 1351 of King Kazimierz the Great of Poland and Charles IV, King of Bohemia and Holy Roman Emperor, which produced a peaceful, albeit temporary, interlude in the long and stormy conflict between the two countries over Silesia.

Although the churches of Wrocław are collectively its most interesting feature, the town contains two secular buildings — ensembles, in fact — of outstanding importance. I am thinking above all of the great Town Hall, or *Ratusz*. Work on it commenced towards the end of the thirteenth century, as Wrocław was beginning to recover from the shock of the Tatar invasion of 1241, and continued well into the sixteenth. Like most town halls of this, or indeed any, period, it was intended to represent the wealth and power of the town burghers, who, as they grew richer and richer, progressively enlarged and embellished the building. Damaged, though not destroyed, during the last war, it has since been restored to its former glory and probably looks better now than it has ever done.

This is without a doubt one of the most magnificent town halls of central Europe, a highly ornate amalgam of Gothic, Renaissance and Baroque styles. Viewed from the outside, it is a picturesque hodge-podge of towers, spires, pinnacles, gables, loggias and windows of every shape and size. Inside, it is richly decorated and contains a wealth of architectural detail. The traditional names of the various chambers such as the Knights' Hall, the Prince's Hall, the Town Scribe's Chamber, the Bailiff's Chamber etc., evoke past centuries when the whole official life of the town, and much of its commercial activity, was carried on within these walls. The building has had a stormy past, though few dates have been so bloody as 18 July 1418, when rioting craftsmen and river fishermen broke into the Council Chamber and killed two councillors, which resulted in the execution of 23 of their own number. Activities are much quieter in the town hall now: much of the building has been turned into a town history museum, there is a Museum of Medals in a ground-floor room of the large Burghers' Hall, while the beautiful vaulted cellars house a pleasant café, the 'Świdnicka'.

The town hall stands in the centre of one of Poland's largest market squares, measuring 173 by 208 metres. Many of the old houses lining the square have been rebuilt in what either was, or has been imagined to be, the original style. The results have usually been successful, and at all events picturesque, particularly No. 2, on the west side of the square. Known as the 'Dom pod Gryfami' ('Griffin house'), it is the largest burgher's house in the city and was built in a Dutch Mannerist style with highly ornamented gables at the end of the sixteenth century. At the north-west corner of the square are two houses known popularly as 'Jaś i Małgosia' ('Hansel and Gretel') from the fact that they stand, brother-and-sister-like, flanking a Baroque gate. The gate formerly led to a cemetery attached to nearby St. Elizabeth's church. The executed leaders of the 1418 riots were buried just inside the gate, so that anyone visiting the cemetery would have to tread on, and thereby desecrate, their remains.

Our second outstanding secular ensemble lies at the Old Town end of the University Bridge (Most Uniwersytecki), a few minutes' walk south-west of Sand Island. This was originally the site of a twelfth-century Piast castle which, together with the city and province, passed first to the Czechs and later to the Habsburgs. In 1659 Emperor Leopold I gave the site to the Jesuits, who eventually erected what is now the university church of the Name of Jesus (formerly St. Matthew's, and not to be confused with the present St. Matthew's in ul. Szewska, one street to the east). This is arguably the best Baroque church interior in Wrocław, with superb ceiling frescoes by the Viennese Johann Michael Rottmayr protraying the 'Glory of Jesus'. To the east, in ul. Szewska, stands another part of this Baroque ensemble, the Ossolineum. The third largest library in Poland, it was founded in Lwów in 1817 by the Ossoliński family and transferred to Wrocław after the last war. The building in which it is housed was originally a hospital of a crusading order of religious knights and was erected between 1675 and 1715, possibly to the designs of the Frenchman Jean Baptiste Matthieu (or Mathey), who had also worked in Prague. Its northern façade, stretching along the Oder and displaying a graceful dome and curved Baroque gables, is one of the most charming views in Wrocław.

For most visitors, however, the most attractive sight in this area is to be found on the first floor of the main building of Wrocław University, immediately to the west of the Name of Jesus church. The Jesuits had founded an Academia Leopoldina here in 1702, and in 1811 it achieved university status. The present building, its great length stretching along the Oder, is pretty and merely competent, and, from an architectural point of view, nothing special. What *is* special is the Aula Leopoldina, a magnificently decorated auditorium now used for solemn university occasions, and also for concerts, because of its fine acoustics. (In fact, the latter are so fine in this trapezoid-shaped room, that if one whispers facing one end, one can be heard at the other end.) The war left the Aula windowless, though not burned out, and the first post-war students attended lectures in their overcoats. It has been restored to show the full grandeur of the decoration, including the large illusionist ceiling fresco depicting the 'Glory of Divine Wisdom' by Johann Christoph Handke of Olomouc, in Moravia, and Joseph Mangoldt's rich stucco work and large-scale sculptures of the Emperors Leopold I, Joseph I and Charles IV. Note, too, the series of niche paintings depicting the Fathers of the Church, the great philosophers, ancient as well as Christian, and the princely patrons of learning.

For the traveller who feels that he has seen enough architecture for a while, Wrocław is extremely well provided with attractive parks, and these, together with the very large number of garden allotments surrounding the city, make it one of the greenest places in Poland. In fact, on 22 July, Independence Day, the whole of Wrocław goes flower-mad, with shows, parades, flower arranging competitions, and even a special post office that sells stamps and postcards featuring flowers and plants. (Polish stamps are usually very colourful in any case.) Letters posted in Wrocław that day bear a special floral postmark. Visitors who cannot wait until 22 July are advised to make straight for the University Botanical Garden, directly behind the Archdiocesan Museum. Open only in the summer months, it contains over 7,000 species, including the most varied assortment of mountain plants and cacti in Poland. A kilometre to the east across a branch of the Oder lies sprawling (112 hectares) Szczytnicki Park. Founded in 1785 on formal French lines, it was remodelled as an English landscape park in the 1860s and, in addition to its 600-year-old oaks (this was originally open countryside) is said to contain a more varied flora than almost any other park in Europe.

When we tire of flora, there is always fauna, and the Wrocław Zoo, only a few minutes' walk south of Szczytnicki Park on the bank of the main branch of the Oder, is — again — one of the largest in Europe, containing more than 3,000 mammals, amphibians and reptiles, representing over 500 different species. Its collection of birds (more than 700 varieties) is the finest in the country.

The main sights of Wrocław can be visited in the course of one long day, although to see everything adequately that we have described will take a day and a half perhaps, or even two. However, our visitor may choose to prolong his stay in order to include some of the very tempting sights that lie within a day's drive from Wrocław.

Excursions from Wrocław

Twenty-four kilometres north of Wrocław through pretty rolling hills lies Trzebnica, famous for its great pilgrimage church, the burial place of St. Jadwiga, known as St. Hedwig in German-speaking countries. A German princess, she was betrothed for political reasons to Henryk I (the Bearded), prince of Wrocław and Silesia, around 1190. A long series of personal tragedies, including the deaths of five of her children and two of her sisters, as well as the banishment of two of her brothers, led her in her mid-thirties to renounce the sumptuous life of the court and to adopt an ascetic life style, eating simple food, dressing in humble attire, and mortifying her flesh, at the same time taking vows of chastity. Her ostentatious asceticism hardly pleased her family, who thought it unbecoming to a princess, but it won her the love and admiration of the poor. Following her husband's death in 1238 she moved to the Cistercian nunnery at Trzebnica, which Henryk had founded in 1202, and where her daughter was abbess. After her own death five years later she was buried in the abbey and, in 1267, canonized by Pope Clement VI, thus becoming the first saint of the Piast dynasty.

Trzebnica is still the chief resting-place of the saint, although a finger lies in St. Hedwig's cathedral in Berlin, and lesser relics have recently been distributed to all 120 Polish churches that bear her name. Her chapel, which lies at the south-east corner of the church, was erected by her grandson, Archbishop Władysław Piast of Salzburg, around the time of her canonization, but her present lavish alabaster and marble tomb was put up much later, in 1679–80 by Abbess Krystyna Katarzyna Pawłowska, whose funds helped rebuild the church after serious damage during the Thirty Years' War. However, the origins of the church are late-Romanesque, as can be seen from the exterior, and also from the inner and outer portals, like the charming one at the west end with its carved tympanum depicting King David playing his lute for Queen Bathsheba. Inside, Romanesque and Gothic is largely concealed by Baroque and Rococo. The rich, creamy walls, Mangoldt's sumptuous high altar, full of statues and gilt, the rich profusion of side altars and the series of 19 paintings by the school of Michael Willmann, one of the best local eighteenth-century artists, make Trzebnica one of the most magnificent of all Silesian abbey churches.

But it is by no means the only one. Forty-nine kilometres north-west of Wrocław, across a rich, fairly flat agricultural landscape peppered with small villages and Baroque church towers, lies Lubiąz, one of the oldest (founded before 1200) and grandest. It is slowly being restored following early post-war Soviet occupation, but even in its present dilapidated state it is most impressive, particularly the long (223 metres) façade created by the church, abbot's palace and cloister.

Another great abbey, now restored and serving as a parish church, lies 56 kilometres south of Wrocław at Henryków. Founded in the first part of the thirteenth century during the reign of St. Jadwiga's husband, Henryk the Bearded (hence its name), it is famous to all students of Polish literature for its *Księga Henrykowska (Book of Henryków)*, begun in Latin by Abbot Piotr, or Peter, in 1268–73 and containing, by way of exception, the first sentence written in Polish. It boasts a fine Baroque interior, but a no less handsome one — also with princely associations, is to be found at Legnickie Pole, 67 kilometres west of Wrocław, and just before the town of Legnica. This was the site of the Tatars' great victory over the Poles in 1241, after which the former turned south, for reasons still not completely explained, leaving the latter to rebuild the shattered southern half of their country. Prince Henryk the Pious, St. Jadwiga's son, was killed at the battle and his body decapitated, so according to legend the only way his mother could identify his remains was by the fact that he had six toes on one of his feet. On the spot where his remains were found the saint erected a chapel, which was replaced two centuries later by a modest Gothic structure, which now serves as a battlefield museum.

Literally just round the corner lies the great former Benedictine abbey (now a parish church) of the Holy Cross and St. Jadwiga, built between 1727 and 1731 by the famous Austrian architect, Kilian Ignaz Dientzenhofer, one of the masters of European Baroque. Do not be put off by the shabby surroundings of the church. After the secuarlization of the abbey in 1810 the monastery buildings were turned into a Prussian cadet school, where Hindenburg was once a student. But our real goal is the church itself. (In case it is closed, the priest lives in the house across the road.) Once inside, we can marvel at Dientzenhofer's extraordinary skill in turning pure mathematical forms — the structure is in fact composed of an elongated ellipse intersected by two shorter crossed ellipses — into a visually satisfying whole. To decorate his church he brought in artists of the highest quality, particularly the famous

Bavarian painter Cosmas Damian Asam, who contributed the ceiling frescoes depicting the discovery of Henryk the Pious' remains on the battlefield, as well as the missionary activities of the Benedictine Order.

Almost all the small and medium-size towns of Silesia contain sights worth seeing, but because of massive destruction at the end of the last war, few now contain so many objects as to justify a special excursion. That is to say, they are well worth stopping to see *en route* from point X to point Y, but few are worth travelling dozens of kilometres out of one's way.

However, one area that is worth a special visit is the Kłodzko valley, that rectangle of Polish territory that protrudes into Czechoslovakia to the south of Wrocław. Formed by several branches of the Nysa river, the valley is rightly considered the most attractive part of the Polish Sudeten range, which here reaches a maximum height of 1,425 metres in Śnieżnik (Snowy Mountain). A border region, it changed hands frequently between the Czechs and the Poles, as is shown by the fact that the Gothic parish church of Kłodzko, the main town of the region (88 kilometres south of Wrocław), was founded by a fourteenth-century archbishop of Prague, Arnost of Pardubice, who is also buried there. Kłodzko, with a population of some 30,000, is built on the hilly banks of the Nysa Kłodzka river, and its location is one of the most picturesque in Silesia.

The surrounding green and rolling hills contain one-fifth of the country's total sanatorium accommodation, including the famous spas of Polanica, Kudowa, Duszniki (where the sixteen-year-old Chopin gave two concerts) and Lądek (where Goethe and Turgeniev were patients). Polish spas deal with a variety of conditions and ailments, and most accept foreign as well as Polish patients, who ordinarily follow a three-week course of prescribed treatment.

The Kłodzko region has some of the most unusual natural attractions to be found in Poland. Amongst the strangest are the Wandering Rocks (Błędne Skały), in the Table Mountains (Góry Stołowe) on the Czech border, west of Kłodzko. Composed of chalky sandstone carved by centuries of weathering into fantastic shapes, they form part of a nature reserve of 21 hectares. It is easy to get lost in them — hence their name — so it is a good idea to stick to the marked paths. Also, some of the passages are so extremely narrow that a really stout person will be able to get through only with great difficulty. Nearby, also on the border and just to the west of Kudowa, is the village of Czermna, famous for its burial chapel of 1776–8, the walls, ceiling and altar of which are covered with skulls and bones of some 3,000 persons, while the remains of a further 21,000 are reputed to lie in the crypt.

A short distance to the north lies the pilgrimage church of Wambierzyce, a Baroque structure constructed in the years 1695–1711 on the model of what the people of those days imagined to be the ancient Temple of Jerusalem. Like Kalwaria Zebrzydowska to the west of Cracow, the village contains numerous Stations of the Cross (in this case, over a hundred) and is still an extremely active centre of Marian devotion.

Cheating a bit, and including a few sights which lie outside the Kłodzko valley but are still within easy reach of Kłodzko itself, we should mention Paczków (29 kilometres to the east), often referred to as the 'Polish Carcassonne'. Actually, it is on nothing like the scale of its French counterpart, nor is it so magnificently situated, but it *is* surrounded by defence walls, which make it very picturesque in its own right. Incidentally, the Gothic parish church has a curious fortified appearance, the result of reconstruction in the sixteenth century, when a footwalk for soldiers was added behind the attic-storey parapet.

Finally, on our way back to Wrocław, let us stop in the small town of Ząbkowice Śląskie, 22 kilometres north of Kłodzko. Here, in a side-street to the south-west of the market square, stands one of Poland's two leaning towers. (The other is in Toruń.) It is actually the detached bell-tower of nearby St. Anne's church, and its stone base dates from the end of the thirteenth century. The ground shifted two centuries later, probably as a result of a minor earthquake, and, as in Pisa, the burghers of the town tried to straighten it by adding a top storey perpendicular to the ground. It did not help, and the tower, which is 38 metres high, now leans 1.5 metres out of true vertical. It can be visited and makes a good leg-stretching stop before our last 65 kilometres back to Wrocław.

6 GREAT POLAND

Great Poland (Wielkopolska), centered on Poznań, is the historical heartland of the country, for it was here in the tenth century that Mieszko I began the long process of unifying the various tribes that were later to call themselves Poles. Yet the history, that is to say the unrecorded history, of this region goes back much further than that, as archaeologists have discovered amidst the hilly, lake-studded landscape near Biskupin, roughly 84 kilometres north-east of Poznań. The story began in 1933, when a local school principal, Walery Szweitzer, out with his pupils on an excursion, noticed some wooden stakes protruding from the shore waters of Lake Biskupieńskie. He learned that a local farmer had unearthed bits of wood protruding from the nearby turf, as well as a number of small, pre-historic articles. In the following year archaeologists from Poznań arrived at the site, and their investigations, which were interrupted by the war, resumed in 1946. What they have unearthed is a fortified island settlement (now a peninsula), established around 550 B.C. by representatives of so-called Lusatian culture, which was probably one of the main components of later Slav civilization. A century and a half later the rising lake level forced the inhabitants to abandon the site, but owing to the specific chemical properties of the water and soil the foundations — building here was in wood — have substantially been preserved. Entrance to the settlement, which was oval-shaped and surrounded by a palisade, was by means of a gate at the end of a causeway some 120 metres long. The settlement was further protected by a breakwater composed of an estimated 35,000 stakes, which would have both repelled invaders and reduced the thrust of the ice pressing against the banks of the island. Inside, there were more than a hundred huts arranged side by side along 12 parallel streets, the whole surrounded by a wood-paved street just inside the palisade. Archaeologists have reconstructed part of the settlement, including pavements, several huts, the entrance gate and some of the palisade; and of course much of the original breakwater, over 2,500 years old is still visible. Artifacts and other objects from the settlement and other excavations in the neighbourhood are on display in a small museum midway between the entrance to the park and the site itself, which is open only between 15 May and 15 October.

From pre-history we move into recorded history at Gniezno, a town of some 60,000 inhabitants roughly midway between Biskupin and Poznań. This was the seat of the early Piasts, although Mieszko I was eventually to make Poznań his capital in 968, also establishing Poland's first bishopric there. But Gniezno trumped Poznań a generation or so later when, in the year 1000, it became the seat of the country's first archbishop and primate, which it remains to this day, although the primatial see is now linked administratively with Warsaw.

One reason for Gniezno's importance was the presence here of the remains of St. Wojciech, Poland's first patron. A Czech, he had studied in Magdeburg, where the local archbishop gave him his own name, Adalbert, by which he is more generally known in the West. His mission to the pagan Prussians in what is now the north-east of Poland appeared to succeed at first, but in 997 he was murdered by them. Bolesław the Brave ransomed his remains, paying (according to legend) their weight in gold, and brought them to Gniezno, where they lie above the high altar of the cathedral in a splendid silver reliquary topped by a reclining figure of the saint, the whole by the Baroque master Peter van der Rennen of Gdańsk.

The cathedral and, in particular, its contents are the main reason we have come to Gniezno, but they are reason enough. The building, its two massive west towers dominating a tall nave, is one of the most monumental Gothic structures in the country and can be seen to best effect from a few hundred metres to the south, across Lake Jelonek, where, rising above a skirting of trees, it looks most picturesque. The third cathedral to stand on this spot, it was given its present external form in the middle of the fourteenth century. In 1942 the Germans turned it into a concert hall, and three years later it was burned out, but it has since been restored, during which time the interior was re-Gothicized. (It had been remodelled in the Baroque style in the seventeenth and eighteenth centuries.) Restoration uncovered some handsome Gothic stone carving (e.g. the tympana of the entrance portals) and even some fragments of wall painting, and against the interior west wall there stand two enormous tomb tops, of which the more important, the one in marble belonging to Archbishop Zbigniew Oleśnicki, dates to 1496 and is by Veit Stoss. But the chief treasure of the cathedral is its pair of bronze doors, now standing in the south-west portal and depicting eighteen scenes from the life and death of St. Wojciech. The series begins with his birth, in the bottom panel of the left-hand door, and concludes with the deposition of his remains at Gniezno, in the bottom panel of the right-hand door. Dating to the second half of the twelfth century, these are amongst the oldest work of their kind anywhere in Europe.

Forty-nine kilometres to the south-west through fairly uneventful scenery lies Poznań, the cultural capital of Great Poland, with a population of over half a million. Poles from other parts of the country tend to be unkind about Poznań. Too German, they say, and of course it is true that the whole of Great Poland was under Prussian rule from the second partition in 1793 to the restoration of Polish independence in 1918. But people tend to forget that this area, and particularly Poznań, was a centre of Polish nationalism. In 1848 the whole of Great Poland rose up against the Prussians, and in 1906 some 75,000 schoolchildren went on strike against attempts by the authorities to Germanize the educational system. Prussian occupation did, however, leave three positive legacies. First, the roads in Great Poland are rightly considered to be better maintained than elsewhere in the country. Second, the Prussians encouraged agricultural improvements, and the farms here are on the average bigger and more prosperous than in most other parts of the country. Third, industrial growth was also encouraged, and nowhere is this more obvious than in Poznań itself, with its vast Cegielski Engineering Works, founded by Hipolit Cegielski more than a century ago and now, like all heavy industry in the country, state-owned. Before the last war it made railway coaches and engines, but in recent years it has expanded production to include ship engines, machine tools and a whole range of other engineering goods.

Poznań is also famous for its trade fair. The first one was held in 1921, and since 1925 they have been held annually, except during the war years. Recently, it was decided that the fair had become too unwieldy, as the number of visitors and exhibitors from Poland and all over the world grew larger and larger, so it has been split in two, with a fair for heavy industrial goods in June, and another for consumer goods in September. No sightseer in his right mind would ever knowingly try to visit Poznań at fair time, for the hotels are over-booked then, and the restaurants impossibly overcrowded. But at other times of the year our traveller is in luck, for because of the fairs Poznań is better supplied with good hotels, per head of population, than either Warsaw or Cracow.

Poznań is more than just industry and fairs, and it is not particularly 'German' either, although admittedly a few of the nineteenth-century major public buildings, like the big Neoclassical Opera House of 1910, would look perfectly at home in a large Prussian provincial town. But the most attractive buildings in town are much earlier, dating from the Romanesque through the Baroque period, and it is these that we have come to see.

The city lies astride the river Warta, which flows 808 kilometres through the heart of western Poland from its origins south of Częstochowa to its junction with the Oder above Szczecin. At Poznań the river was formerly a tangle of meandering channels, and it was on one of the small islands rising above the surrounding marshes that the ancient town developed. A princely residence once stood here, even before Mieszko I made it his capital in 968, but the most important surviving structure is the cathedral which gave its name to the area, Ostrów Tumski (Cathedral Island). Like so many major Polish buildings, it has had a chequered career. Originally a Romanesque stone basilica, of which the crypt and the base of the south-west tower survive, it was rebuilt in red-brick Gothic, and then damaged on several occasions, most notably during the Swedish 'Flood' of 1655–60, which reduced the population of the once thriving city to a mere 300. Eighteenth-century reconstruction left much of it covered in plaster, in which state it remained until the end of World War II, when, along with three-quarters of the historical heart of the city, it was largely destroyed. Post-war rebuilders have made the exterior Gothic once again, except for the Baroque tops of the west towers, which rising elegantly above the surrounding trees, dominate the area. Inside, the cathedral offers a motley collection of Renaissance tombs, some old frescoes of the Apostles in the entrance to one of the south chapels, a collection of coffin portraits in the ambulatory and, at the far east end, the neo-Byzantine Golden Chapel (*Złota Kaplica*) of 1835–41, containing monuments to Mieszko I and Bolesław the Brave, who are putatively buried in the crypt.

Opposite the west end stands the Gothic church of the Blessed Virgin, a steeply gabled red-brick structure, which has remained undamaged through the centuries. Every time the cathedral was damaged or destroyed, its congregation temporarily moved here. It looks a bit peculiar, a mere half of a church, for it is no more than a choir and ambulatory resting on six stout pillars. But it can never have had a nave, for athwart its west end, paralleling the river, stands another late-Gothic red-brick structure, a psalterium, or residence for the chantry priests of the cathedral. Before leaving the area, be sure to note, in the outer fabric of the south wall of the church, certain small, round indentations about the size of a thumb print. According to legend, garrulous women were once punished by being forced to dig out these holes with their tongues. Legend also says that the shallow gashes at shin-level at the south-east corner of the church were made by the devil trying to tear down the building, but they were more likely left by medieval knights thus sanctifying their swords before going off to war.

Two or three other interesting churches have survived in the old suburbs to the east of the cathedral, particularly the tiny Romanesque church of St. John of Jerusalem, founded by the knights of the same name towards the end of the twelfth century and now sandwiched between a number of main roads and the artificial Malta Lake (Jezioro Maltańskie), excavated by Allied prisoners during the last war. Beyond lie new suburbs, many of them constructed of pre-fabricated modules, for Poznań is now erecting two vast housing estates, Rataje and Winogrady, capable of accommodating over 220,000 persons, and all this on top of the 180,000 new rooms built in Poznań since the war.

But now we shall turn our attention westward, across the Warta, to the new town centre established a few years after the Tatar invasion, in 1253. A grid surrounded by a roughly circular wall, bits of which still survive, particularly the north-west portion, it is centred on a large market square measuring 140 metres on each side. In the middle stands one of Poland's most famous town halls. There had been a Gothic town hall on this site as early as the beginning of the fourteenth century, but in 1550 Giovanni Battista Quadro from Lugano, an area that spawned many of Poland's major architects during the next two centuries, began a thorough Renaissance remodelling of the structure, adding a grand east façade featuring three storeys of arcades shielding external loggias, the whole surmounted by one of the country's tallest towers. From the pair of doors above the clock on the same façade two mechanical goats emerge every day at noon, bump their horns together 12 times and then go back inside. This commemorates two animals of long ago who, according to legend, got lost in the town hall and started fighting. The commotion roused the locals, who ran into the square just in time to notice that fire was about to engulf the whole area. Nowadays the sounds issuing from the building are generally more melodious, particularly on week-end evenings during the summer, when public choral and vocal recitals are presented from the loggias.

The interior should be visited, partly because much of it has been turned into a museum devoted to the history of the city, and partly for the magnificent first-floor rooms. The Renaissance Hall is especially stunning, with its vaulted and coffered ceiling full of intricate stucco work. Hardly less impressive is the richly painted ceiling of the Court Chamber, with its coats of arms and numerous portraits of ancient Polish princes.

In the front of the town hall stands an ancient pillory, while to the south there extends a row of narrow brightly coloured houses, from the arcaded ground floor of which herring-sellers once hawked their wares. The houses are so very narrow—only one or two bays wide—because in olden days one was taxed according to the number of windows one had. Originally dating from the sixteenth century, they were demolished in the nineteenth and reconstructed after the war. Also of interest is the statue of St. John Nepomuk, on the south side of the square. A medieval Czech who refused to betray the secrets of the confessional and was drowned in the Vltava (Moldau) for his stand, he has become, not altogether surprisingly, the Church's favourite protector against floods. The precaution of erecting the statue was taken after the disastrous flood of 1736, when bodies floated out of the crypt of the parish church, and the waters reached a height of two metres, as can be seen from the mark incised on the front of one of the houses on the east side of the square.

A couple of houses to the north at No. 45 stands Poland's only Museum of Musical Instruments, which is well worth a visit. Its three floors contain instruments from all over the world—some bizarre, like the Tibetan ritual horn made from a human tibia and the Chinese lute covered with snakeskin, and some of more general interest, like the valuable Amati and Guarneri violins and the pretty French clavecin, the cover of which is painted on both sides with charming mythological and hunting scenes. There is also a Chopin room, with a photogravure of the famous pianist in Prince Antoni Radziwiłł's salon, *circa* 1829, as well as a life mask and a cast of his left hand.

The Old Town of Poznań lends itself to strolling, and because it has largely preserved its original grid system it is fairly difficult to get lost here. Little churches, and a few very big ones, are tucked away amongst its picturesquely dilapidated streets, and some of the houses—massive sixteenth-century structures—are buttressed for support, as in Cracow. Here and there, statues of patron saints watch over passers-by from the corners of houses, and courtyards beckon, particularly that of the mammoth Górka mansion, with its rows of restored Renaissance arcades. The family, one of the most powerful in Great Poland, died out almost four centuries ago (their grand chapel and ceiling-high monument lie off the north aisle of Poznań cathedral), and their house is now an archaeological museum, with a rich collection of material from throughout the province.

Of the Old Town churches, my personal favourite is the parish church in ul. Gołębia, two streets south of the market square. A Jesuit church until the temporary suppression of the order in 1773, it is the grandest Baroque church in Poznań and was begun in 1651, though work continued on it for nearly a century. Its architects were a series of Italians, men little known outside Poland, though they have certainly left their mark on Poznań and throughout the Great Polish countryside, in splendid Baroque churches like those at Grodzisk, 48 kilometres south-west of Poznań, and Sieraków, 72 kilometres north-west, both by Christoforo Bonadura; at Holy Mountain outside Gostyń, 70 kilometres south of Poznań, by Giorgio and Giovanni Catenacci and Pompeo Ferrari; and at Ląd, 76 kilometres to the east, largely by Ferrari. Each of these churches is, for a keen church-crawler like myself, well worth a special trip from Poznań, but for those who lack the time or energy to make the necessary detours, the parish church at Poznań is just the answer, for all the above-named architects worked on it. Full of warm *trompe-l'oeil* marble colours and huge baldacchino-type columns framing massive side chapels, it contains one of the country's largest pulpits, a dark-brown and gilt giant that stretches out deep into the body of the church from well inside the chancel. Yet, possibly because it is rarely well lit, I have always found this, despite its rich Baroque decoration, a surprisingly quiet, restful spot and a good place in which to pause between spells of sightseeing.

Unless one has very special interests, most of the important sights of Poznań can be seen within the space of a day, although one would need somewhat longer for leisurely strolling. Visitors in search of excursions out of Poznań will probably have guessed from the geographical introduction at the beginning of this book that the scenery in this part of Poland is pleasant rather than spectacular, with the flat or gently rolling landscape offering quiet surprises, rather than sudden thrills. Buildings, and not landscape, will therefore be the main goal of our excursions here. For readers who want a rest from churches, Poznań has two attractive country houses practically on its doorstep, or at any rate less than half an hour's drive out of town. One is Kórnik, 20 kilometres to the south-east. Originally the property of the powerful Górkas, it passed to the Działyńskis in 1675, and to the Zamoyskis in 1880. Finally, in 1924, the Zamoyskis gave it to the state.

It is a curious building, more picturesque than beautiful, and even — perhaps — more eccentric than picturesque, particularly its exterior. Surrounded by a moat, it was rebuilt in the middle of the last century to modified designs by the famous Neo-classical architect, Karl Friedrich Schinkel. From the front, with its turrets and crennelations, it resembles an English neo-Gothic castle, despite its coat of whitish-grey plaster, but its back, or garden elevation sports a huge recessed arch more than a little reminiscent of Persia or Central Asia. But it is bizarre fun, and well worth the trip, and not least because of the varied collection of pictures, furniture and ethnographical objects, many of them acquired by Władysław Zamoyski during his expedition to Australia and New Guinea in 1879–81. Much of the collection is housed in a vast Moorish Hall, repeating the oriental motif of the garden façade. The Zamoyskis and the Działyńskis were all great patriots, suffering much for their adherence to the national cause during the Partitions, with the neo-Gothicizer of the house, Tytus Działyński, escaping from Prussian troops after the 1830–1 insurrection only by hiding in one of the ground-floor fireplaces. It was he who began the famous Kórnik library, which now contains over a quarter of a million volumes, a large proportion of which are housed in the mansion itself. It was he, too, who greatly enlarged the beautiful old park that stretches to the south and east of the building.

Thirteen kilometres to the west of Kórnik lies Rogalin, the Raczyńskis' former country seat. Begun in 1770 in a gently Baroque style, it had acquired a Neo-classical interior by the completion of building a generation or so later. Outside, it is a pretty cream colour, the curved wings of the entrance elevation giving it a handsome depth and scale. Inside, it is full of furnishings from the seventeenth to nineteenth centuries, largely brought from other houses, for Rogalin lost its own treasures during the last war. An outbuilding behind the left wing of the house has been turned into a gallery of pictures by important Polish and lesser-known French and German artists of the nineteenth and early twentieth centuries. The large park surrounding the house contains, to the right of the main entrance, the most famous trees in the country, three ancient oaks with circumferences ranging from 6.70 to nine metres. They are known as Lech, Czech and Rus, after the legendary founders of the Polish, Czech and Russian nations, though to my knowledge nobody has ever definitively determined which is which, and I have even heard it rumoured that Polish guides, tactful to a fault, will tell Czech groups that the biggest oak is Czech, and a day later tell Russian groups that it is, in fact, Rus. But I daresay that, deep down inside, every Pole knows very well that the biggest one is their own legendary ancestor, Lech.

7 THE NORTH

The Polish North, roughly corresponding to the ancient provinces of Pomerania (west of the Vistula) and Warmia and Masuria (to the east), is as picturesque as it is today thanks to the ice sheet that covered much of the country during the last Ice Age, many thousands of years ago. Every time the glacier paused in its movement southward, it left behind an east-west moraine, that is to say, a ridge of debris — rocks and soil — that it had scoured out of the earth's surface. The north of Poland is full of parallel moraines, many of which are richly forested, and most of which are of fairly gentle elevation. (The highest point here is a mere 329 metres above sea level.) Later, as the glacier retreated, it left behind great hunks of 'dead' ice in hollows nestled in amongst the moraines, and as the climate grew warmer, this 'dead' ice melted, thus creating the several thousand lakes that are such an attractive feature of this area. Many of the lakes are fairly small, often little more than woodland pools, but some are very large indeed, the largest of all being Lake Śniardwy in Masuria, with an area of 107 square kilometres.

With a few exceptions, such as the lower Vistula valley, the soil here is relatively poor. Consequently, the area has never been densely populated. So the landscape — this charming combination of lakes and rolling hills, so romantic particularly in the autumn, when the deciduous trees change their colours against a backdrop of evergreens — is largely unspoiled. To be sure, the North is experiencing a certain amount of tourist development, but it is so large an area (roughly a third of the entire country), that the tourists still appear to be vastly outnumbered by the trees, which is not always the case elsewhere on the continent.

This is an area for outdoor holidays, and it is particularly well supplied with camp sites. The whole of the North is criss-crossed by literally hundreds of crystal-clear rivers and streams, and also by a number of canals, probably the most famous being the Elbląg Canal, which extends from Lake Druzno, just south of Elbląg, to Lake Drwęckie, near Ostróda. Constructed in 1845–76, it follows a

144-kilometre course through lakes, rivers and artificial channels; and, for dealing with differences in water levels, it has adopted the solution (unique in Europe) of moving boats across dry land on rollers, rather than relying on locks. The region is perfect for canoeing, and craft can be hired at the larger holiday centres. Probably the favourite route is Masuria's Krutynia River, which connects a score of lakes along its 100-kilometre course.

Thinly populated and still predominantly rural, the North is rich in game, including deer and boar, as well as the usual pheasant and duck. ORBIS organizes hunting and riding holidays, one of the most popular centres being Biały Bór, 76 kilometres south of Słupsk. There is also a rich variety of fresh-water fish, such as carp, bream, tench, perch, eel and pike. However, certain other types of animal are carefully protected, like the 300-odd elk in the Czerwone Bagno (Red Swamp) sanctuary near Rajgród, south-west of Augustów, and the tarpans, the smallest horses in the world, at Popielno, also in Masuria. But perhaps the most famous of all Poland's protected species are the *żubry*, or European bison, to be found in the Borecka Forest, west of Suwałki, and also to the south-east, in the Białowieża Forest, on the Soviet border. The latter has been turned into one of Poland's most unusual national parks, unusual partly because it is the only surviving primeval forest in the lowlands of Central Europe, and partly because, to preserve this unique characteristic, no motor vehicles are permitted, no flowers may be picked, and no 'tidying-up' operations are carried out. If a tree falls over, it stays where it falls, and so on. A hotel and tourist hostel stand near the entrance to the park, and visitors may take a four-hour cart journey through the most interesting parts of the reserve.

As a result of the post-war boundary changes, Poland has acquired a Baltic coastline more then 500 kilometres long, compared with the tiny 'Polish Corridor' between German Pomerania and East Prussia which had previously been its sole access to the sea. Sopot, formerly on the territory of the Free City of Danzig (Gdańsk), has been a fashionable resort since the last century, and although now it is more 'popular', it still possesses a smart-looking old-style Grand Hotel, as well as several modern ones and a 512-metre-long pier, a favourite strolling spot. New resorts have also sprung up, like Świnoujście, on the island of Uznam, directly on the East German border at the mouth of the Oder. Across the river lies Międzyzdroje, on the island of Wolin. Besides the sea, the main attraction here is Wolin itself, with its great beech and oak woods, interspersed with lakes, swamps and moraine-type hills. Now a national park, Wolin is generally reckoned the most beautiful area along Poland's Baltic coast, and on balance I think I would agree.

Throughout the North, as in Silesia, the Germans fiercely resisted the Soviet and Polish advance westward in 1945, and the towns of the region suffered enormous damage. Destruction was particularly severe in Pomerania, and there are no centres that merit a detour from Warsaw, and only a couple that might merit one from Poznań, although if one is already in the area, there are a number of sights well worth visiting, such as the restored Gothic churches of Słupsk and Kołobrzeg, both town centres having been almost entirely destroyed in the final days of the war. Szczecin (in German, Stettin) was also heavily damaged, both by Allied air raids — it was part of Germany at the time — and during the Soviet Army's struggle for the town, which lasted more than a month. Originally a Hanseatic town ruled by a long line of Slavic princes (the last, Bogusław XIV, died in 1637), it passed to the Swedes initially before becoming Prussian in 1720. Its most famous citizen was Sophia Augusta Frederica, the daughter of the commander of the local garrison, Prince Christian August von Anhalt-Zerbst, who, like many another German princeling of limited means, had been obliged to enter the Prussian service. At the age of sixteen she was betrothed to the Russian Emperor, Peter III, becoming, after his murder, the Empress Catherine II (the Great). The house where she was born at ul. Farna 1 is gone now, its place being taken by a modern block of flats.

Szczecin is by far the largest city in Pomerania, with a population approaching 400,000. It is also Poland's largest port in terms of tonnage handled. The city is handsomely situated along the banks of the Oder, while its Parisian-style boulevards and squares, laid out after 1875 on the site of a Prussian fortress, give it a special elegance and scale which war destruction and fairly uninspired rebuilding have somehow managed to leave more or less intact. Luckily, some of the Old Town has been restored, such as the Gothic hall church of St. John the Evangelist and the Gothic cathedral of St. James. The latter had been left in a ruined state as a war memorial until 1972, when the creation of the new bishopric of Szczecin-Kamień led to the restoration of this huge church as the seat of the diocese. An even larger task has been the restoration of the massive Castle of the Pomeranian Princes, in the centre of town overlooking the river. Begun in 1346 on the site of an earlier fortress, it was remodelled on a number of occasions before its partial obliteration during the last war. It has now been rebuilt to house a number of lecture halls, a theatre (700 seats), a film room, a café and a concert hall, as well as providing space for temporary exhibitions. From an historical point of view, perhaps its most interesting feature is the sarcophagi of many of the Pomeranian princes preserved in the vaults of the late-Gothic east wing.

Thirty-six kilometres to the east lies Stargard Szczeciński, an ancient Slav stronghold still surrounded by much of its thirteenth-century walls despite heavy damage suffered at the end of the last war. What makes a visit here particularly worthwhile is its magnificent hall church of the Blessed Virgin Mary, arguably the finest Gothic church in the whole of western Pomerania. It is certainly one of the largest, measuring some 80 metres in length, which is also the height of the north tower, while the nave is over 30 metres wide. On sunny days, light pours in through the ambulatory windows, suffusing the whole choir in a lovely golden yellow; but probably the most attractive feature of all is the superb nave vaulting, each bay following a different geometrical pattern.

Lovers of organ music will want to head for Kamień Pomorski, 82 kilometres north of Szczecin and 84 kilometres north of Stargard. A bishopric was founded here as early as 1176, and the town was more important than Szczecin, but it now has fewer than 6,000 inhabitants, and the bishop resides at the last-named town. However, Kamień still possesses a cathedral, a squat stone and brick structure, in parts as old as the diocese. Its main attraction is the magnificently exuberant gilt organ of 1669, one of the best in the country, which is the work of Michel Berigiel of Szczecin and is used for recitals by the most famous Polish and foreign organists throughout the summer months.

To the east, in the Vistula valley and beyond, the attractions lie much thicker on the ground. The landscape looks richer, farming is more intensive here, and crop yields are greater, particularly in the lower Vistula region, which contains some of the best agricultural land in the country. This has always been a more prosperous area than Pomerania, so even allowing for the very considerable damage wrought by World War II, there is more to see here.

The chief reason for this is historical. The 1220s saw the arrival here of the Teutonic Knights, a crusading order which was ultimately to prove far more of a threat to the Poles than the pagan Prussians whom they had originally been called in to subdue. Over the next two centuries, i.e. prior to their resounding defeat by Polish, Lithuanian and Tatar forces at Grunwald in 1410, they managed to spread their power across the greater part of northern Poland, at the same time erecting a score of fortresses and castles to keep the region in check. Many of these are now only ruins — but what ruins! — like the massive remains at Radzyń, 18 kilometres south-east of Grudziądz. One sturdy brick wall stands more or less intact, with its long, narrow windows and two tall square towers, perched on a hillock just outside town. Gniew, to the west of the Vistula roughly midway between Grudziądz and Gdańsk, also has a castle, a chunky red-brick box, its four walls pierced by the same long, narrow windows that we have seen at Radzyń, and in a much better state of preservation.

But the finest of all the castles of the Order stands at Malbork, on the river Nogat, a branch of the Vistula. It was begun in 1274, and in 1309 the Grand Master of the Order moved here from Venice. However, as a result of the defeat of the Order in the Thirteen Years' War (1454–66), it became Polish and a royal residence. Later, at the time of the First Partition (1772), Frederick the Great acquired it, turning it into military barracks. A century ago it was rescued from an alarming state of decay and neglect, but World War II left much of it devastated, and restoration had to begin all over again.

What the restorers have put back together is one of the largest medieval fortresses in Europe. It is also one of the most impressive and beautifully situated, with the best view of it to be had from across the river. Actually, Malbork is not a single fortress, but three (an upper, lower and outer fortress), the whole consisting of dozens of grand and less-grand chambers, many featuring the beautiful vaulting, in fan or star patterns, which we have come to expect in the grander buildings of North and West (i.e. German-influenced) Poland. During the summer months, the great main courtyard is frequently used for musical and theatrical events, while part of the middle castle now houses an Amber Museum, for the Baltic coast, a mere 36 kilometres away, is one of the traditional sources of this beautiful material.

The Church was no less a builder than the Teutonic Knights, although nothing it has left behind is on quite the scale of Malbork. The richest bishopric in the whole region was that of Warmia (in German, Ermeland), a triangle of the richest land in the whole of Prussia, and the only part of the province to remain loyal to Catholicism after the Reformation. The bishops' chief residence was at Lidzbark (or Lidzbark Warmiński), and their moated castle, an imposing rectangle more than a little reminiscent of the

Knights' fortress at Gniew, survives to this day. Its most impressive features are undoubtedly the great Council Chamber, with its remains of late-fourteenth century frescoes and the coats of arms of the bishops of Warmia, and the massive vaulting of the cellar and armoury, which resembles nothing so much as great spiders perched on stubby pillars.

The chief religious centre of Warmia was Frombork, a small town perched on a hill overlooking the Vistula Lagoon. The setting is picturesque in the extreme, with a beautifully restored late-Gothic cathedral, bishop's palace, chapter house and canonry all grouped together in a charming wooded setting. The best building is the cathedral, a red-brick structure with fine Gothic vaulting and much rich Baroque decoration, like the splendid organ at the west end. In 1497, Copernicus became a canon of Frombork and lived here until 1512, and when he died in 1543, he was buried in the cathedral. A museum devoted to the life and work of the great astronomer has been set up in the canonry.

Another Warmian town with Copernican associations is Olsztyn, a provincial capital of some 120,000 persons, and, as it is well supplied with hotels, a perfect base for excursions. Olsztyn lies on both sides of the river Łyna, whose banks now form one of the prettiest parks in the whole country. Dominating the town is the great fourteenth-century castle of the Warmian chapter, which has been converted into a regional museum containing interesting exhibits of paintings (many from the local manor houses abandoned in great haste by their German owners in 1945), medieval sculpture and folk crafts. Between 1516 and 1521, Copernicus was administrator of the chapter house, and the sun dial on one wall of the castle gallery is said to have been designed by him.

Yet another town with Copernican associations is Toruń, on the Vistula midway between Warsaw and Gdańsk. The astronomer was born here in 1473, and his birthplace at ul. Kopernika 17 has been turned into a Copernicus museum. Once a great Hanseatic river port, Toruń gradually declined to the advantage of its great rival, Gdańsk, downstream, and bitter religious disputes in the seventeenth and eighteenth centuries — Toruń was Poland's chief Protestant political centre — only accelerated the process. A number of fine old houses and churches survive from earlier periods, however, particularly the Old Town Hall, a dark-red brick rectangle begun in the middle of the Market Square in 1393 and subsequently embellished during the Renaissance. It now contains a fascinating museum devoted to medieval art, with a particularly rich collection

of old Polish stained glass, very little of which was survived elsewhere as a result of Poland's turbulent history. Of the churches, by
far the greatest are the huge Gothic halls of St. Mary's and St.
John's, the former lying at the south-west corner of the Market
Square, and the former to the north-east, in ul. Żeglarska. Both
churches contain a rich display of tombs, altar furnishings, frescoes
and even a few bits and pieces of old stained glass.

Toruń has always been famous for its gingerbread, which comes
in various shapes, including hearts, and much of which is exported.
It is widely on sale in English delicatessens. For visitors who wish to
buy it where it is made, there is a shop that specializes in it on the
east side of the Market Square.

Much of Toruń's old thirteenth-and fourteenth-century walls
survive, particularly along the Vistula. Three of the old gates still
survive — the Bridge Gate, the Seaman's Gate and the Monastery
Gate — and several of the towers, including a Leaning Tower, which
is lower than the one at Ząbkowice Śląskie, but only slightly less
askew at 1.40 metres out of true vertical. Local guides always ask
visitors to stand with their heels and backs firmly against the tower,
but of course it is impossible, and one invariably falls forward
inelegantly.

Gdańsk, once the greatest port on the Baltic, lies 177 kilometres
to the north. A member of the Hanseatic League as early as the
thirteenth century, it belonged to Poland from 1454 until the
Second Partition in 1793 and provided her chief maritime access to
the rest of Europe. German cultural influence was very strong, and
the town was largely Protestant after the Reformation, but it
remained loyal to Poland, at least in part because of the many
freedoms and privileges it had extracted from the Polish kings. It
was, in fact, to all intents and purposes a city state within the
kingdom, and the arrangement seemed to suit everybody. It certainly suited the burghers of Gdańsk, whose town enjoyed a Golden
Age of prosperity during the sixteenth, seventeenth and eighteenth
centuries.

Evidence of this is to be seen everywhere in the city, despite the
massive damage at the end of the last war, which left 55 per cent of
Gdańsk in ruins. Rebuilding has been going on much more slowly
than in Warsaw, and for this reason it is even more satisfying,
particularly in details, which give a third dimension to the 'new-old'
buildings of Gdańsk, which those in the capital sometimes lack.

Despite war damage, fine Gothic churches and Renaissance and
Baroque mansions can be found throughout the Old Town,

although the restorers' great masterpiece is the 'Royal Route' that stretches roughly half a kilometre through the heart of Gdańsk along the Long Market (Długi Targ) and Long Street (ulica Długa). Burghers' houses reminiscent of their great counterparts in the rich merchant cities of Holland and Flanders line the route, their chief peculiarity and attraction being the charming entrance terraces that have been virtually rebuilt from ground-level since the war. The dominant structure, however, is the great Town Hall, built in dark-red brick at the end of the fourteenth century, with a disproportionately tall spire tapering to a height of 82 metres above the street. Next door is the Dwór Artusa (Artus' Mansion), a late-Gothic structure that now wears an elegant, almost Dutch façade of 1616. This was the chief meeting point of the rich burghers of the city, and the headquarters of their powerful guilds. Following restoration, the mansion now functions as a gallery of contemporary art. In front stands what is perhaps the most famous fountain in all Poland, the Neptune fountain, the work of Peter Husen and dating to 1615. The great sea god, formed of bronze, holds a trident in one hand and a sacrificial bowl in the other, emphasizing Gdańsk's great dependence on Neptune's watery realm.

In many ways the greatest building in the whole city lies just to the north of the 'Royal Route', at the end of a narrow side-street. This is St. Mary's, the largest Gothic church in the country and also the largest in the entire Baltic basin, measuring 105 metres in length and 29 metres to the top of its vaults, while its great tower is an impressive 78 metres from top to bottom. For grandeur, this is like most of the other grand Gothic churches that we have visited in Poland, only more so. It is claimed that half of the population of the city, which is approaching 450,000 persons, could fit into the nave, aisles and transepts, and I am prepared to believe it. The church was formerly richly decorated, but its proliferation of altars, statues, pictures etc. was largely destroyed in the war, leaving only the vastness of its space and the grandeur of its proportions.

The other churches of the city are too numerous to list here. Rising high above the city, their red-brick profiles are easy to find, and each visitor will doubtless find one or two favourites of his or her own. It only remains for us to mention the rich collection of the National Museum in a building adjoining St. Anne's church, in the south of the city on ul. Rzeźnicka. This is one of the best museums in Poland, both for the quality and the variety of its holdings. Probably the greatest of all its pictures is the Last Judgement by

Hans Memling, which formerly hung in St. Mary's, but the museum is also rich in the works of other Dutch and Flemish masters, such as van Ostade, de Hooch, Jordaens, van Dyck and van Goyen, and it also contains numerous fine works by local painters, as well as artists from elsewhere in Poland and the continent.

8 EATING AND DRINKING

Polish food is hearty and filling, as might be expected of a northern country with fairly long winters, though it is far from being stodgy—certainly no more so than traditional British cooking! One of the finest features of the Polish culinary repertoire is its scores of different soups, including numerous varieties of *barszcz* (a beetroot soup similar to the Russian *borshch*), some of which are almost a meal in themselves. Other excellent soups include lemon soup, sorrel soup, mushroom soup, *chłodnik* (a cold, and very refreshing, summer soup, made with lashings of sour cream, cucumber and veal or—rarely, but more traditionally—crayfish) and tomato soup. Always home-made, tomato soup is one of the first things a Polish cook learns to prepare. Another favourite 'starter' is fish, which is often served cold, such as carp, perch or pike in aspic, or salted herring in sour cream, with chopped apple and onion.

Pork is the favourite meat, followed closely by veal. Little lamb is eaten, while Polish beef is rarely of the quality of its British or American counterpart. Polish poultry, on the other hand, whether chicken, duck, or goose, is generally free-range and full of flavour, while Polish hams and sausages (*kiełbasy*) are world-famous. Traditional dishes include *bigos* (hunter's stew), made of sauerkraut, cabbage, pork, sausage and bacon, and reheated frequently over several days to enhance its flavour; *kołduny*, which is actually a Lithuanian dish, consisting of lamb-and-beef dumplings flavoured with marjoram and served in beef broth; *zrazy* (rolled beef fillet), usually stuffed with mushrooms, ham, or dill cucumber and served with *kasza* (buckwheat groats); *gołąbki* (stuffed cabbage); and *flaki po warszawsku* (tripe Warsaw-style), a highly spiced dish beside which its French and English counterparts pale to insignificance, and which is guaranteed to convert even the most inveterate tripe-hater into a fervent devotee of the food.

The Poles are passionate carnivores, and when meat is available, many eat it three times a day. Unfortunately, the production and distribution of meat in Poland is extremely inefficient by Western standards, and this, coupled with the need to export it in order to earn precious foreign currency, has led in recent years to a chronic meat shortage. (Long queues of customers outside butcher shops are a not uncommon sight.) But, however trying this may be for the Poles themselves, it does not affect the traveller, for hotels and restaurants are invariably well supplied.

The Poles are also very fond of pasta and batter dishes, such as dumplings (filled with curd cheese, meat, mushrooms, cabbage or fruit), noodles and pancakes (usually fruit- or cheese-filled, and served with a dollop of sour cream). They are naturally full of calories, but well worth sampling. In any case, Poland is not a country for dieters!

Polish meals usually end with compote, ice cream (almost always superb), *kisiel* (a sort of blancmange served with cream or a fruit sauce), or a cream cake or slice of torte. Polish breads and cakes are usually very good — and often excellent. They are also fairly cheap. The word to look out for is *cukiernia* (cake shop). Here one can buy individual cream cakes and doughnuts for the equivalent of a few pennies each, or huge slabs of cheesecake and torte for slightly more.

Polish tea is ordinarily served plain or with lemon. In either case it is usually weaker than the English variety, because it is not intended to be drunk with milk. The visitor would be well advised to follow the custom of the country, because the Poles almost invariably boil their milk, and the addition of the latter to Polish tea produces a pretty strange concoction. Polish coffee is usually either much better or even worse than the murky liquid one gets in an average English restaurant. Coffee is frequently, and tea usually, served in a glass. The trick is to hold it by the fingers as close to the rim as possible. Polish tap water is safe to drink, but it is often heavily chlorinated, so it is no wonder the Poles themselves prefer soda or mineral water. Refreshing soda water, either plain or flavoured with fruit syrup and costing next to nothing, can be bought from numerous street vendors in all the cities and towns of Poland, particularly during the summer months.

Visitors in search of stronger drinks have come to the right place, for nobody, except possibly the Russians, produces better vodka (in Polish, *wódka*), This is doubtless why, according to recent statistics, the Poles hold the world record for the per capita consumption of spirits. Polish vodka comes in a number of varieties, including *wyborowa* (the plain vodka most commonly exported to the West), *żytnia* (rye vodka, probably the best of the unflavoured varieties), *myśliwska* (hunter's vodka, flavoured with juniper berries and reminiscent of gin), *jarzębiak* (rowanberry vodka), *wiśniówka* (cherry-flavoured) and *żubrówka* (flavoured with a blade of sweet-scented Hierchloe grass, said to be a favourite nibble of the *żubr*). Polish beer is not of such uniformly high quality, although two brews — Żywiec and Okocim — are particularly worth remembering. As for wine, the Poles produce virtually none of their own and are therefore obliged to import it, which may explain why it is fairly expensive, particularly in hotels and restaurants. The Eastern Bloc countries are the chief suppliers, the best reds coming from Hungary, e.g., Pinot Noir and Egri Bikavér (Bull's Blood), and also from Bulgaria. Good fairly dry whites come from Hungary and Yugoslavia, while Hungary (Tokay) and Rumania (Cotnari) produce fine dessert wines.

Although Polish hotel eating times are roughly those of Britain and America, the Poles themselves, and most non-hotel restaurants, are geared to different hours. The average Pole is already at work by eight, and even earlier in factories, so breakfast (*śniadanie*) is eaten early and generally consists of bread (not toast), butter and jam, and tea or coffee, plus at least one of the following: cheese, eggs, cold ham, sausage, tomatoes, dill pickles and cake, often cheesecake.

The Poles are compulsive tea- and coffee-drinkers, consuming seemingly endless glasses of one or the other, along with perhaps a sandwich or a piece of cake, to sustain them until lunch (*obiad*), the largest meal of the day, which is eaten fairly late, usualy between one and five in the afternoon. This is because many Poles — who, as they begin work early, also finish early (often by three o'clock) — wait until they reach home to eat lunch. This usually consists of soup or another form of starter, a main course (meat, potatoes and a vegetable or salad — often cole slaw), followed by something sweet. The third meal (*kolacja*), which is eaten towards mid-evening, usually takes the form of supper, rather than dinner, and may include cold cuts, cheese and tomatoes, or perhaps a hot dumpling dish, and possibly cream cakes.

Poland has no equivalent to the English pub, while its beer taverns are, on the whole, scruffy. The growing number of cocktail bars are fairly soul-less places of little character, pushing Western (or Western-style) drinks at ridiculously high prices. (A word of caution; in Poland, 'cocktail bar' is also used to describe a place where fruit-and-milk drinks are sold, but one can usually tell from the outside of a bar the kind of refreshment one is likely to be served inside.) On the other hand, Polish cafés, whether indoor or (in the summer) outdoor, can be extremely pleasant, particularly in Cracow and Warsaw, and also in the numerous restored castles and town mansions now frequently housing some of Poland's most attractive cafés and restaurants. The one drink which is usually unavailable is beer, which Poles tend to consider 'low class' and not the sort of thing one should order in a café.

The Polish restaurant situation has improved considerably in recent years. There are more of them, many being privately run on license from the state, and they are better decorated than formerly. Some even provide menus in foreign languages. Service can be fairly slow, but not much slower than in an English restaurant on a busy evening. A useful institution is the *bar mleczny* (literally, 'milk bar'), which is basically a self-service dairy and vegetarian restaurant offering a wide range of soups and egg, pasta and batter dishes. They are rarely much to look at, but the food is cheap, plentiful, usually well prepared and very authentic.

Of course, the best place to sample Polish food is in a Polish house. This is by no means impossible, for the Poles are a hospitable people, and in Poland a chance encounter is more likely to lead to an invitation home for dinner than in many other European countries. If such an invitation comes your way, be sure to take your hostess a few flowers (always an odd number, though no Pole has ever been able to tell me why), some chocolates, or, best of all, something from your home country. Arrange to arrive a bit late — certainly not early — and shake everyone's hand. The Poles themselves generally kiss ladies' hands, but unless one can do this smoothly and naturally, a single handshake is probably better. The Poles are warm and generous hosts, and always loathe to let their guests depart. Who knows, you may even decide to return to Poland one day . . . I am sure you will.

INDEX

INDEX